Unconformity

A novel by
John McLellan

With best wishes
John McLellan

This is John McLellan's second novel, building on the success of his first - The Faultline, which was launched in 2022. Unconformity is a stand-alone novel but readers of The Faultline will also be able to enjoy the continuity of both narrative and characters.

Before starting to write novels, John McLellan had a long career in management and consultancy, in the logistics industry, within the BBC and for the NHS. Since graduating from Swansea University with a geology degree in the late seventies, he has maintained a life-long interest in the subject. He now undertakes voluntary fieldwork in southern England and northern Scotland, whenever he can. When not writing, he also volunteers in his local NHS hospital. He lives in Bristol, with his partner David.

Unconformity, first published in February 2024 by the author, with the print support of Whitehall Printing, Bristol.

Gratitude is once again given to Dave Cousins of The Strawbs for the use of one quote at the beginning of part one of this novel.

Paperback ISBN: 978-1-3999-7756-2
A catalogue record of this book will be in The British Library and the national legal deposit libraries, during spring 2024.
#faultlinenovel
Email:faultlinenovel@gmail.com
Find The Faultline on Facebook.

The cover photo is with the permission of Ross Davidson Photography, and is taken on the Beinn Eighe ridge, looking north.

To all the people with whom I have been privileged to share friendship and affection that lasts for years, through thick and thin. Thank you.

Foreword

None of the characters in this novel are real people, and any resemblance to anyone living or dead is coincidental. All the characters are hybrid assemblages of memory and imagination.

As in my first novel, the scenery and geology are portrayed as accurately as I can manage. Their beauty and wonder form the ever-present backdrop to this story.

John McLellan
February 2024

Part One

Chamonix, 1983

"Sunshine and the tender flower, both melt the young man's heart. But he who lingers waits his turn, must learn to play his part."
From The Flower and the Young Man, on the album, Grave New World, by The Strawbs 1972.

Chapter 1

Fifteen hundred feet above the alpine valley and suspended in the air, the cable car pods had been stuck for ten minutes, unmoving except for the gentle rocking from side to side in the breeze, and a slight up and down movement in the warm air rising from the ground below. The intense afternoon sun had quickly turned the glassy pod into something like a greenhouse and even with the ventilation windows open, it had become very stuffy.

The feeling of being trapped and out of control was overwriting any sensible thinking for Peter. He could feel his chest tightening and his throat felt constricted. He also felt like just wrenching open the door and jumping out. It was probably a hundred feet or more to the ground, which, at this point, was a steep slope of rock outcrops interspersed with scattered pine trees. Somehow, this seemed a plausible escape route to him right now.

'How long has it been Simon?' He thought his voice sounded like someone else's, stretched and a bit too high.

'Come on Pete, take it easy. Asking every thirty seconds isn't going to make it magically start going again!' Simon looked at his friend sympathetically and put a hand on his shoulder.

But then, just as Simon did this, they both felt a sharp jolt and then heard the mechanical whirr of the cogs and machinery above them picking-up speed again. The tiny cabin, supposedly made for six, but feeling cramped enough with just two and their climbing gear, lurched forward as it started its downward journey again.

'I wish that wouldn't happen' said Peter, 'I know it's just a problem at the station at the top or the bottom, someone falling over or something, but it freaks me out so quickly. I was just starting to fantasise about shoving the rope out, tied to that central pole, and abseiling off.'

Simon felt quite shocked by this remark and could see his friend really had been starting to panic. He sighed and rubbed Peter's shoulder again.

'Don't be daft Pete, you would die! Anyway, you can be calm again. We are fine now and will be down and out of this box in a few minutes. Doesn't it feel better with the air coming in through the window again? Just breathe it in.'

When they reached the ground at the town end of the cable, the cabins slowed down so abruptly they bumped into each other and jostled around a little, reminding Peter of fairground rides, like the waltzers with their unpredictable lurches. He didn't really like those either.

Then everything was moving very slowly, the doors automatically sprung open and out they stepped. It felt so good, reassuring and solid, to Peter. He grabbed his rucksack in his hand and darted out, Simon followed with his pack already halfway on his shoulders.

It was a shame, thought Peter, that had happened just at the end of a great day on the mountains. Hours earlier, they had been at the same spot, setting off upwards for the day, on the cableway station platform as soon as it opened. A number of other walkers and climbers had been doing the same. It had run uninterruptedly then and the three thousand feet of ascent to the top station had taken just minutes it seemed. Getting out at that point had been to arrive in a different world. The feel of the sun, the clear cool air and the glacial glitter on mountains all around was completely intense - and he loved it. He knew Simon had felt the same.

He thought about that now, thinking that much of the weight of the rucksack on his back was the clothes needed in the frosty early morning. Those down jackets, breeches and fibre-pile jackets had been replaced by shorts and T-shirt attire in the mid-afternoon fry, as they had come to call it. He had decided to just manage with running shorts, a favourite lightweight pair, while Simon's were more a cut-off denim. Both of their T-shirts were from a concert they had attended together, earlier in the year – part of U2's War tour – Simon's in grey and Peter's in black. It was a casual thrown-together look that they both liked and could also see marked them out as Brits as they strode through the streets.

They set off down the short hill from the station and headed left into the busy road that led to Rue Docteur Paccard, which they considered to be, and referred to as, the main drag. It contained most of what they wanted and needed from Chamonix . It was a colourful and bustling town, nestled into a steep-sided Alpine valley, with lots of hotels, restaurants and shops. But for them, the only places they tended to visit were a supermarket to get desperately required bottles of mineral water, a bountiful patisserie and, of course, the Bar Nash. They required all three of these, and in that order.

It must be impossible to walk down this road, Peter thought, without constantly looking up to left and right. Each side of the valley quite different from the other. The darker and rugged Aiguilles Rouges range forming the northern flank, from which they had just descended, and the southern slopes dominated by the much higher Mont Blanc and its outliers of snowy, white and crystalline peaks.

They soon arrived at the Brasserie Nationale, as the bar was properly known, after a litre of water each and a wedge of a very sticky and chocolatey cake. They stopped to look at the notice board by the doors. There were dozens of pinned pieces of paper with brief sentences, names and campsite locations, mostly British but some French and Italian notes as well. Most were addressed at the top to a named person. Some simply just had a date, a name and tent location. One or two revealed brief chapters of life such as: *NWMC Greybeards group! Thurs 16th August. We had a problem with the car and have had to go down to St Gervais. Back tomorrow at the campsite. Paul and Glyn.*

Peter perused them for a while, but there was nothing for him or Simon. He wasn't expecting anything but 'you never know' he thought to himself. Simon had already gone off to the bar to get a couple of beers.

They thought it was unlike most French bars, having a large, open area where people could just stand, a bit like a pub back home. Right now the area was pretty full, mostly of men but some women too. Most people were dressed in a very casual style with shorts, vests or T-shirts being commonplace. Others were still in climbing gear, looking hot and heavy in thick shirts, salopettes, breeches and solid leather mountain boots. A distinct whiff of sweat mixed in with the more prevailing scent of tobacco smoke. Nearly all the men, including Simon, had full-face beards. The minority were clean-shaven, like Peter. He admired some of those beards, the neater, shorter ones – and wished he could be patient enough to grow one too.

What was different to any pub back home, was the array of picture posters which adorned the walls. A number of the climbing gear manufacturers used high quality photos to advertise their wares – everything from ropes and chocks to ice axes and helmets. Most of the shots were of climbers on famous climbing routes, some others were more arty images of hard-looking guys eyeing-up mountains. The latter were the ones that tended to attract graffiti, mostly multilingual, in slang and usually indecipherable.

The sound of the bar was more uniform though. English language prevailed, but from all parts of Britain. Because most people were on trips with friends or climbing clubs, it meant there were blocks of regional accents in different places around the bar. And in the background to this was a distinctive pop soundtrack on the PA system, so much more distinctive, they all thought, to the more melodious French music in other bars around town. Right now it was Heaven 17's Temptation and he knew the tape well enough, after just a few days, to be certain this would be soon followed by

Blue Monday by New Order. The latter seemed very popular out here and this one could sometimes be heard drifting out from the doorways of more definitively French bars too.

'Hey Pete', he was hailed from somewhere in the back of the bar and although it was a bit muffled he could tell it was Dougal and that he would be with Keith. In a quieter spot, the former had a clear and bright-sounding Scottish accent. From Fife, as it had been pointed out more than a few times. Simon picked-up on it too on the way back with the drinks and they both made their way through the cigarette fog and the crowded tables to greet their friends, ensconced at the back of the bar, glasses and bottles fully littering the table. The two were part of that constituency still in their climbing clothes and they were definitely part of the more sweaty crowd.

Peter noticed they looked quite distinctive though, in a way that hadn't struck him so clearly before – both taller than him and Simon but also compared with many in the bar. They had much more of a rough and ready look than most, somehow giving them a self-assured appearance. 'So, you made it down in good time then?' asked Peter, his eyes flitting across the faces of his friends and then along the table.

'Yeah, we've not been here long. Just into our second pint, or half-litre thing anyway.' Hesitating, he looked down at the table. 'And this lot aren't all ours, if that's what you think!'

Peter asked how it had gone and Dougal gave a lengthy description of the early morning, pre-dawn, start from the Albert Premier hut, their wanderings over the Glacier du Tour and their attempt on the line of their chosen mountain. For the second time on this trip, they had been unlucky. Peter loved listening to Dougal's stories, he just would launch into a long monologue, usually with pretty colourful language and descriptions, all underlain by mostly hidden good humour. Out here, the target of his frustration and jokes was usually the local population.

'We're starting to think now it must be a seasonal thing, or this season anyway. But we have twice encountered these bergschrunds and by the time we navigate them, we've lost the time to do the route. I'm getting pee'd off with it, to be frank.' Dougal removed and rubbed his glasses with a grey and threadbare handkerchief. An action Peter thought, and knew really, always indicated some degree of irritation.

'It's also the bloody French!' Dougal continued. 'The endless faffing around, stomping around in their new plastic boots from midnight onwards. Stomp, stomp, stomp. Those boots are all the rage up there. Don't know where they all get the money. You don't need them! What's wrong with leather? Nobody back home wears them, even in the Cairngorms in winter. The noise on the hut floorboards, hard boots hitting harder wood. You can't kip through it. They can't bloody talk quietly either, not if they tried. They spend the evening stuffing their faces, knocking back the wine. They might as well put a tricolour on the bog – nobody else can get in. And then there's the women! Not that many, but! Preening around. Oh aye, nice talent some of them, you have to say that, to be fair, pretty tasty actually, but the blokes are pandering around them the whole time, and the birds themselves must have half their rucksacks full of bloody make-up. Jesus. Honestly…'

The other three watched this tirade and said nothing. When Dougal paused and took breath though, they all burst out laughing. They thought there was a kernel of truth in what Dougal had said and he was funny with it.

Keith said, 'You know what Dougal, there were actually a fair few Brits up there too. We weren't the only ones.'

'Yeah, all keeping quiet cos they're trying to get to bloody sleep.' Dougal finished laconically.

'Why don't you ask around here?' suggested Simon, after a

moment's thinking. There must be plenty of routes that are pretty doable just now. Everyone here looks and sounds like they are having a good time. I mean they have all had a drink or two but also look as if they have got up something too.'

'Aye, that's true enough.' Said Keith, sounding a bit like he didn't really want to know that fact.

Dougal thought it was a neat idea though, just needed the prompt and he suddenly jumped up and off he went. The remaining three talked about the day.

'Well we know the Aiguilles Rouges are lower, and tamer, but we have just had another good day haven't we Simon?' Peter went on to explain getting the first télécabine and then the walk east up and onto the rocky ridge at the Col de la Glière and two small summits reached by a hard snowfield that had needed crampons and roping-up, for a little while anyway.

'Those bloody télécabines though. They freak me out, always stopping, suspending you in mid-air.' Peter rolled his eyes and supped his beer.

'Well at least you two are getting to the top of something.' Said Keith. 'We will have another go tomorrow, while the weather holds. I suspect Dougal will be back in a minute having found that he would rather we make up our own minds than rely on the judgement of someone else we don't know. He might get some bergschrund insights though! I had previously thought of them as large crevasses but out here, they form wide and deep gaps that are bloody hard to deal with. We must be doing something wrong.'

A while later and after more rounds of beers, they all broke up and headed back to their respective campsites, for Peter and Simon via the supermarket. The other two hadn't been to this part of the Alps previously and had dismissed the campsite preferred by Peter and Simon as 'packed' and too busy, ending-up at the much larger site north-east of the town centre. They also had said they thought their girlfriends would prefer it, when they eventually arrived. Conversely, when first entering Chamonix, Simon had just driven straight into their campsite and found an ideal spot immediately without even looking around the rest of the grounds. Afterwards, he had considered it just good luck and good timing.

Leaving the Bar, Peter nodded to another guy about his age, just outside the main door, and got a friendly nod back. He didn't think he knew him but had felt his glance had lingered. The man was also about the same height as Peter and was one of the clean-shaven ones although he had a darkish swathe of fine bristles, a little bit more then a five o'clock shadow. It was a hairiness that continued on his chest and down his bare abdomen to his green, slightly shiny, athlete's shorts.

Peter needed to do something and decided to hang back a bit, leaving Simon wandering off ahead. He could maybe say anything, but what? This happened with him occasionally, he recognised it immediately, knowing there was the potential for a thing to happen but having no idea how to precipitate it, nor even feel sure that he wanted to anyway. The fear of taking a chance and getting it wrong. In the end they exchanged a few words about where they were from, the bar and, inevitably, the weather. Peter risked taking the chat a nudge further.

'Well, you did the right thing coming outside here, it is pretty hot and stuffy in there.'

'Yeah,' said the stranger 'I like a ciggie occasionally but it's just too foggy in there for me.'

'Sure, it is a bit unhealthy to be fair. Hmm – you look like a runner?' Asked Peter.

The other men frowned slightly, looking curious now. 'A bit I suppose, out here though? No, just doing the climbing and walking. Oh, did you mean the runners' shorts?'

Peter had been thinking of nothing else during this conversation.

'Yeah – a bit like mine I suppose. In the afternoon heat, they just seem fresher don't they – just being so light?' Then he couldn't think what else to say. Wanted to ask where the guy was staying but thought it might sound too obvious. 'Well, better get on I suppose. Catch-up with my mate. Might see you around again?'

'Yes, sure.' said the man. 'Hope so.'

Walking away, after a few steps he looked back round, the other guy was still watching him. The words "hope so" ringing in his ears. Simon asked who it was that Peter had been speaking with. Peter felt like he had been caught out and was conscious of blushing slightly and tried to stop it.

'No idea, but he had looked familiar at first – as I said to him. He's from Reading – near where I was brought-up as it happens.' He hoped this covered what he was really thinking, which was how good the guy had looked, fit, lean and attractive. Peter wondered whether this was an opportunity he had passed-up again, but couldn't think what to do about it.

'So, Dougal and Keith said they will see us tomorrow afternoon in the Alpenstock Bar or the evening if they do better.' Simon stated, changing the subject, as they set-off down the main drag. 'Unbelievably, you know, they are going back now for a quick sorting out and then getting the train up to the Mer de Glace and stopping at a hut this evening to have a go at something else. They want to keep-up momentum, that's the way Keith put it.'

'Blimey. They have the bit between their teeth don't they! Straight from one route to another. Hope they do ok this time.' Peter gave a slight shake of his head. 'What do you think is the issue for them?'

'Well, we have a lot less experience of big glaciers don't we? That's one of the reasons the Aiguilles Rouges are so good – we don't have that worry and problem. Those two know what they're doing, more than us anyway, but I picked-up that this summer has been particularly hot, so the bergschrunds are maybe more open and therefore trickier?'

'Don't know Simon! The back ends of glaciers are so massive, I really don't know if those chasms in the ice can expand so much in just one season. Whatever though – it's causing them some problems.'

Their conversation turned to food, what to get at the supermarket and what to eat that night. Simon thought Peter should just leave him to get on with this, as he had thought about their meals all the time so far anyway, and was happy to do so.

On the way back to the campsite he remarked that it would soon be coming up to the anniversary of starting at University. They shared a few moments of memories quickly culminating in a rapid review of the summers back then. As was normal, Peter chatted about the geology field work in Kinlochewe in the summer of 1977 and other trips to the North West Highlands.

'You were lucky really weren't you Pete? Liking walking in the mountains, and climbing, and then getting those trips to Torridon and stuff?'

'Yeah, I was. I didn't know that would happen when I went there though. To University I mean. It was all announced in the first year and I didn't know then that I would make it through to the second year at that point. It turned out well in the end I suppose. My life completely revolved around the climbing club and the geology department.' Peter sighed. 'As you will remember.' He paused. 'And the tea bar of course! And the drinking bar…' He shook his head. 'Would have been better spending more time in the lecture theatre though.'

This made Simon turn to this friend while they were walking down the approach road to the campsite. 'It has turned out ok Pete – you got a job easily. You sound like you are going to go off into one of your thoughtful modes though! Talking of your field work always does that to you, you know! I don't think I have ever got to the bottom of it.' He paused. 'Then there's that woman friend you used to have, you met back then I think – the one who hasn't been around the last few years. The one I've never yet met, if she exists!'

Peter thought it was unusual for his friend to comment on women at all. Quickly scanning through history in his head, he couldn't recall Simon with a girlfriend ever, although he was also pretty certain he wasn't interested in guys either. While ruminating on this, Simon's last remark was left hanging in the air and Peter could feel he needed to say something but then he thought it was hot, sunny and he had been out on a great day in the Alps and didn't really want to get too reflective about the past. His friend maintained a silence though that was hard to ignore and in the end he simply said, 'You mean Sue, yes, I haven't seen so much of her. She got married.' He hesitated, deciding whether to say more or not. 'The thing about Kinlochewe… well, a lot happened! I think I became an adult there too, you know. That's the truth of it. I think.'

Simon thought this was typically enigmatic but knew it would be all he would get right now. As it was, they were approaching the campsite gate. Camping Les Arolles had a welcoming feel, not too big and therefore not too noisy. The whole site was looking full though, but with the trees and bushes around, it didn't have the impact of a camping city like the one the other side of Chamonix. When they first arrived, a lot of French people were packing up and heading back home after their long holidays but much of their place had seemingly been taken by British campers, and a few Italians too. Tents seemed to be grouped but they hadn't bothered looking around, just using the site as a washing, eating and sleeping base – and they felt very content with it.

'Right,' said Simon. 'Showers, change, pack for tomorrow? Then a quick dinner and back to the pub?'

Peter nodded and smiled. 'Sounds like a plan!' He could always rely on Simon for that.

Chapter 2

As it turned-out, the next day was pretty much a repeat of the previous one, as far as the climbing and walking went. Peter and Simon had another successful venture out onto the mountains on the north side of the valley. They had done a scrambling route on the Aiguille de Charlanon, mostly on rock warmed by the sun, with one high icy stretch of snow where they had roped-up as well as using crampons. The efforts had been rewarded with more spectacular views south to the Mont Blanc massif and all the mountains and glaciers to the east of it, including where they believed Dougal and Keith to be again. Being a shorter route than previously, they found they had a lot more time for photos, which they enjoyed.

Peter thought the trickiest bit of the day, for him, had been negotiating the same cable car again, with its inevitable mid-air hesitations. He got through the journey this time by distracting himself and concentrating really hard on his Zenith-E camera and asking Simon to explain once again how to use the telephoto to get foreground as well as distance. He thought he had remembered it but Simon's calm and patient explanation had a soothing effect on his claustrophobic concern.

This time, on returning to town in the mid-afternoon, they were going to go straight past the Bar Nash, as they had a different rendezvous in mind – their one other haunt in the town. Peter insisted on going across the road though, ostensibly to check the noticeboard, but really he was in search of the man in green shorts. He didn't know what he would say, if he had the guts to follow-up on that "hope-so" comment. But the guy wasn't there anyway. He felt a mixture of feelings at this realisation, most noticeably he felt butterflies in his stomach.

Along from there they went to the main Place du Marché and turned down the road towards the station but also, more importantly, to their objective, Le Bar d'Alpenstock. It looked a bit cheap and tacky from outside, and appeared as if it was a small element of the largeish hotel which rose above it, but they could never see any sense of a hotel reception. This rather plain exterior belied a large and smarter inside area with two levels of tables, some comfy seating in places and, they had discovered, some friendly service from Pierre and Maurice. They always felt welcomed even when a bit worn-out, dishevelled and wearing just their scruffy, British-defining mid-afternoon kit.

The two waiters seemed to be on duty whenever they arrived, both this year and last, the tall and aquiline Pierre behind the bar and the shorter, stockier and moustached Maurice serving the tables. Both were always in black trousers and white shirts - Pierre's sleeves habitually rolled-up above his elbows and Maurice's just turned back at the cuff.

They were supported by a waitress who mostly appeared with food orders. She was quite taciturn and slightly offhand, not just to the Brits, they noticed, but to everyone. She moved slowly and deliberately with the food orders, wore a tight-fitting black skirt with a white blouse, and clearly was proud of the way she looked. She was quite petite, had tied-back black hair and the overall effect, they had all agreed, was quite sexy. Peter liked her and thought that she had a great way of being aloof to the attention and looks she generally received from men. Not exactly disdainful but something quite knowing and a touch of justified superiority. Not hearing, or ever being able to solicit, her correct name, they had instead christened her Yvette.

As on this occasion, it was seemingly always busy in a steady sort of way. Watching the two male staff take, shout and exchange information, line-up and then serve drinks to tables inside and out, seemingly faultlessly. It was like looking at a work of art at times, Peter thought.

For some reason, this was also the place where Brits tended to hang-out other than the Bar Nash, but it was more mixed too. It was possible to hear Italian, Spanish, French and English being spoken at the different tables. Whereas the Bar Nash could feel like a Snowdonia pub at times, the Alpenstock always retained a distinct continental flavour – the style and arrangement of tables making it quite unlike anything back home in the UK. That's what they all thought anyway.

This time, they had a friendly greeting as usual, were given a nice table with a banquette one side and immediately had their order taken for croque-monsieurs and beers.

'So…' Simon wondered aloud '…do we think Dougal and Keith are going to be here shortly or later?'

They didn't have to wait long for an answer. Yvette had only just delivered the food when the other two arrived. They threw down their rucksacks, pulled-up two chairs opposite and Simon and Peter saw straight away that their day had also been a bit of repeat, and not necessarily in a good way. They looked the part though, Pete thought, hard hats dangling off their rucksacks, mirrored glacier goggles loose on their necks like an adornment, and Dougal in his dark-blue salopettes. He thought they could get away with being taken as hardened French climbers this time, but knew better than to say this.

'Right,' said Dougal. 'Don't ask! All we want to say is we are coming-out with you two tomorrow, it looks like weather might change after that, and we have to get up something. We are right fed-up…' Maurice arrived, making a welcome interruption to the flow, to take orders for large beers.

'What was it?' asked Peter. 'Bergschrund trouble again?'

'Aye it was, well …we had decided to tell you that' said Dougal. 'But it wasn't that really. It was just too hard. Too icy. Think the warm spell has stripped off snow and left a lot of the route with real ice or, worse, verglas. We got going on the route but we had to back down. Over ambitious.'

'Well, black ice I can certainly understand. Too many French on it too?' enquired Simon, smiling.

'Yeah, well, it would be great to blame them, but we can't. Same crap in the hut at night but, no, it's just us, we've decided. So, we are coming with you tomorrow, if you let us, and then get back on the harder routes when the rain clears off, or if it doesn't come. Although that will no doubt mean fresh snow up high if it does rain down here. Oh, you know what I mean.'

The beers arrived and they all chinked their glasses, knocked back their drinks and quickly ordered another round. Dougal went off to the loo and coming back and sitting down, noticeably more cheerful, launched into a description of another group of British climbers, so he thought, in the back of the raised part of the Bar.

'They look like a club meet. You can tell. Best thing though, at least two good-looking birds in amongst them!'

Peter shook his head and made an exaggerated rolling of his eyes. 'You two have your girlfriends arriving soon!!'

'Yeah, but they're not here right now, are they!?' said Keith. 'And looking isn't cheating, is it!' Then he and Simon went off for a pee and to check-out what Dougal had discovered. They came back in full agreement.

'We got a couple of nods – friendly like.' said Simon.

'Not from the women though.' Added Keith. 'You're right though Dougal. It would be good to go climbing with the two lasses we got a look at. Better looking than present company! No offence lads!' They all laughed. 'One of them did follow me with her eyes though, I thought, all the way back here.'

They all looked sceptical about that. More beers arrived, more croques, for Dougal and Keith. There was an attempt, from Dougal, in his best schoolboy French, to engage Yvette in some chat but she remained cool, perfunctory and pretty much ignored him, but gave a sly wink and smile to Simon and Peter as she went off. Peter found himself blushing a little and saw the same thing had happened to Simon. Peter thought to himself the smile had been a small reward for not overtly flirting with her like the other two.

'Hey up though!' said Dougal. 'Something's happening'

They followed his eye and saw one of the other group of Brits was on her way, seemingly towards them, or in their direction certainly. Maurice arrived back with the tab at that point, coming behind the banquette to save interrupting their conversation, and Peter turned around to him to sort out the payment, rifling in his pockets and rucksack for some Francs.

'I told you she had given me a look.' Suggested Keith. 'That's one of the nice-looking birds with that other lot.'

'Nah,' said Dougal, 'she just saw us here and thought "now they're a group of guys I could spend time with." Maybe anyway!'

The woman from the other group of British climbers now indeed came straight up to their table. She would be about chest height to Dougal, slim, wore pinkish, dusty-looking denim shorts and a black and white, fitted, check shirt with the sleeves rolled-up. She had long, bronzy coloured hair, hanging back over her shoulders and further down her back. All of them watched her arrival with increasing anticipation, with the exception of Peter who was still distracted with lost currency and the bill.

'Hello darling.' said Dougal in what was, for him, a genuinely bright manner. 'Got bored with your club and want to join ours?' The woman didn't say anything straightaway but smiled. Dougal and Keith looked her up and down approvingly. Simon tried to just give her a friendly smile.

'You are welcome to sit and have a drink and a natter if you like...?' continued Dougal, hopefully, and trying to sound genuine.

'I will.' She said after a moment's hesitation. 'But...' A longer pause. '…only if it's ok with Pete!' And she nodded her head in Peter's direction.

There was a slight hesitation as if they hadn't quite heard properly, and then all at once Simon, Keith and Dougal's heads turned to Peter, some astonishment in their faces. Peter had only half-heard their conversation and turned back from finally settling the bill with Maurice. He at first saw the woman's boots, socks, tanned legs and the shorts. When he then looked up at her face, his jaw dropped open and it was his turn to look astonished.

'Well, is it ok Pete?' she said, head tilted to one side, a broad smile emerging on her face.

Peter could hardly speak, floundered a bit trying to move along and then he and Simon squeezed along the banquette to make room at the end. But the woman stepped over the legs of the latter and simply wedged herself in between him and Peter.

'I can't believe this' he said to her quietly, and then to everyone. 'Er guys…' he pointed at them in turn, 'Er, Simon, Keith and Dougal, this is Sue. I don't know how we are meeting like this, but Sue is an old friend.' They all nodded to her, leaning forward, eager and anticipating more from Peter.

'Oh yeah…' said Dougal, after a second or two, getting back into his usual jokey mode. '…what sort of old friend is what we're all wondering!?'

'Stop it Dougal.' Half-whispered Keith.

'No, it's fine.' said Peter, taking Dougal's comment at face value. 'Erm…' a pause. 'Er – well, the very best sort actually.' Peter said finally. He and Sue looked at each other's faces while this was being said, smiling, both shaking their heads lightly and slowly.

'Well' said Dougal, recovering, 'Sue! Old friend of Pete. Of the very best sort. Something we need to hear more about as soon as we can; would you like a drink?' And without waiting for an answer, turned, caught the waiter's attention and signalled the request for another beer by holding up his own glass.

Keith, Dougal, and even Simon, had eagerly leaned in and it was clear to Peter that Sue was both flattered, but also a little unnerved, by being the focus of this fairly intense attention. They all stayed like that while Peter gave a few words about how and why he and Sue knew each other.

Simon had been at university throughout the same time as Peter and knew that this was about the geology mapping project again. It seemed to him like an incredible bit of serendipity after the earlier chat at the campsite. Hearing now that this was the very Sue who had been there too that summer, was a surprise and gave some insight to him. He knew that Peter had been going through a troubled spell with his university girlfriend at that time and wondered what sort of relationship he might have had with Sue. He saw they seemed very comfortable with each other and couldn't help feeling this chance meeting was going to be significant for his chum.

After a while, Dougal, who always liked to get facts straight, summarised. 'So, you two met about eight years ago then, flung together in Kinlochewe with a load of other geologists like Pete. Essentially, all in Torridon. One of the greatest parts of one of the world's greatest countries, by the way.' He paused for, and got acknowledgment, mostly as guffaws. 'Anyway, geologists… that is to say, like Pete was trying hard to be at the time!' There was a bit more laughter, including from Peter.

'He was trying to get his mapping project done and you kept distracting him Sue, and I can understand, well-enough, how and why that might have happened! and…' not allowing Peter or Sue to jump in with their protests '…then after you finished with university life in different places, you kept in touch but not so much recently. That about right?'

'Yeah,' said Peter. 'It must be two or three years, maybe. How amazing to meet out here, and even to spot each other.'

'You haven't changed much Pete and I would have spotted you anywhere.' And with that, Sue lightly touched Peter's leg. A gesture of affection not lost on Dougal, who raised his eyebrows quizzically.

There was a bit of a lull and Sue felt the need to fill the gap.

'I got married back around the time we last saw each other and we sort-of lost touch.' She had been speaking to them as a group but now turned more towards Peter. 'Things have changed for me a bit recently. I needed a good trip to the mountains.' Choosing to change the subject, she continued, 'How about you all? From what you said Dougal, I assume this is some sort of club trip too? That's the people I'm with over there – all from South Wales Mountaineering Club.'

Dougal relished the opportunity to tell a story, and he expanded at length. How they were indeed all from another climbing club in Bristol and getting to the Alps was also an annual event. They weren't very organised though and had camped at different ends of the Town, having travelled separately. More were coming in a few days. He wanted to know if Sue was a climber.

'Not really,' she said. 'I love the environment, getting up as high as I can but I'm not really into ropes and the two-in-the-morning starts from huts, falling into crevasses and all that.'

'Well, we try to avoid that too.' Joked Keith

'Not very well though.' Replied Simon.

'And you can piss right off Simon!' continued Keith, to laughter from the four men. 'You sound more like these two Sue, more like Pete and Simon. They are getting in some good days by not being too ambitious. Meanwhile, we are doing those hut starts you mentioned and not getting much done. Bergschrunds seem to be our problem though, not crevasses. Maybe that's just a matter of scale though! What about your crowd?'

'I ought to be getting back to them actually, I guess' said Sue. 'They are a mixed bunch too. There's about ten of us and I've realised from this chat we are on the same site as you Pete. Must be in a different bit of it. It's been getting quite full hasn't it? I have a friend here, sharing her tent, and she and I go walking a lot together. It has been ok on this holiday so far, like you, so we'll see how it goes.'

She was finishing her drink and clearly intended to go back to her friends in the other part of the bar. Simon, who had been mostly quiet throughout the whole conversation and had been studying, and thinking about, Peter, suddenly said, 'If you and your friend fancy joining us tomorrow Sue, you would be welcome.' He paused, hoping he was doing the right thing. 'Pete and I want to go up the road to the téléphérique de l'index and on to Lac Blanc and up behind there onto the ridge. And then back the same way, more or less. It's about ten miles and three thousand feet of ascent. A good Scottish day. Equivalent.'

'Hmm, sounds like it is.' Said Sue. 'I know those a bit, as Pete will tell you. That's very kind of you Simon.' She looked at Pete and saw him nod his head encouragingly. 'I'll check with Sheena. What are we talking about time-wise?'

'Seven, by the reception kiosk ok? We need to drive and aim to get the seven-thirty cable cabin.' Simon confirmed. 'We can all go in the one car. Dougal and Keith can meet us at the base station, if they decide to come.'

While Sue went off to check, the other guys all turned to Peter.

'You. Dark. Horse.' said Dougal, slowly, shaking his head and grinning. 'She's really fit-looking and sounds nice. Just how well did you know her before she got married, eh?'

Peter shrugged. It was too complicated a story to share lightly and he was feeling distinctly off-balance from the encounter. Simon sensed this and cheered him by simply saying, 'She just seems smashing Pete.' The other two nodded assent. And at that point, Sue returned.

'OK, we are up for it. Thank you. We are all going for a pizza this evening at that place up the road at the edge of the woods, so can't see you later but will see you in the morning.' She leaned over and gave Peter a quick kiss on the cheek. 'So incredible to bump into you like this. Nice to meet you all.' She added, nodding to each of them in turn. 'See you later.' She waved and walked off; half way back she turned and blew another kiss to Peter who was still watching her.

'Come on then.' Said Dougal, not wanting to let it go. 'Tell us the rest of the story of you two…'

Peter chatted with them all a bit longer, talking more about those times in general, the importance of the fieldwork for his degree, the mountains, the other geologists. He still didn't want to say much more about Sue or the other things that happened years before, but which were often on his mind and which he felt too private to share. Not only private. He actually feared being truly honest – feared even good friends would turn their backs on him if they knew what had happened back then.

On the way back to the campsite and their tent, he found himself and Simon were unusually quiet. Peter felt his mind was having a memory cascade. When they got to the tent and Peter gathered his wash-kit and towel, Simon said: 'You know Pete, you've talked more about that those Scottish trips more than you probably know. Most times we go out for a walk or on a meet, you know there's always a point where it occurs. Twice today!'

'Oh God, I'm sorry Simon. Banging-on about the past. It's too self-indulgent. Sorry.'

'Hey! There's nothing to apologise for. It always intrigues me. I'm just saying it was obviously a big thing in your life and whatever happened up there…' he paused, '…well, it seems it is part of you.'

Peter smiled and nodded, rooted to the spot for a few seconds. 'Hmmm. I don't know what to say Simon.' Then changing the conversation, 'We don't know Sue's friend yet, but it was so nice of you inviting them both like that. Really great you thought of doing that, in fact. Thank you. I'm looking forward to it – a lot!' He realised just how much this was true and went off to clean-up.

CHAPTER 3

The following morning, the two women and the two men met on time. There were shared introductions with Sue's friend Sheena, who was similar in height and stature to Sue, with black, shorter hair and looking fairly equally tanned by the Alpine sun. Trying not to shiver in the cold morning air, they quickly jumped into Peter's Vauxhall Viva for the short trip up the road to the cable car. It was slightly higher up the valley and still in shadow, and as a consequence, was even chillier. All four of them were dressed principally for a hot summer day though, but starting-off with jumpers and fibre-pile jackets on top. Dougal and Keith were waiting for them at the cable station.

'What kept you?' asked Keith, making a joke of it. 'We are usually halfway through the route by now!'

'Struggling halfway across the first glacier don't you mean?' teased Simon, who received wry smiles in return.

They all piled into the cable car with several other people. About half-way up the ten minute ride, the téléphérique cabin came out of the shadows and into the full glare of another bright mountain morning. The interior of the arrival station was still very cold but when they emerged onto the trail, the sunlight and warmth was both strong and instantaneous. So, before getting going, they all had to pack away their jackets into rucksacks, and an hour later, the jumpers went too. By that time, they had also started to climb up the rocky and lengthy zig-zag track to the lake.

Peter felt, as he always did, truly alive in this mountain environment. Clear, crisp air that he could taste it was so fresh, stunning views all around, the warmth of the sun on his skin. He extolled these virtues of Alpine walking right out loud. Sue, Sheena and Simon all agreeing at once.

After that they were mostly silent on the way to the Lake itself.

It got hotter and sweatier, being fully exposed to the south. They passed a few people and everyone was polite and cheerful, at least as far as minimal French and English could convey. Being higher up, most people it seemed were now in the same attire. Vests, usually skimpy for the women, mostly shorts for both sexes, big boots, sunglasses and various forms of canvas hat. The only obvious difference was that a lot of the French just looked smarter and also used ski poles as walking aids. Something never seen in Britain, thought Peter, but seemingly ubiquitous out here. He thought they looked awkward and couldn't see how they helped much and doubted he would ever want to use them. To him they looked more like a fashion item than an aid to walking.

The six of them changed positions on the trail at various times. The well-worn path was really only wide enough for one person, so any very early risers already coming back down the trail had to be given space to pass. Sometimes this proved to be a useful moment for photos of Mont Blanc, the Aiguille Verte and the other big mountains opposite, or just a pause for a breather.

Along the way, it happened that for a long stretch, Peter and Sue were together, alternating one behind the other occasionally. They initially just were happy with not talking, just absorbing the sounds of the mountainside. But after a while they caught up a little with some of each other's histories. Mostly it was Sue speaking and she sounded quite terse as she summarised a short marriage, an abrupt end and already acrimonious proceedings with solicitors.

'It's a shame it has fallen apart Sue. I thought you and Colin were going to be really happy together. You seemed to be so certain he was the one for you – and you fell for him so quickly.'

The reply from Sue took a while to arrive. The ground was quite steep and Peter thought Sue must be saving her breath. Then she said, 'There's a lot more I could say Pete, but you know what? It will spoil this gorgeous day out.' Another break in the flow. 'So do you mind if we leave it there?' The last part of this was delivered quite abruptly.

Peter felt doubly surprised now, and a bit pushed-back. He had remembered Sue as being very open with him, so he hadn't expected the discussion to close down like this. Nor had he ever imagined the sort of things Sue had started to say. He felt amazed that Sue would get involved with someone, let alone marry him, leading to such an outcome. Sue getting divorced!? That was news and a shock to him.

'Come on Pete.' Sue said, stopping briefly and taking Peter's hand for a moment. She spoke more cheerfully. 'What about you and your love life?'

They walked on a bit before Peter could organise his thoughts properly, both about her story as well as his own. Sue was right though, he thought, it is a gorgeous day.

'Actually Sue, I agree with you. It's too nice up here for this sort of conversation. Look at that stunning view!' They halted and looked south. It was a clear day, not yet hazy at all and the air seemed particularly transparent, looking across to the Mont Blanc massif, the Mer de Glace glacier and everything around. They took some more photos, but mostly just looked, a bit awestruck.

'Come on, we had better catch-up with the others. But I know you are still really waiting for me to say something at least. There just isn't much to say really Sue.'

Peter went on to explain that he still had contact with Penny, but that she was now married. That had also been quite a quick development. He felt over the relationship now but it had taken a while. He explained that for him it had become more of a habit and, like any habit, it was painful stopping.

'You haven't rushed into anything with someone else then?' Sue asked. She was leading on the path now but turned briefly, to ask him questions.

'No. I have quite enjoyed the sense of being on my own really.'

'That's a nice thing to say. I will remember that thought. What about…you know what I'm going to ask Pete, what about Steve? He never came back into your life did he?'

'You see, I knew where you were heading with this talk Sue!' He smiled at her. 'No, I haven't really been with any men either, if that's what you want to know. That was very much a one-off experience. I liked Steve but contact seems to have drifted away now – I never did see him again.'

'Was it a one-off?' She sounded a bit disbelieving. 'Still?'

'Come on, let's park this talk. Like we just agreed! We're nearly at the Lake.' Peter felt the need to get off that topic as quickly as possible.

Sue shrugged, nodded and they passed the last mile quietly, with just the occasional whistle from a marmot to keep them company. They found the charming rodents were very hard to see unless you looked really hard.

They found themselves amongst quite a large number of people at Lac Blanc. It was a friendly spot, with lots of conversations going on around them, nearly all in French. They all decided to keep up momentum, get crampons on and ice axes out and as soon as they started off, they were on their own and it became very still and quiet. They headed straight up several hundred feet of hard packed snow immediately behind the lake, on an increasingly steep slope to a ridge just south of the peak called Aiguille de Belvédère. That soon led to a short, sharp and very exposed ascent to the peak of the Aiguille itself. All of them felt very pleased with themselves, all feeling the joy of getting to a mountain summit, albeit a relatively straightforward one compared to those on the Mont Blanc side of the valley.

Dougal said, 'I have to hand it to you guys. This wee route is classified as an F, just a Facile grade. Keith and I thought we would be doing a bit of AD as a minimum out here, Facile being dismissed in our heads as far too easy. This is maybe where we've been going wrong! I have to say, and it's worth at least a pint later lads, this has been brilliant. Just brilliant.'

'It's a bit like climbing back home isn't it guys?' Sheena asked. 'I can hardly get up any rock climb, but V Diff always strikes me as a bit of a misnomer – usually easier then it sounds. Out here, it seems the opposite? I would assume Assez Difficile would be the equivalent of British Very Difficult but it must actually be incredibly hard, if that Facile we just did is anything to go by.

'There actually is a French Very Difficult, Très Difficile, Sheena.' Explained Simon. 'No idea what it's like to do one.'

'Aye, well it should be BH, that one Simon.' Dougal chipped-in. 'Bloody Hard. And that's about the limit of my French lingo too.'

Everyone joined in with the chuckle. 'Don't listen to him Sheena.' Simon added. 'Keith and Dougal are much better at French than they let on! They just don't like to admit it! In fact, they secretly love the country and the people!'

Simon ducked as Dougal did a pretend lunge at him with his ice axe. There was then a bit more joshing, with jollity masking the anxiety about the drop back down. The descent was essentially a reverse of the way up and it was here that all of them felt much more exposed. Not just to the full-on glare and heat of the sun, but also to the dangers of being on the slope in the early afternoon. Now tired from the effort of climbing to this point, everyone felt a bit intimidated.

'We're a bit crazy doing this.' Said Dougal at one point. 'Once we are off the ridge section, stones are going to be flying off from above as we hack our way down the snow flank…' He shook his head. '…we shouldn't be doing it really. Bigger rocks above start thawing or part of the snow begins slabbing away – we could find ourselves back down by Lac Blanc pdq!'

They all ploughed on, having no choice, keeping fingers crossed and concentrating on keeping upright, one steep crampon placement at a time. Peter was at the back and at one point stopped and just looked ahead, thinking that the image would be imprinted in his brain for years to come – sun blazing down on a diagonal line of five friends ahead of him, each several yards apart, ice axes angled across their bodies, held in readiness for a slip, edging their way down a forty-five degree slope of brilliant white, hard-packed snow.

Once down by the lake and taking the easy trail back to the cable car station, there was a shared sense of relief and camaraderie. Sue found herself alongside Dougal – or more likely he had engineered this position in the line of walkers.

'We could do with more like you over in our club in Bristol.' Dougal said. Sue wondered if he meant as some sort of capable scramblers or did he mean just as women. She guessed the latter. 'You know what I mean I'm sure.' Dougal continued, as if reading her mind. 'We have far too many beards and nowhere near enough people like you two.'

'I think I will take this as some sort of compliment.' Sue said, a bit guardedly.

'You should! Pete and Simon might be nice looking guys but they've not got your looks! You brighten-up any vista, even one like this!' and he swept his arm across the snowy and icy mountains bathed in sunlight.

'Are you chatting me up Dougal? Have you ever wondered…?' she turned to face him. 'Could this be connected with why you don't get more women joining-in with your Club?' She meant this to sound friendly and not too heavy.

'Yeah, fair enough Sue – I ken what you're getting at there but I meant it honestly enough. I know I have a reputation for trying it on with every new bird that comes along, but it's not true.' Sue looked at him a bit doubtfully. 'Not completely true anyway! In your case, honestly, you just look great. I don't know your situation but it sounds like, from what I've earwigged, you have had, or are having, a bit of a choppy time with your hubby. Well, he's a fool, that's what I'm thinking.'

Sue felt she could hear the genuineness in this conversation now and lightly touched Dougal's arm. 'Thanks for saying that. It's fine, you get a bit used to blokes being a bit over-attentive – that's all.' She sighed.

'It's understandable to me Sue, but I ken it's not always welcomed by women like you.' He paused, thinking of something he wanted to say, wanting her to know he was black and white on this subject. 'Where I am with women right… Where I am… is that I love their company – makes me feel good. Makes me feel whole. Makes me feel like that - just to look at a woman like you.' He paused a while as they walked on, then added. 'I would defend you, you know!' Sue stopped and looked at him a bit quizzically. 'A woman like you. You know, if you were being hassled by a bloke, someone really pestering and not getting the message, I would, I really would…in fact I do… I do stick my oar in! I don't like seeing that!'

Sue smiled at him and laughed lightly. 'That's sweet Dougal – I take that at face value too. If I ever need defending, I know where to come.'

'I mean it – I do. Honestly.' Said Dougal.

'I know.' She touched his arm again, lightly. They held a look at each other and exchanged smiles.

Eventually they arrived back at the campsite in the mid-afternoon. Dougal and Keith having driven off straight back to their own tents. All of them were tired, hot and thirsty. None of them felt like doing it, but Sheena eventually volunteered to make a cup of tea for everyone and so they gathered around the tent she shared with Sue.

'How did you two meet then?' asked Peter, suddenly realising that although it felt like they had been chatting all day, a lot of it had been of the moment and he needed to fill-in some gaps.

'Just through the Club really. Sue came along after Uni, didn't you Sue? Like me really. But she was stopping in South Wales for teaching work and in my case, it was the other way round - I was returning to the town from Uni in Aston.' The two looked at each other, quick smiles. 'Now I work down the new Swansea Leisure Centre,' Sheena added.

'Then I dropped-out, mostly, after marriage really.' said Sue, joining in the chat again. 'But got back into things more recently. There's always a Club meet to the Alps in August, so I was pleased to come along – this year especially.'

'You remind me a bit Sheena, of a friend of Sue's from years back. A good friend of hers called Julie. And that's a compliment by the way.' Said Peter.

'He means you just make good tea,' joked Sue. 'I am still good mates with Jules actually Pete. I lost a bit of connection with her, the Colin thing again. I thought she was a bit negative, then it turned-out she was right all along.' Then Sue gave a long sigh and drooped a bit. Peter saw what he had been noticing during the day, that Sue was actually pretty unhappy right now, hard to hide it though she was trying. This was a state he hadn't really seen in her previously.

Sheena put her arm around Sue's shoulders for a moment and gave her a brief squeeze. 'So, that's where you two met then wasn't it?' she asked Peter, turning to him. 'Up in Kinlochewe, when Sue was up there that summer?'

Peter felt she was being polite in the conversation as he felt certain Sue would have told her something already – they seemed so close and at ease with each other. 'Yep, that summer.' He confirmed. 'Sue and I met when I was doing geology fieldwork and she was working at Julie's Uncle's campsite. We were all there that summer and in a few weeks became good friends.'

'The very best, actually, was what you said in the Bar' intervened Simon.

'See, you've made Simon a bit put-out now Peter!' suggested Sue, smiling. 'You've been close mates for years and then this girl turns-up out-of-the-blue after a long time and you assert her as your best friend!'

'No, I haven't. Well, I mean, yes he is a best mate. Er… Look – you're both really good friends ok!?' He chuckled, pleased to be having a bit of banter suddenly and seeing Sue perk-up again – wanting to keep her on the bright side. 'Oh, Simon and I started walking and climbing together at Uni but he didn't do geology. We have settled into living and working in Bristol, as everyone seems to, you can't escape, and now both in the local climbing club.'

'So, you and Simon have been friends a long time then by the sound of it.' Stated Sheena.

'Pete came to Uni the same year as me and we both got involved with the mountaineering club and have been out on the hills and mountains together ever since.'

'Eight years in fact Simon,' added Peter.

'Gosh' said Sheena, 'you've seen a lot of life together really.'

'I don't know about that,' said Peter, looking wistful. 'Not sure that journey has really got going.' And Sue looked at him, giving him one of her lingering looks that Peter always experienced as if she was rooting around a bit inside his head. He realised how easily and quickly he was reconnecting to her and the amount of time passed seemed to be shrinking away.

'How long have you known the other two then?' asked Sheena.

'A couple of years I suppose. And there will be a couple more people too, this week.' said Simon. 'Dougal is from Scotland, as is obvious. He came south for work in the defence industry. We have a lot of that in Bristol. Keith is in the same sort-of field and they climb together all the time. Dougal's girlfriend is coming out with a mate of hers, who's now become Keith's girlfriend. They're really good friends, bit like you two maybe, I suppose. They're all camping the other end of town as you saw.'

There was more conversation about Alpine trips, climbing clubs, the sort of people, similar types and groups and so on, which was pretty much what they had been talking about all morning on the mountain, at least when they had the spare breath. Peter found himself dropping out of the conversation occasionally; becoming absorbed with how Sue was going quiet again, quieter, distracted, contemplative. She seemed to be far away for some moments and the episodes of cheeriness he remembered so well from the past, and as she had been in the Alpenstock the day before, those moments seemed to be quite fleeting.

Chapter 4

Nobody was in a rush the next morning. Low, growls of thunder rolled around the valley and misty clouds now cloaked the forests and slopes of the mountains. It looked like it would hang around all day or develop into rain, but the Metéo weather notice board in Town said the afternoon would be clearer and dry. They all discussed it over steaming mugs of tea and coffee.

The South Wales crowd and Peter and Simon huddled around the campsite office having a discussion in zipped-up fleeces. Dougal and Keith had driven over as well to see what was going on, if anything. The consensus, and the combined efforts to read the weather notes on the office door in French, was that the weather change would be short-lived and then a storm would come. There was a table and a bench under an awning, currently occupied by Sue and Sheena.

'Same as last year' said Simon, 'after mid-August, all the French starting clearing-off home and the weather goes downhill.'

'Yes, but if you remember Simon, after a day or two we will hopefully wake-up to brilliant sunshine, the mountains cloaked in fresh snow and then it will settle until we all go home. I reckon the weather does it just to help the Froggies feel better about going home after the holidays.' This was Dougal's contribution.

'I hope so, for the others arriving tomorrow.' Peter was thinking of Dougal and Keith's girlfriends.

There was a pause in the conversation. Peter's attention was drawn to Sue who had been brushing her hair, which dangled down onto the map she was studying at the same time. She suddenly stopped doing that and looked around. Peter felt pleased for her as she looked so much more at ease this morning. She had the look of wanting and needing to do something though, rather than fester in the Town.

'Well,' she said 'how about we all get our act together and go out for the afternoon? We can get a train around midday, I think, up to the Mer de Glace. If it does brighten-up, then we will be in the right spot. If it stays looking like north Wales weather, we can have an expensive coffee and come back down. But, look.' She pointed at the map. 'We could walk up from the glacier train station, then walk west along the balcony path to the Aiguille du Midi midway cable station and get the cable cabin back to Town. Looks alright, ish, on the map – but I'm not the expert here.'

Everyone turned to look at Sue. Peter felt for a moment like some of the guys were all a bit shocked that it was a woman who was the one provoking the group into doing something. They all clustered around for a look at the IGN map. Simon summed it up, tracing a line with his finger across the unfolded sheet. 'OK. Well, Sue's route, from the Montenvers train station, Pete and I did a variation last summer. It looks like firstly up a steep zigzag, then a contour round this mountain behind us,' He pointed vaguely over his shoulder at the hut roof but in the direction of the slopes behind, 'and up another steep slope to the edge of the Glacier des Nantillons, over another bit of contouring to this second glacier – the Blaitière, then along a bit and drop down to the cable station.' He looked-up, checking he was getting nods from people. 'It's only four miles or so, tops, but some killing slopes plus we will be exposed to stone-fall all afternoon. Hopefully fab views though – looking back across to our much-loved Aiguilles Rouges.'

'Aye, you're right Simon – and Sue. We should just bloody well get on with it. We'll end-up festering around Cham' spending cash otherwise. I'm up for it. Fifty-fifty the weather will turn out ok' said Dougal. 'We'll need crampons and axes for the wee glaciers to cross. I haven't done them but they look short.'

'Well, we did this last year.' said Peter, 'like Simon mentioned. Just hadn't thought about it for today. It was hot last summer too, an afternoon again. It's hard ice on the glacier bits but not crevassed anywhere, not as far as we could see anyway, and a clear track. There is quite a lot of rock and stone shooting down from the peaks above, as Simon said. We just went across as fast as we could.'

Sue giggled. 'Let's be optimistic then. I haven't come all this way to wear breeches and cagoule though. So, if I can't strip off a bit, we're not doing it – are we Sheena? Well done Pete – you have made my mind up.' Sheena was smiling, feigning a shocked look at Sue.

Actually Sue - it's your idea, you should lead!' Peter objected, but teasingly.

In the end, the group comprised Dougal, Keith, Simon, Peter, Ian, Tony, Sheena and Sue. The two additional men being from the South Wales club. After a brisk and chatty walk to the station, they boarded and found a scattering of seats on the glacier rack railway to the Mer de Glace. The train was busier than expected and while most passengers were in a mix of overcoats, duvet or quilt jackets and ski trousers, the group felt distinctly under-dressed in their mix of shorts and fibre-piles.

But after alighting, and as they ascended the steep and rocky path from the station, they found themselves once again above the remaining valley clouds and the air was very warm. The terrain was rough going but with a distinct path weaving its way through boulders and rocks with mountain sides towering above. Whistling marmots once more accompanying them.

Sheena and Sue had managed to manipulate the grouping so they were for a while together at the back of the line filing up the slope. Sheena said she wanted a chat and suggested they stopped for some water and then take their time catching-up the others again. Sue readily agreed. The two of them smiled broadly at each other, enjoying the unexpected afternoon in mountain sunshine.

Sue spoke first, while repacking the water bottle and putting the rucksack back on. 'What do you think then – us being up here with this lot as company?'

'I know! It's like being escorted a bit.' Stated Sue, with a brief giggle. 'I think I like it!'

They started walking again, but deliberately slowly. The men were all now a couple of hundred yards away.

'Well, would you rather be leading?'

'No fear Sheena – I don't know what I'm doing when we get to the glacier bits. I really just didn't want to stay around Town, making myself a bit depressed.'

Sheena put her arm round Sue's waist and gave her a squeeze. 'I know. Even if we did only resort to having a rip-off coffee at the station back there, I thought it was good to get out too.'

'What do you think of them all then?' asked Sue, tilting her head forward and nodding at the line of men up above them on the trail.

'Oh – right, are we going to do a ranking then?' asked Sheena, both of them starting to giggle again.

'Yeah, actually!' Said Sue, determined sounding. 'Let's do that!'

'Oh, well, look at them, right now they all look quite similar don't they? Think they all score quite highly actually! Dougal and Tony are taller. None of them are fat yet. Your Pete hasn't a beard, nor Tony. Simon, Dougal and Keith's beards are all a bit rugged, Ian's closer and neater. I think they all pass muster pretty well. Mostly eight out of ten.'

'I agree, but he's not my Pete Sheena!' exclaimed Sue.

'He is though Sue, isn't he? A bit anyway? You and he seem pretty close – you can see it and I can feel it in you. Plus you have talked about him quite a lot, to be fair.'

There was a pause while they negotiated a clamber over some boulders and large natural steps which were a stretch. Tony, who was the nearest of the men, shouted back to check they were ok and the two women assured him they were and also manged to persuade him they didn't need any fuss and were happy at the back having a natter.

'So…?' asked Sheena, returning to the theme. 'The thing is I don't see it. What you told me about him. You wouldn't know! Is he really?'

Sue looked enquiringly but knew what Sheena was asking, and answered eventually. 'Yes, he is.'

'It's not obvious is it? I suppose I wondered if him and Simon… you know. When I asked them yesterday how long they had been friends, I think I was looking for a hint of something else. But then again they are the same as a lot of other climbing club guys aren't they! They form bonds with their buddies that are quite close.' She paused, thinking about that. 'I guess when climbing they have to place complete trust in each other don't they?'

'Yeah, that's true. Hmm – all that time ago, Pete had this other friend though. Another geologist. That's how it was to start with anyway. They helped each other with their geological mapping. It never occurred to me and Jules that they were also sleeping with each other. I've told you about it before – and now you've met him! Uncanny how this has happened! That thought though, that they might be gay, never occurred back then – and doesn't crop-up much now either, does it?'

'He's fond of you.' Sheena said. Sue nodded her head in agreement. 'Is he in denial then? I've other friends from college who use that psycho-babble term in other ways. Sorry, what am I trying to say? I suppose I mean, if Pete is like that – well, he doesn't exactly do anything about it does he? He doesn't give off those signals I mean. In fact, he strikes me as fancying you, to be honest, not some other guy!'

They could see now that on an obvious rise on the mountainside, the men were stopping for a breather and that their little chat would have to finish before too long.

'You must have seen how he looks at you?' continued Sheena.

'Yes, I know, I know – I do probably fancy him too. In a way, you know. He's really kind and just nice.' Sue found herself hesitating to say more.

'Plus he's at least eight out of ten.' Sheena said, then stopped and held onto Sue's arm to bring her to a halt too. She looked straight into her friend's eyes. 'Hold on…I think I've just learned something from you Sue! Did you two do something together in Scotland then?' Her voice rising with the surprising realisation this was perhaps true.

'No!' Sue paused, taking a deep breath, looking back down the path they had been following. 'Well, yes actually.' she continued, feeling a little sheepish, being drawn into a confessional moment. 'Before I discovered the other thing about him. We did go pretty far one day. In broad daylight I remember, on a mountainside. He really wanted me and I felt the same about him, but didn't want to get pregnant. You know…' Sue pursed her lips. Now looking at Sheena for reassurance.

'Wow!' exclaimed Sheena. 'Sue, you sweetheart. That explains what I'm noticing' They fell into a hug. 'On my God – you two nearly having it off and then finding out he was doing that with another bloke!' she shook her head. 'Gosh Sue, you are going to have to tell me the whole story about this.'

'I will. But it's going to have to wait – the guys are watching us and waiting!'

Sheena wanted to ask more, but the closeness of the others now brought the conversation to a necessary close. Sue took Sheena's hand and gave it a tight squeeze, which was immediately reciprocated.

When the two women reunited with the men, they had all now arrived at the edge of the boulder-filled moraine running alongside the narrow tongue of blueish ice now right in front of them. This first glacier, the Nantillons, appeared tranquil at first glance.

Ian commented on the view ahead of them. 'From what Pete and

Simon have been saying, when we were back at the campsite, we are going to have to go for it at some pace. There might be some fresh snow on the ice but it's not supposed to be crevassed, you can see it's clear but you never know. As it's early afternoon, it could be like a shooting gallery.'

Simon nodded. 'The ice is steep above and below the path, but last year the track across was well travelled and flattened by crampon wear. You're right though Ian, stones can shoot down like bullets from three or four thousand feet above. You will see them lying around on the ice as we get going'. Everyone grimaced at that point and looked from one to another. 'So, we just have to do it quick, like you said!' he concluded.

The little glacier was sitting in a scooped-out hollow of the mountainside. To get on it involved a fairly steep scramble down loose moraine, stones and boulders of all sizes mixed with coarse grit. They could see it would be the same up the other side. Even as they considered it, they watched amazed as one rock trundled down at some speed and they actually saw another stone fly straight over the end of the glacier.

'We should have brought helmets.' Said Sue.

'No point' Dougal suggested. 'Any of these hit you then a helmet wouldn't stop them. It's a bit nuts doing this!' The last bit spoken softly, almost to himself. 'But we just need to get crampons on and go for it. It will be five minutes and then we are relatively ok.' Peter admired Dougal's old-fashioned gallantry that he thought emerged at moments like this. Even before he said anything, he just knew Dougal was going to take care of Sue and Sheena, which in this case he did by getting Keith to lead across the glacier, getting the women to walk close in line, while positioning himself slightly above them on the ice, seemingly to be hit first by any stones, or at least to provide some sort of early warning.

It made Peter smile. He realised though that all of them, since leaving the campsite, had been attentive to the two women when given the opportunity, although in truth they were more than capable of looking after themselves. He could see that Sue and Sheena had quite enjoyed the attention of the six men though and he hoped the day would especially cheer-up Sue, especially as this mini expedition had been her idea.

The crossing was done in next to no time, then there was a half-mile trudge over a very stony trail to the next one, a bit less steep but consequentially a bit broader. None of this made them feel any safer. They took a break and admired the Aiguilles Rouges chain opposite. Ian and Peter had binoculars and they took turns to identify routes across there that they had done or could still do.

Peter pointed out Lac Blanc to Sue, to which she said. 'Wish I had been in a better mood! It looks more special now than I felt at the time.'

On the way across the moraine of the second glacier they encountered a group of a half-dozen French climbers going the opposite way. Presumably coming off the Aiguille du Midi and heading to a hut on the Mer de Glace, Peter reasoned, or maybe the train station just suited them better. They looked like hard climbers to him – some in their thirties maybe, some their own age, tanned, lean, muscley, mirrored goggles, tall back packs piled high with gear, and so on. Their conversation was loud and they sounded exuberant.

'You can hear them coming a mile off.' said Keith. 'No chance of peace and quiet with that lot on the path.'

'This looks like a group of the sort that talk that loudly at two in the morning,' agreed Dougal.

The path was really just a person wide at this point but they could all see a broader and flatter area ahead, roughly equidistant between the two groups. It would be an obvious point for them all to pass each other.

'What's the betting they don't stop at that lay-by when they get there first?'

'That's a dead cert Tony.' said Ian. 'Well we're nearly there too.'

As had been predicted, the group of French alpinistses showed no awareness of the approaching British group. came straight past the flat area and met the party head on, just a minute or two later, acting then as if it was all the fault of the others, not them. After a bit of shrugging and fussing around, the French made a deliberate show and effort of turning back to the flat area – so it seemed to Peter. It meant there would be a short moment where the two groups were alongside. Peter knew that both nationalities amongst climbers were more than capable of being rude about each other. This time, it seemed some of them made it as awkward as possible for the Brits to squeeze by. Peter could sense that Dougal, in particular, was feeling riled. There was some jostling and feigned sighs of frustration and some muttered comments on both sides.

It could all have been ok though, but as the French party moved off to continue their journey east, the one at the back turned and shouted something. Peter could roughly make out words that sounded like "cease bronlers ay ler poots". He didn't know what it meant but felt it sounded rude.

Dougal waved his arm at them dismissively and received the gesture back from the same French climber who then also clutched his left arm, turning up his forearm and extending his index finger.

'Yeah, whatever, same to you too.' Dougal said, rather than shouted – partly to himself. And they all started to walk along the trail again. 'What did they say Keith – any idea?'

Peter interrupted and said the words he thought he had heard. Keith, who was pretty good at the language having done some grape picking in the past to finance a previous trip, explained that Peter's pronunciation wasn't too bad and that the Frenchman had effectively described the Brits as six wankers.

'Oh! Very nice!' said Dougal. 'We're eight though!?'

'Yeah' said Keith. 'That's the poots bit. Ermm' he hesitated, already anticipating Dougal's reaction. 'Er, the word poot, as Pete said it, that's French slang for whore. It's a very common put-down bit of slang language out here. From blokes anyway. So it was, the whole sentence, more or less - six wankers and their whores.'

Dougal stopped, looked at him, almost in disbelief, mouth dropped open, his face flushed and then his lips pursed as he swung round and started marching quickly back down the track towards the French group. 'Oi, messieurs!' he shouted very loudly.

'Oh God, there's going to be a diplomatic incident' said Keith, quickly stepping onto the trail and then equally rapidly deciding it was better not to make it a group on group confrontation unless it turned nasty. Peter and the rest of them really only had time to react enough to simply watch as Dougal actually caught-up with the other climbers in about a dozen very long and very fast strides – almost bounding along the path. The one who had said the offending words had turned around to face Dougal again, had folded his arms and had his head and shoulders back – defiant-looking.

'Qu'èst ce que vous avez dit?' Dougal asked him, tilting his head slightly to one side and fixing direct eye contact, essentially demanding the Frenchman repeat it.

The guy instead nodded his head back aloofly and, after a deliberate pause, then shook his head very slowly and just laughed. It was cut short though as Dougal grabbed the front of the man's salopettes and yanked him forward, knocking him off balance and causing him to flail his arms trying to keep upright. Dougal struggled to find enough French but wanted clarity of what he was about to say. In the end there was no doubt for either group what he meant. Keith found himself muttering simultaneous translation to the completely silent British group.

'Monsieur! Nous ne sommes pas branleurs, wankers, mais peut-être vous etes! And...' at this point he pulled the climber right up to his face, you could see his bicep braced under his tee-shirt.

'Oi mate, we aren't wankers, but perhaps you are!' said Keith, whispering.

Dougal continued, red-faced now...Elles...' actually shouting, he pointed with his free hand roughly behind him, broadly in the direction of Sue and Sheena, 'Elles sont nos amis. Of the mieux sort in fact! Elles ne sont pas pûtes.' He half spat-out the last bit.

'Those women are our friends, of the best sort in fact. They aren't whores!' Keith's lips hardly moved.

The Frenchman's face tightened and yet he continued to look resolutely, refusing to let himself be intimidated, at Dougal, who responded by shouting even more loudly, 'Quoi!? Qu'ést ce que vous voulez un piolet dans votre tête!?'

Keith took a deep intake of breath, before translating, 'What? Do you want an ice-axe in your head!?'

By this point two more of the French had managed to get control of themselves and the situation – and they dragged the confronted climber backwards. The oldest-looking of them, a bit silvery haired, was clearly taking charge of the situation and, it turned-out, spoke very good English. He had both his hands up in front of him, palms upwards facing Dougal, as the mouthier one was being bundled along the path by his mates. 'Monsieur.' he said very deliberately. 'Monsieur. Desolée. Très desolée. I am very sorry. 'e thought it was a little plaisanterie – a little joke. But 'e is an idiot. I am sorry.'

'The nice bloke is saying he's very sorry, it was just a little joke etc.' said Keith.

Everyone could see Dougal's tension start to dissolve, his shoulders dropped down along with his arms. 'Aye, well, that's as maybe. We are all out enjoying the mountains. There's no need to be bloody offensive.'

'Je suis d'accord monsieur. Encore, I am very sorry. To you and especially to les deux mademoiselles aussi.' And he looked towards Sue and Sheena. He said to them, directly, 'Very, very sorry. 'e is very stupid – and, may I say, selon moi,' and here he tapped his own chest, 'yes, for me you are very beautiful. Both of you. Il me semble que vous;' he motioned his arm indicating all of the men, 'you guys – you are very lucky.'

'Right, nice bloke says he agrees with Dougal and in his opinion us guys are very lucky to have you two women along with us.' Keith smiled.

Bloody charmer, what a diplomat! Peter thought to himself. But he also thought it was nice and also clearly well meant.

The French leader now lowered his up-spread hands slowly, making sure the situation had been defused, and then offered one to Dougal. They shook hands for several seconds and gave each other a bit of a slap on the shoulder. Then just before he turned, the Frenchman looked again at Sue and Sheena, almost clicked his heels, Peter noticed, gave a slight bow to them, and then finally waved at them and then to everyone else. He turned round and trotted off down the track to rejoin the group who had moved some way down the path.

They all suddenly realised they were breathing again. And there were some comradely pats on the back for Dougal. Keith said, 'I think it was that bit of French with the threat of an ice-axe in the head that got the sensible ones into gear.' All of them chuckled, a bit nervously.

To everyone's surprise, Sue squeezed past then, gently pushing them all aside, went up to Dougal, stood up on her feet, put a hand behind his head and gave him a kiss on the cheek. And to the further surprise of everyone, Dougal actually blushed.

Turning round and seeing everyone was looking at her, Sue put her hands on her hips, stared back at them all and said. 'God, you guys!' She shook her head. 'Blooming heck. No wonder the Hundred Years War lasted so long!' She smiled broadly then. 'Well, I don't know about Sheena, but I have to say I think feel a bit like Guinevere now!' They all laughed a little. Tension dissolved completely. Peter just thought she looked radiant in that moment.

Sue and Sheena gave each other another hug, the group sort-of shook itself and they all restarted the walk. Continuing the gradually widening path to the téléphérique station.

After a few yards, Ian weaved amongst the others and came up alongside Peter near the front.

'I don't know about the rest of us but Dougal gets full marks for the Lancelot impression!"

Peter laughed. 'Yeah, that's really good Ian. I liked Sue's quip about Guinivere. Chivalry was definitely in full force back there. He only needed a sword and a shield!'

'Yeah, well, threatening to use his ice axe in that way was maybe a new take on that idea.'

They laughed together, enjoying the moment. Still feeling the release of the tension of the situation.

'You know what though Pete?' Ian paused and stopped walking a moment. 'If he's Lancelot, I reckon you could be Arthur.'

Peter looked at him, figured-out slowly what he was suggesting and shrugged it off.

'Don't know about that. We're just old friends Ian.' Then, thinking this didn't really cover it, added 'she helped me a lot one time, quite a few years back.'

'Erm, maybe Pete, I don't know your past, but when her Colin came on the scene, she brought him on a meet once. Wasn't his thing, you could see. Think a lot of us were a bit wary about him – bit too full of himself. Personally, I thought he was wrong for Sue.'

'Did you? Just on one meeting like that?'

'I suppose so, given it was a Club meet for a weekend, we were all there, crammed into a mountain hut, and he seemed a bit of an outsider straightaway. But he didn't reach out then either - a bit smug or aloof about it. The thing was, in the Club, some of us saw Sue by then, very much as an insider. If you know what I'm getting at.'

'I see what you mean,' said Peter 'the thing about Climbing Clubs though Ian, is a lot of the blokes like having the women along, like Sue and Sheena, but aren't really interested in relationships.'

Ian chuckled a bit. 'That's true. They turn out to be grey-bearded bachelors don't they!' he paused. 'not me though! I liked her from the first time she turned-up in the pub. I would never have wished it on her, but for some reason I imagined myself picking her up if the marriage ever fell-over. I wanted to be Arthur! But you've turned-up now and taken on that role as far as I can see! That's what I reckon anyway – from her reaction to you. I can see it from the way she looks at you.'

Peter wondered about that. He thought Ian was being light-hearted but could hear a real honesty behind the words. 'I don't know' he said. 'I don't think I'm cut-out for quite that role.' And he looked at Ian who had stopped and regarded Peter quizzically. A lot of thoughts ran through Peter's head then, about chivalry and he remembered being concerned for Sue years before. He could see the image of her crossing a scree slope and him guiding her, even though she didn't really need it. 'Maybe I am a bit of a protector at times', he said to himself as much as to Ian.

They both continued the walk, side by side, each in their own thoughts. Peter thought Ian now felt like someone who had been a mate for longer than a day. The conversation had caused him to think. One thing he saw was that Ian was a bit like him, not just a similar height and build, but maybe in personality? Ian had seemed a mix, so far, of being comfortable in his own skin but amiable and chatty too. He had a solid, gently self-assured feel about him like a lot of engineers, so Peter thought.

After another couple of hours, having finished the walk, and taken a busy but easy big cable car descent to the valley, they were all back in the campsite again. After a bit of banter, they went their own ways for showers and suppers, agreeing to go down the bar together later, with whoever else was up for it.

Chapter 5

In fact, when they regrouped later, Peter counted the number going into town was ten people again, including himself and Simon. All of them, without exception, had dark blue fibre-pile jackets on – pretty much the uniform of British climbers, Peter thought, especially in the evenings – the only time they appeared cohesive and sartorially smart. He could see Sue wasn't really in the same place as the rest of them in terms of her outward projection anyway. It wasn't so much a matter of clothing, he felt she just looked a bit sad and could sense this was true. The two of them found themselves side by side, in the middle of the group strung out in pairs walking along the narrow pavement of the main drag leading alongside the river to the bar.

Peter took a deep breath and said, 'You ok Sue? I don't think you really feel like going down the pub do you?'

'No, not tonight Peter, I don't actually.' She gave a bit of shrug and crossed her arms. Their pace slowed down immediately.

'I'm sorry. I thought we had a good day and you seemed bright and cheery earlier. It was great you persuading us all to go out like that. It was funny you being defended by a knight in shining armour!'

She gave a short laugh. 'Oh, I've liked the day. It was fun, really it was. I'm glad we didn't have Keith's diplomatic incident! I was relieved.' She seemed animated one moment than dropped down again the next. 'it's just . . .oh, I dunno. it's just been a bit overwhelming recently really. You asking me about it isn't the problem. Seeing you though…it has reminded me how much my life had become disordered. I hoped this trip would begin a reset for me.'

Peter noticed she had called him by the longer form of his name, which had only happened rarely in the past. It had the effect of making him feel paternal, or fraternal, he wasn't sure which – mostly he felt he wanted to help, to fix things, make it better. He wasn't sure he knew how nor if it was his role to do that. So, quickly finding some inspiration from somewhere, he just said, 'tell you what… how about we buy a bottle of wine in the supermarket? There's the one just coming-up, you know, L'Eclerc, and then go back to the campsite with it? Or I will just walk back with you, if you prefer to just have an early night? Maybe you need some time on your own.' The last bit more of an observation than a question.

Sue stopped walking, hesitated then took Peter's hand and said, 'yes please. Would you mind? Can we do that? We'll have to be quick to go into the supermarket right now though. It will close at seven, any minute. Pete, it's a nice thought - I would really like that.'

The others seemed disappointed but amicable. Peter felt he could discern a concern for Sue from Sheena and others, and he felt like an interloper. Who was he to be acting closely with Sue, when this was mostly her group of friends she saw every week or so? He noticed Ian was looking straight at him though, nodding slowly with eyebrows raised, saying everything without speaking.

Twenty minutes later, they were back on the ground in front of the door of Sue and Sheena's tent and Peter was opening a bottle of the local Savoy red. The temperature was falling away quickly and it looked like being a cold night coming up. They still had their fleecy jackets on but Peter agreed readily when Sue suggested sitting inside the tent. Sheena, he found out, had brought a couple of large, sturdy candles with her, which were placed on old saucers in the door area of the tent. With the flysheet closed, they actually produced some welcome warmth as well as light. They were sitting cross-legged and Peter noticed, and liked, the extra head height in Sheena's tent compared to his own.

'I think we should finish our chat from the other morning.' Sue looked at Pete and she gave a wan smile.

'Are you sure? I was concerned about you. I had such a strong memory of you and me talking on the mountains right back in Kinlochewe days. I know we met quite a bit after Uni, those winter trips to the Cairngorms and so on, before Colin came along, but it reminded me of that time in the far north-west. Because of how you seemed different today, not how you were the same.'

'You've lost me a bit there Pete. What do you mean?'

Peter realised he felt a bit unsure of what he was trying to say, wanting to say. 'Hmm – yeah, that was a bit muddled. Well… back then, you were so open. We talked about so many things, even though we had only known each other five minutes. You had this ability to get me, and others, to open up and share stuff – and you did the same in return. I have never seen you do the opposite; just clam up a bit like you did on the way to Lac Blanc.'

'Yeah?' Peter stayed silent then as he saw Sue thinking about the conversation they were having. It looked to him as if she could be upset and he was rapidly trying to think how to manage the flow, deciding staying quiet was the best thing, if he could.

'Well, it's just been pretty awful Pete.' Sue said, eventually.

Peter could see now she looked and sounded sad. Her head dropped a bit, and a swathe of her long hair fell forward. He put his hand on her upper arm.

'You go first Pete.' She said, without looking up. 'Come on, let's finish the history bit.'

'Ok, if you're sure'. He took a deep breath, a bit exaggeratedly he realised, 'but there's not much to add really to what I said. You know some of this. After Uni, as predicted, we all got involved with working lives didn't we? Penny and I were apart and we became more like that. She got involved with one or two other men and eventually married one of them. You know that far in the story now.' Sue still didn't look-up. 'That was the end of a long on-off-on-off relationship for me, as you will remember. Shall I keep going?'

'Yeah. It's fine. It's funny though, I hardly ever smoke now, but I really want one.' She did glance up briefly then. 'It's talking with you in a tent that's brought it on! You used to feed them to me all the time back then.' She suddenly looked-up fully, smiled, and Peter felt the whole interior of the tent became brighter immediately.

'I have a packet of Marlborough, for emergencies, but try to avoid them these days too.'

'French Marlborough?'

'Yes. I know what you mean. They taste different and are better than the UK ones.' He thought about going to get them, but didn't want to break the conversation.

'Anyway, I had a short and intense fling with someone – on the rebound I suppose. Met this person on a club trip, and we had a really passionate thing but when she came to see me in Bristol, it didn't work-out – two different worlds I suppose. It was ok when we were both in the one, but not when we were in the other. I'd never done anything like that before. You know, chat to someone in the pub, then going straight to bed and stuff.'

'Nice for you while it lasted though. Eh?' asked Sue. 'I am making an assumption about how physical that relationship was. That's how Colin and I were at the start, you know? But, unlike your description, I thought we actually were in the same world. Only realised our worlds were different a while later. But carry on. Please.'

They were sitting cross-legged, facing each other. Peter experienced another flashback to an intense conversation about the same things really. Love in its manifest forms. The mental image he saw now though – both he and Sue were so young then – and yet, she hadn't changed much physically and now the emotion of the conversation also felt so familiar. He felt as if he just was back there and could remember the scene so readily. He would have felt comfortable just staying with that memory, but Sue was watching him, with that look again, waiting for him to continue.

'It's something about pubs I think! Hmm – there's one I went to when I started management training. I was sent here and there to get different work experience. Anyway, in this one place, there was a Trophy Tavern. I was only staying there a night. The two blokes running the place were very friendly. Locals muttered about them at the bar I noticed. "two blooming poofs" one of them said. But it also appeared that anything's excusable if you run a good pub, which they did, so they got away with it.'

'But they were a gay couple then?'

'Yeah, they were. Nice people, one older and one a fair bit younger.'

'And you found out for sure they were gay did you?'

Peter found himself blushing. Why did that reaction happen? Sue knew about this from the whole thing with Steve in Kinlochewe, so it wasn't really revealing a secret, and yet he felt like he was disclosing something – something he had kept to himself. He also realised there was probably nothing he could, nor would, keep secret from Sue though. It struck him how uncanny it was to have met her again out here like this.

'Yes. I haven't told this to anyone. Bit of a confession I suppose. Not happy about it really. But it was obviously around the time we were less in touch with each other Sue – getting on with our lives. And it was a real one-off with them. They got me very drunk. Or I allowed it I suppose. I stopped the night with them. Was sick as a dog in the night and in the morning. I regretted the alcohol.'

'So, is that it then? Steve and you never got back together, I know. No other gay adventures anywhere?'

'No!' He found himself feeling a bit prickly now, uncomfortable about the memories he had surfaced. 'I don't think it's me. It's just a thing. Something I did. It's in the past.' He looked at her, found himself trying to be defiant but failing rapidly. 'I was so drunk, I don't even know what happened that time – you know…in bed. Of course, it was very different to what happened with Steve… that was, well, you know!' He found himself faltering, saying too much. 'It happened then but hasn't happened since – not like that.' Sue returned his look with one that seemed to Peter a mixture of concern and confusion. He actually felt pretty confused about what he had been saying too.

'This is what I think Pete; I don't believe people go through a phase with this sort of thing. You know, some people say "it's just a phase, he or she will grow out of it". I think it's pretty remarkable though what you have said. I wonder why there hasn't been more? I saw you turned inside out by the relationship with Steve all that time ago.' She paused. 'I still think that's you.' She put her hand on his leg for a moment and then reached over and poured some more wine. Handed a glass to Peter. Instead of picking up the other glass, she just sighed deeply.

'But with you in front of me again now Pete, I also remember just feeling close to you then too.'

'Sue, you need to know – I have never forgotten the affection with you, that I felt we shared. Still share? You were also the emotionally intelligent one amongst a group of juveniles. This is how I remember it.'

She took a deep breath. 'I don't know about that – we were all just growing-up. I felt this attraction to you though Peter.' She sighed again, reached for a tissue and blew her nose lightly. 'And it's just so lovely you are here right now talking with me, listening to me…' her voice drifted off.

Peter had been reflecting on all they had been saying and was sinking into a deep memory when he suddenly saw and heard Sue make a funny noise in her throat a little and he was moved to see a few tears starting to run down her face. She dropped her head and then started to cry more freely, some of the tears dripping onto the foam sleeping mats and groundsheet. He rushed to put his wine glass down and put his arms round her and gently pulled her forward so her head was against his chest. He felt himself starting to well-up a bit too as Sue just settled there.

'Oh Sue…' He was panicking now, trying to think what to say. 'I can feel it.' Then he decided any words just risked being clumsy, and his heart went out to her. He just continued to hold her, feeling choked and unable to think clearly what else to say or to be able to say it.

After a few minutes, Sue recovered a bit, still had her head lowered and was running her hands through her hair, sweeping it back repeatedly over her shoulders, finally holding it all there with her two hands locked together on the back of her neck.

'Bloody hell Sue. Think this is one of those emergencies I mentioned! If this isn't time for a fag, I don't know when is. I'll be back in a minute.' And Peter rushed out of the tent.

Returning with the Marlboroughs, he lit two and gave one to Sue. She looked tensed-up, her face streaked, still snuffly and trembling a little. Peter thought she was cold and put his jacket round her.

'You know, I can remember you lighting a ciggie for me like that in your own tent that time.'

They smoked the cigarettes quietly, sipping the wine. Neither speaking, but it not feeling uncomfortable for either of them. Peter felt pretty shocked to see Sue like this. He realised how close to her it made him feel, and he wished he could just put a sticking plaster over it or something, whatever it was.

Sue suddenly started speaking again. 'I was knocked-off my feet by Colin, that's for sure. He was so physical and it had an effect on me I never expected. I wanted him as much as he wanted me, at first anyway. This is the short version Pete – I need to do this quickly, or I won't get it out at all.' She sat up straight and Peter saw some tear tracks and noticed she still sounded nasal like she had a blocked nose.

She continued, speaking quickly. 'At first I couldn't do enough for him, and then I realised he just expected it. I started doing things for him, food, washing, breakfast in bed, you know - to be nice. But he more and more expected me to do those things. The word please went from the conversations. "Please could you get me a tea sweetheart" became "can you get me another tea then?". That sounds so small, doesn't it? But it was hundreds of things. I had a job too, but that made no difference. It started to make me resentful and that put me off him a bit in bed. A big no-no.'

'Was it?'

'Oh yeah. He wasn't having that. We would go out, maybe for a drink, come back and he would want it straight away – lounge, kitchen, wherever. If I tried to wriggle out of it, he would use his strength of will to make me give in. Again, these things progress, don't they? So, for a while it seemed easier to go along with it but then I became resentful of that too.' She paused.

'Do you want to stop Sue?'

'No, please Peter, just don't speak. Just shut up, please. I need to keep going. I just need to draw breath.' She reached and used another tissue. 'I tried to talk with him about all this, me being the do-everything housewife, but he didn't care. Shrugged. Would walk off and go down the pub, expecting me to clear-up. Talking about the sex thing was hopeless. He actually said "I'm your husband. What the bloody hell do you expect to do?" He didn't hit me, in case you're wondering, but did push himself on me – usually with a smile, but it was impossible to stop him to be honest.' She looked away towards the dark end of the tent.

'He could…oh, I don't want to tell you. I sometimes found it really uncomfortable, painful sometimes. He never noticed. Didn't care when he was like that.' She paused. 'Recently I have found it he was seeing his old girlfriend too, had been for some while. Still is, in fact.'

She stopped then, her face crumpled again for a moment. Just a tear or two this time. Peter found himself tensed-up like a spring. Sue lifted her head to look at him, biting her lower lip a little. 'What do you think? I'm stupid aren't I?'

Peter felt himself almost rigid, with an intensity of emotions. 'I think if he was here now…If he was just out there, then I would just go straight over and hit him, full on, no hesitation.' And he felt shocked at the force of his reaction. He found himself fumbling for another cigarette and realised he was now the one shaking.

'Oh Peter, are you wanting to be my white knight now? Gosh!, I can't remember seeing you bristle like this before.' She leant back then, arms at her sides, leaning on her hands. 'Oh, don't get angry, I'm just feeling sorry for myself. I don't know why I didn't see what he was like from the start.'

'Don't blame yourself Sue. He took advantage of you. The bastard.' He tried to order his thoughts. 'I'm angry because you just deserve better.'

She reached over and stroked the side of his face gently. After a moment she said 'I need to move. To do something I think. Shift myself and the mood. How about we walk down the road a bit? Maybe we will meet the others coming back?'

'Because it's bloody freezing Sue!' But he could see she was right about needing to change the scene. 'Oh, alright then, of course, you're right, it will clear our heads. And our lungs.'

They met the others but only after walking nearly all the way back into the centre of Chamonix. Peter chatted to Simon on the return and got to speak with a couple of the others in Sue's Club – Ian again and his climbing buddy Tony. Everyone was in good spirits and Peter was pleased when he looked around and saw Sue had linked arms closely with Sheena and another friend, Wendy, seemingly cheered-up a bit. It really had been a head-clearing exercise, just into Town and straight back again.

Once not walking, back at the campsite, everyone noticed how cold it had become – too chilly to hang around much. Everybody was in a hurry to say good night and get settled. After a very rapid teeth cleaning, coming out of the loo block hut, Peter was surprised to bump into Simon carrying a rolled-up sleeping bag, which he then realised was his own. 'There's been a change of plan Pete. Not quite sure what it's about but it looks like I'm on my own tonight.'

'Eh? What's that about then. It's my tent, you can't evict me!' Feeling a bit irritated, Peter decided it was best to just go along happily with whatever was happening, really though just wanting to lie down and rest. Sue came up to them at that point and Simon stepped back into the shadows a bit.

'Pete.' Sue said quietly, standing very close. 'It'll be ok with Wendy, that's my other friend, she doesn't mind. Sheena will go to her tent.' Peter knew he looked a little perplexed. 'Simon's got your sleeping bag there.' She now looked right into his eyes and he remembered her ability to speak visually like she was now – encouraging him to do something. 'Would you come and be with me in the tent tonight? Please?'

Even though the exterior neon light on the hut was quite dim, he could see it reflected on Sue's eyes, now looking a little moist. He knew that she knew, he couldn't, and wouldn't, refuse the request. He nodded to Simon, took his sleeping bag from him and went with Sue back to Sheena's tent.

Inside, he found himself feeling time compress around him again as he had the sharp memory of a conversation with Sue in his own tent years earlier. Back then, having just effectively come-out to her, she had spent two or three nights with him and they had hugged through all of them, or so it felt to his memory. Now Sue was asking him for the same thing.

'Come on Pete. We can put one bag open on top of the other. We'll keep our undies on though, ok? Like we did that time before. And T-shirts. Quick, it's cold.' And she had pretty well stripped-off while talking. Peter did the same.

'Loose boxer shorts now eh?'

Peter felt a bit self-conscious at that. 'Er - I just like these – they're the thing now aren't they? I blame the bloke in the launderette. You know? The TV advert.' Sue laughed at that. Again Peter felt the mood lift instantly as she smiled. 'They are alright in the evenings but I can't go clambering around in them or climbing. You know - things get caught-up if you're stretching or clambering around...'

'Stop! No, I don't know Pete - and that's enough information, thank you! Just get in. Come on. That's it. We'll be snug in a minute.'

Peter was amazed how cosy he indeed felt as Sue wrapped herself around him and they held a long hug. No sooner had they started the cuddle though, he could feel a couple more tears emerging again from Sue and he hugged her a little bit tighter. It seemed to settle after a while, her face buried into his chest, her hair half-smothering his face and mouth. He found a tear of his own emerging, in sympathy with hers.

It shook him how much the moment caused him to recall the intense hugs of what had until now felt like a different age. In some crazy way to Peter it seemed like the present and past were on top of each other at this moment. He recalled now how upset he had been trying to figure out what he felt for Steve and what that meant for who he was. How brilliantly Sue had helped him confront the reality of what was going on then and how she had befriended and supported him when he felt at sea with his own emotions.

Now here was the same woman, this time confronting the reality of her own life and looking to him for comfort and support in turn.

And he found himself wanting to provide it in abundance. He felt grateful to have been put in this position by chance. They went on hugging until at some point Sue noticeably relaxed, blew her nose quite a bit, snuggled into him again.

'Thanks Pete, this is just the most comfortable feeling right now. How strange us meeting again. I'm sorry for all this pathetic crying though. You have brought it out of me.' There was a long pause. 'That's probably a good thing really.'

After a while, Peter wasn't sure how long had passed or how much he had been asleep. He awoke, lying on his back, Sue facing away from him but her body pressed closely along the length of his. He just listened to her steady breathing and wondered dreamily about the way life could take unexpected turns. He liked to feel in control of what he was doing but in the middle of the night like this, could feel surprisingly calm and relaxed even when dramatic things happened, right out of the blue.

He was enjoying the sleepy reverie when he realised Sue had woken too. She turned round and put an arm across his chest. He turned to face her and then they were wrapped in a close embrace again. After a moment, she lifted her head from his chest. He could sense, more than see, her looking at him. Their mouths found each other's and they kissed on the lips, at first tentatively and then a bit more fully. Peter felt dizzy and giddy as the pleasure and sensation of the kiss united with one in his own tent, in a similarly tight hug, eight years previously. In fact, it felt uncannily like the same one had never really stopped.

Chapter 6

If any of the others felt it had been odd that Sue and Peter spent a night together, nobody said anything. Peter had only received more raised eyebrows and another piercing look from Ian, and Simon had given him a friendly, but largely silent interrogation over breakfast. Mostly this was about concern for Peter and checking he was ok and still happy. Sheena and Sue, they had seen, had gone off for a little mooch.

It was an in-between day again, the bad weather still in abeyance. All of them assessed it was a deterioration from the previous day but it could easily feel wasted if they just hung around the campsites. Cloud was pretty low, so nobody wanted to do anything that would require an overnight in a hut, nor going too high. Peter knew that Dougal and Keith's girlfriends would be arriving at some point and that would be an excuse to meet at the Alpenstock early. Simon and he conferred over the 1:25,000 map and then quickly rounded-up interested people for a walk up to the Glacier de Bossons, no more than a two mile walk each way, and straight from the campsite itself.

A small crowd of them converged onto the start of the steep but well-used path mostly in amongst tall trees, that also crossed, three times, the approach road for the Mont Blanc Tunnel. Simon navigated, although it was straightforward most of the time. After the last bit of road they made a brief stop to view the Tunnel opening itself, which they agreed seemed so small compared to the vast bulk of mountain which it penetrated.

After that. the route took them over a large stile off the Tunnel road, and then to La Buvette de Boissons, a small snack and drinks hut, where they had coffee from a woman who looked and dressed like a climber herself. She was both surprised and pleased to see them, on what was obviously a very slow day for her. Ian insisted on paying for everyone, saying he had just had his first-ever bonus at work and felt like sharing some of it. An offer that was gratefully accepted by all of them.

Then they passed a vicious-looking dog chained-up to a woodland hut that barked incessantly, before finally making a horizontal approach to the glacier itself. At that point, the ice was very massive and rose above them, split by many crevasses of various sizes, some proper chasms looking incredibly blue in their interior. So, even though they were still quite close to the valley floor, the place had a high mountain feel about it and a tangible sense of danger. They explored around a bit on the glacier, at least where it looked safe and watched amazed when a large collapse of seracs occurred, just a short, but mercifully safe, distance from them. The massive towers of ice must have been hundreds of tons each thought Peter.

The dramatic fall of the ice put them off further wandering around and they soon reversed the path back down the way they had come, once again both aggravating the dog and then pleasing the buvette woman a second time by having another round of hot drinks and sitting at the rudimentary assemblage of chairs and café tables amongst the trees. Despite protestations from Ian, everyone paid their own way this time.

'Wendy and I have been talking about next summer.' Announced Sheena, somewhat out of the blue. 'I wonder who else might fancy a change from the Alps and go up to Scotland instead? What do you think? Why not go to the Highlands?'

Nobody had really expected a conversation about what to do in twelve months' time, so there was no reaction for a moment or two.

Simon broke the silence first, answering Sheena's question. 'Er, two reasons I can think of! Midges is one thing…and rain another.' He received affirmative nods from others.

Sheena persisted. 'Well, out here the weather yesterday and today hasn't been reliable either, has it? It doesn't have to be like that up there.' She paused. 'I'm talking about the far north by the way.

As far as you can get without swimming to Orkney.' Sheena had everyone's attention now. 'My Mum has a cottage right up there and Wendy and I think it might be a change from the Alps. It's windy most of the time – tends to keep the midges off.'

'I've heard you talk about it before. Yeah – I might be interested.' Sue chipped-in.

'Sounds like a girls' trip developing.' Suggested Tony.

'I don't know,' said Peter. 'I could be up for that too. I would miss the sunshine and shorts maybe but there's other attractions.'

'Ha! You mean the rocks!' Simon quipped, to laughter from others.

'That's true Simon. They are great rocks up there!' Peter said, realising he was immediately attracted to the idea.

Ian looked at him curiously. 'There's a lot of rock here, you'd think. Over on your Aiguille Rouges, there's no trees up high, not much ice, but plenty of rock everywhere.'

'Ahh Ian. There's rocks and there's rocks.' Said Sue. 'You don't know Pete! He's going to tell you in a moment that the north of Scotland has the best rocks in the world…'

'Sue, you stole my line. I was just going to say exactly that…' replied Peter. 'I love them but understand they might not fire everyone's passion. They do happen to make great mountains though.'

'That's true, and it's not great weather here just now is it?' said Wendy. 'It might be nice to explore up there. Plus I think a holiday that isn't entirely focused on mountaineering, all the time, day in, day out, might be nice. I fancy devouring a load of books for one thing. Never seem to get the right time for that. It would be very different for me.'

'Well, you could stay at home and do that – if you just want to read!' said Simon, hoping he didn't sound dismissive.

'Oh, come on Simon,' Peter interjected. 'the last three years, it's been Cairngorms every winter, Alps in the summer – we could all do other things. That's all. We do all have other interests after all!'

'Thanks Pete.' Said Wendy, puckering her lips and blowing him a quick kiss.

'It's not all about rocks for me either,' continued Peter, and it doesn't have to be all about books, or anything else. I'm perhaps a bit biased though. I love it up there, as everyone probably knows by now.'

The discussion continued a bit, but then largely broke-up as people made the descent back to the campsite. The four who had been enthusiastic so far, stayed back and had a talk about practicalities. Peter thought it sounded good but realised it would almost certainly mean letting down Simon, as he wouldn't have the holiday time from work to do both things. He spent much of the rest of the walk quietly thinking to himself and trying to get his head around the question of what he really wanted to do in life generally, not just summer holidays.

Ian came alongside him though as they reached the broader path across the fields towards the campsite. 'Persuade me then Pete. I've never been north of Fort William or Inverness. Tell me about Suilven or something.'

'I've not done that one Ian. Looked at it from the road. There's a geological viewpoint nearby – looks out across a range of mountains, including Suilven, Stac Polly, Quinag – others you will know by name. Nothing like the height of the Alps, but wonderful in a very different way. And once you go north, beyond those places you mention, you enter into…well it feels like a different country. There's an emptiness – no, not empty, a wildness. That's a better term. It's the oldest bit of the UK too, oldest bit of Europe in fact. Geologically. It calls to me, to be honest.'

'I can hear in your voice Pete – you could sway me, I think.'

By mid-afternoon they were, as they had intended, all back in the Alpenstock – completely taking-over the raised area of the bar. Everyone who had been out in the mountains had returned safely. Dougal and Keith's girlfriends had arrived and the combined grouping of climbers was keeping Maurice and Yvette very busy. The two new women settled in immediately, ensconcing themselves with Sue, Wendy and Sheena and pushing-out the guys.

It meant Peter found himself talking with Simon a lot again and planning what else to do before they had to go home. They still had a week or more left but the next two days were confirmed as 'orageux' on the météo sign. All other detail had been omitted but for this single word, gloomily alerting everyone to a period of storms. People knew it would last a couple of days and in fact the rain was starting by the time everyone got back to campsite in the gathering dark, having spent a large part of the afternoon and early evening chatting. Many routes had been described, relived or planned over beers and various hot and cold delights from the Alpenstock team. All of them were tipsy and heading for a good night's sleep and an unhurried morning.

By daylight it was lashing down. Peter and Simon resisted stirring as long as possible. It was hell going out for any necessity, and the coming back was all about trying not to bring water into the tent. On one occasion, Simon had taken his ice-axe outside and dug a number of drainage grooves in the ground around the tent, to stop the copious rainfall accumulating too rapidly and potentially flooding them.

It went on a whole day and before they knew it, everyone was settling in for another damp and desultory night, with a likely repeat the next day too.

Peter couldn't stand it and, on the second stormy morning determinedly got himself up and organised to go into Town for a morning coffee, maybe a cake or something to cheer himself up. Simon joined him and they went round the Welsh crowd to see if there were any other takers. The three women came along first, with Ian and Tony and a couple of others threatening to join in later, if it stopped raining for a bit. Peter thought there was no chance of that happening. The storm had got stuck in the valley, thunder was rolling around the whole time and the rain had only just moved from being torrential to steady, but looked like staying that way for hours.

Dougal and Keith's girlfriends, Heather and Linda, were in the bar already. So, it meant Simon and Peter were now with five women, and both of them found themselves feeling pleased about it, both of them guessing they might talk about more than mountains and climbing. Conversation was actually very animated and Yvette and Maurice fussed around them bringing cakes, which they went to get from the patisserie, baguette-sandwiches and coffees. Peter thought they were pleased to have their custom, as they were pretty much the only ones in there.

Heather said she thought it typical for the weather to do this, almost sounding as if it was a personal punishment. Linda and her had been in Annecy just a couple of days before coming here, enjoying the sun and even swimming in the lake, in warm sunshine. Now she said, they had left Dougal and Keith planning climbs in one of their tents, maps spread all over the groundsheet – something they could easily do, and were happy to do, all day long.

'I sometimes think they are better at planning the climbs than actually doing them!' said Linda.

'They've struggled a bit to get up stuff so far,' said Simon, 'but I know what you mean. It's the same for us all though.' He looked at Peter. 'The scale of the Alps is a lot different to anything back home.'

'Another reason for considering northern Scotland then!' Suggested Wendy.

'Oh, I don't know about that. I quite like it in winter when, in a

65

way, you are going there for bad weather! The more snow, the better on Cairngorm. But warm and wet days on the hills don't have the appeal of the mountains out here. The fine days make up for any bad ones.'

'Yeah, but right now Simon, you could be ensconced in Sheena's cottage – you've been screaming to get out of the tent the last twenty-four hours!' said Peter.

'Maybe, that's just sharing with you.' Suggested Sue, to giggles from the others.

'Well, Linda and I have taken action,' announced Heather. 'We can't come from sunny Annecy to this in one go. I'm not sure the boys will like it, but on the way here we stopped and just booked ourselves into the hotel across the street from the campsite, just for a night. Dougal will complain about the cost but secretly he will revel in it after sleeping on those high altitude climbing hut floors.'

'I'd never have thought of doing that! What, stay in a hotel - just to get away from the tent?' asked Peter, feeling a bit incredulous.

'You make it sound like it's a daft idea Pete!' Linda said. 'You might want to think about it though. The hotels are in a bit of a dip now – all the French have gone back after Assumption Day and they won't be doing so much business until skiing starts. I've done it before elsewhere, because this always happens doesn't it, with the weather?'

'You and Simon could get a twin room for a night - nicer than the soggy tent.' Suggested Heather. 'Or you three girls could get a room?'

Peter noticed Linda look at Heather and then they both glanced at Sue. He wondered how and when they had become aware that another possible pairing was not him and Simon but him and Sue. And now the thought had come into his own head too, Peter realised he liked this nascent idea. He was cheered by the thought of a warm bed and the memory again came into his head of spending time with Sue, years back, in a tent, reading books together, drinking tea and hugging the afternoon and a night away. He looked up at Sue and found her looking at him. Was it conceivable, he wondered, that she was thinking the same thing?

Simon, perceptive as ever, and no doubt also thinking of the cash, said 'I don't know Heather, I'm happy enough in the tent I think. I've diverted all the water now. Managed to build a mini dam. I even got a thumbs up from Ian for my engineering skills! So, I'm ok actually. Others can do it if they wish.' He made a point of looking at Peter encouragingly.

'Well, for me, I think that sounds great!' said Wendy, with Sue and Sheena nodding agreement. Then, being practical, added, 'But your hotel Heather would be that big Alpine chalet-style place near your end of town, right?'

'Yeah, they have loads of rooms empty. But look, don't worry about that. All the hotels are probably in the same position aren't they? Why not try one of the ones nearer where you are?'

'We'll book into a restaurant too.' Added Linda. 'Decided to make a whole evening of it. Bit of a splurge on money, but gets us away from the blooming rain!'

There then ensued a conversation, mostly for Linda and Heather's benefit, about places to eat, and where was good value, or not from what they collectively knew. However, Sue, Wendy and Sheena all dipped out of the conversation after a while and slipped off to the women's toilet together, leaving Peter to speak with Simon about leaving him for an evening.

The Ladies' loo and washroom was quite cramped, but roomy enough for the three of them to have a talk. Wendy immediately leant back on one of the two hand basins and Sheena settled beside her, practically sitting on the other one. Sue faced them and said, 'Looks like you two are about to give me a questioning.'

'Maybe we are!' said Sheena, sounding friendly but concerned.

'Look, you told me about Scotland. Are you really thinking you are going to check-in to a hotel room with Pete?'

'Well, we haven't decided that have we, I thought the three of us might share.' Said Sue, trying to protest but knowing her heart wasn't in it.

'Hold on!' said Wendy. 'Is there more to this than I know? I thought the three of us might share a room too, but I saw just then in the bar, Sheena flitted her eyes from you, Sue, to Pete and back, am I being slow on the uptake? What's this about?"

There was a moment of quiet while the three women exchanged slightly quizzical looks with each other. Sheena broke the silence.

'Sue and I had quite a talk on the glacier walk the other day Wendy. Is it alright to say Sue?'

Sue nodded and Sheena continued, fixing her attention on Wendy. 'This might surprise you, but Sue and Pete got to know each other pretty well some while back.'

'What!' Wendy knew she sounded disbelieving, but that was how she felt. 'You said the hug in the tent the other night was just that! A hug.' Wendy noticed her voice and hoped she was coming across as surprised, not hurt.

'It was Wendy.' Said Sue, reaching across and touching her friend's arm. 'I haven't been keeping anything from you really. Pete and I kept our pants on and it was a lovely cuddle with him because it made me feel safe and comforted. But…'

'…But, back in the past, it was quite a bit more than that. One time anyway.' Explained Sheena.

Wendy looked confused now. 'You slept together? I mean, properly slept with each other? How's that happen? I thought you said he was gay?'

Sue ran through the story briefly and brought both of them up to speed with the conversation she'd had with Peter. She also said that she thought another reassuring, comfortable, hug with him, in a hotel room would be nice and would continue to help her feel good about herself again.

Sheena spoke for both herself and Wendy, who both now looked at Sue with concern. 'Come on, don't be silly. It's not the room Sue, it's the bed! You told me Peter fancied you probably and this is not like being in my tent with a joined-up sleeping bag and him in his boxer shorts. He's spent the last five years convincing himself that he's not gay, cuddling you probably reinforced that. It's not going to be the same thing in a hotel bed. You've already gone nearly all the way with him, even if it was a long time ago. You know that! So, is that what you want?'

Sue took a while to answer, looking at her two friends, feeling a bit embarrassed for the focused attention she felt she was receiving.

'I love you two!' Sue said, and they all fell into a brief hug. She took a deep breath. 'I don't know …Whenever I have thought of being laid again, since Colin, it's mostly made me feel a bit yuck! But, I want to get over that feeling.' She said eventually, casting her head downwards a little. 'Do you know what I mean?'

Sheena and Wendy both immediately reached out an arm and pulled Sue closer towards them again.

'Of course we do pet.' There was a lull in the conversation for a moment or two. 'Right, well! Practicalities then.' continued Sheena, softly. 'Number one – you're not on contraception, so you need to get something. Préservatifs is what johnnies are called out here. You need a pharmacist – there's a few and they have a big green cross outside. That sign is illuminated if they are open.'

Sue took in this information and nodded, wondering where that bit of knowledge had come from but with no time to ask.

'And number two,' said Wendy, 'I don't want this to be a downer. You've said Pete does nothing about his gayness. I hope that's true, because in the lab at Uni we are hearing a lot of strange stuff coming out of the States just now. Particular groups of people are being struck down by this new apparently sexual disease, the one they're calling HTLV3, or some now calling it AIDS – don't worry about the technical abbreviations though. Nobody knows why it's affecting certain groups. Homosexual men is one of those, but I guess if he's not doing anything, then there's no risk.' She paused, aware of the strong attention of the other two. 'Sheena's préservatifs, if I've said it right, possibly are a barrier anyway.'

'I've just thought of a number three!' said Sheena. 'What happens after?'

With both pairs of eyes of her friends upon her, Sue had to think. 'You mean, when we're all back at home?' Nods from the other two. 'I really don't know. I'm not a one-night stand girl.'

'And he's clearly not that sort of guy either. Awww Sue, what's going to be best for you?' Asked Wendy.

The conversation went round for a few minutes more, until they all become conscious of having been away from the others for what now seemed a very long time.

'I've made my mind up!' stated Sue after a moment or two of silence amongst them. The three of them had a close hug together again, exchanged quick kisses on the cheek, and then returned to the bar.

Simon and Peter thought they had been away for ages but were both too polite to comment. Sitting back down, the three women settled-down and after sipping the recently arrived second round of coffees, Sheena spoke first.

'Look, we're not, hopefully, embarrassing anyone here,' she looked at Peter, 'but Pete, you and Sue have already stayed in my tent together. So, why don't you two treat yourselves to a room? Wendy, if you don't mind love, you and I could maybe share another?' These comments were put as questions but Peter could see the three women had worked-out what they wanted to do already.

Heather said, 'That all sounds fine then.' She had picked-up on the what the loo conversation must have entailed, and added, 'Just think of it as a tent Pete – just one with more solid walls, and a much comfier groundsheet.'

But Peter started to think that a hotel was very different to a tent in more ways than the walls. He realised Sue and her friends must have talked about it and they had probably assumed he would go along with the plan. He didn't mind that, but he was just running through his mind what might happen in the hotel.

He and Sue had spent some time out in the wilds of north-west Scotland and in one afternoon had got to know each other pretty intimately, without consummating their friendship completely. Contraception had been the issue. He remembered Sue was maybe surprised it hadn't been followed through later though. Leastways, she might have been a little perplexed for a while, until she figured-out what was really happening between him and Steve! After that, the possibility of fuller relations had evaporated he thought. But now? Was it the same? It was a long time ago. 'Maybe this will stop me thinking of other stuff,' Peter started to consider how he would feel later.

There was a discussion about which hotel to select and to make an enquiry. Heather and Linda's hotel choice was definitely too far to walk from the campsite being used by the others. Peter looked at Sue. He had his arms on his thighs, lifted them slightly and opened his hands in a gesture of enquiry to her. Sue pursed her lips, appeared to think about it for a second and then nodded her confirmation.

'That's it then.' said Peter. 'How about we try that big place near Le Brévent cable station? That tall one with the balconies and the big sloping roof. It has a sign saying something about views onto the Bossons Glacier and Mont Blanc. You might have to pay more for those rooms though I suppose.'

'Don't bother', said Simon, who had otherwise been quiet

through all this. 'You're not exactly going to get any view are you? Not in this weather!?' They all laughed.

'OK, we don't want to spend money on a room with a view, that's true. But if we're going to do it we might as well be comfortable. I don't want to stay in one of those crappy places like we might stop in for a night on the way to and from the ferry.' Peter asserted, to nods from everyone. Then everyone started to chat at once – the women mostly.

'You really sure though Simon?' asked Peter, quietly, thinking that once again Simon's planning ability was to the fore.

'Yeah of course. I can spread out for a night, for a change. Look…', he said, lowering his voice and just speaking with Peter, '…you and Sue are obviously close. You told me you spent that night before last just hugging her in the tent. Whatever your friendship is, it can only help, can't it?'

Peter wondered if this was true. He realised he was starting to imagine in his head, that this hotel stay could be the moment he and Sue did more than sleep and cuddle together. Right now he wasn't sure how he felt about it all. Simon was right, he thought, "whatever your friendship is, it can only help." Peter had never considered, since Kinlochewe, that he and Sue could be girlfriend and boyfriend. And it was obvious why!

His mind drifted and then focused in on a warm morning, in his tent. He and Sue had the most intense discussion. They were both just twenty. He could remember nearly biting through his lip, trying to hold back the overwhelming emotion as Sue got him to admit to the relationship he had been having with Steve. So, why would she want to sleep with him? Sue was there! She knew what had happened and had treated him since as a good friend, a really good friend at times, but! There is a but, Peter could feel a big but about the boundary between being a friend and being a lover. Weren't he and Sue just affectionate about each other. Affectionate friends?

Simon knew none of this of course. Maybe just wanting to see Peter contented? Peter's mind then went back to the more recent night in Sheena's tent. Without any embarrassment, Sue had invited him into sleeping with her the night. But literally that! Sleeping. They had hugged and kissed a fair bit. He had felt aroused at first but not all night. She had been too upset, apart from anything else. And they had done that before too. But back in Kinlochewe again, they had been very tactile, kept their underwear on the same. And he had been obsessed back then with what had happened with his other friend – another guy. But that was then and this was now. And what was then, hadn't been repeated much. Leastways, other than in his head.

He found himself sighing. He didn't know if he had done this in his mind or audibly, right now he was oblivious to the presence of the others. He knew he was surely kidding himself. The thoughts of other guys were often in his head. The latest was the bloke down the Bar Nash, a few days ago now. However, he wondered - why I am contemplating something happening with Sue in the hotel? It made him realise just how drawn to her he was. Then he knew he couldn't ever be the one to start anything. He wouldn't want to hurt Sue's feelings, nor their friendship. Sue would likely enjoy being close to him all night, would feel comfortable with him. But that's all. Right, he thought, if that's how it is, that's fine.

He looked up then and saw all the rest of them looking at him, six pairs of eyes looking friendly and thoughtful, slightly concerned. How long had they been doing that?

'Blimey Pete! Penny for them?' said Heather, speaking on behalf all of them. Everyone laughed a lot at that. 'God - you were deep in a world of your own just then!'

'Was I?' Peter felt himself feeling caught-out, knew he was really blushing. 'Yeah, sorry folks.' Peter shrugged it off. 'Right, I'm back with you.' He took a deep breath. 'Shall we get going then?'

Chapter 7

When they arrived at that hotel, at first there was no one around and the rather swanky and shiny reception area seemed deserted. Peter realised then that it was three, maybe even four-star and he looked around for the official confirmation notice. The exterior was slightly weather–beaten and a bit faded, so it was a bit of a shock discovering it was smarter than he expected once inside. He then wondered about affordability, but more than that he worried it would all be a bit pretentious – more style than substance.

However, just at that point a rather rotund and happy looking man turned-up in black trousers tucked under his belly a bit, a white shirt, black waistcoat. He looked about fiftyish. In broken English he introduced himself as Le Patron and asked how he could help them.

Sheena and Wendy went first and were offered a twin room with a bath, also a view, together with an immediate apology for the likely absence of the latter. They were given the low-season rate too which the rather bureaucratic reception notice actually suggested didn't start for a few more weeks. The whole transaction had been very affable and Peter noticed that Le Patron seemed pleased to have some business just drop in like this, and also that he was very polite and clearly enjoyed turning on the charm with women.

In his mixed French and English, he had been chatting-up Wendy and Sheena a bit, had them saying what they thought of Chamonix, the mountains and the change in the weather. He had them giggling when he said that had they walked past his hotel in the sun, he was sure he would have remembered them. He said he liked English women because they were more naturelle than the French, more approachable and friendly. He then had Wendy and Sheena blushing a bit.

The man understood the need for people to go back to the

campsite to collect things, followed the bits of mostly English discussion and gave the two women the key anyway. He told them to just let themselves back in and up to their room, to ask for anything else he could do, they were welcome to dine in the restaurant and need not worry about booking ahead. In amongst the attentive charm, Peter also discerned that the manager had seen it all before and seemed at ease, and unsurprised, with people just turning-up like this.

Which was as well for Peter, as he had realised he was now feeling anything but calm. As it became his and Sue's turn to speak, the man now introduced himself as Phillipe. As he started to describe the room options, Wendy, Sheena and Simon interrupted the flow, saying they had decided to head back to the campsite right away. Peter wondered if they had made a discreet departure to make it easier for him and Sue.

The interaction from the patron was very respectful of Sue. She didn't get the same degree of chatting-up, but instead received a slightly more formal charm. He commented on her hair, that it had the light of the high mountains in it, as did her complexion. He suggested that the Chamonix mountains and air were particularly suited to someone like her, if he might say so, someone who, like the surroundings, had a natural beauty of her own. Peter saw Sue flush a little, but he knew she would feel good about the Frenchman's charm. The comments would have seemed more flirtatious back home but conveyed no sense of that here.

As a consequence of all the compliments, Peter couldn't help finding himself feeling very proud at that moment and then also very responsible. The manager turned his attention to him to complete the formalities of checking-in, making Peter feel he was somehow in charge of the stay but also, therefore, of whatever happened next.

Phillipe had assumed they wanted a grand lit, which Peter knew meant double-bed, as well as bath and a great view, which came with a repeat of the apology that this might be missing on this occasion. The patron shrugged at that and perused the thick hotel ledger on the counter. Finally he declared he had a room, très éspecial, assez grand, tout confort, tranquille, - parfait for them, he suggested. 'It's special,' he repeated, 'mais le mème prix, just for you two.'

Peter thought the manager was laying on the charm a bit heavily, but it seemed genuine and it sounded like they were going to get something special at a good price. The manager's willingness to be nice to them as a couple made Peter feel comfortable on one level but added to his nervousness on another.

Philippe wouldn't let them have the key and explained he wanted to take them to their room personally whenever they were ready.

They did a quick trip back to the campsite, talking excitedly about getting out of the rain and treating it as a bit of an adventure. After retrieving over-night essentials from the campsite, Sue and Peter soon found themselves back at the hotel and being escorted by Phillipe to the lift. It was one of those metal boxes that French hotels seem to specialise in, but this one felt lass claustrophobic to Peter as the doorway was a metal grill that pulled across, matched by similar ones on the landings that it slowly glided past up through the middle of the rather grand staircase. On it went, up to the seventh floor and eventually into what Peter thought was indeed a pretty special room. He could see it was really comfortable, but also seemed welcoming – it wasn't too fussy or pretentious like some places he had been with work and he could feel himself smiling and relaxing a bit.

It was very wide and the ceiling sloped away on one side, suggesting they must be up near the roof somewhere. The warm and welcoming bathroom was all fitted-out with chrome, with a small pile of white towels neatly folded. The large bed, of course, was the central focus of the room with the corners of its cover turned-down smartly and little chocolates, wrapped in the paper of the local patisserie, placed on each side. If there had been a fabulous view, occupants would be able to see it from the bed via the ceiling to floor panoramic window which went nearly the entire width of the room.

Phillipe asked if it was acceptable, but must have seen that Peter and Sue were delighted and a bit surprised. Peter recognised this was entirely as the man had hoped and intended, and he believed a lot of this was probably due to Sue. The manager had taken a shine to her, he thought. They were again assured that they only had to ask for anything. Leaving them in the room, Phillipe gave a nod to Sue with a genuine smile, did a little bow to her and gave Peter what he felt was a longish look. One that had just the tiniest hint of a knowing smile to it.

With the manager out of the room, Peter found himself feeling unsure what to do next. Sue broke through the hesitancy they were both experiencing and took Peter's arm and pulled him across to the window.

'It's a shame. Maybe the cloud will lift at some point, it seems to be hovering just above the hotel. It makes it feel really precipitous looking down to the town doesn't it?'

Peter agreed and they talked about what they would have seen if it was clear. This led to a bit of a chat about being out on the mountains, things they had already done and still hoped to do before returning to Britain, although Sue's group would be heading home all too soon now.

He wondered how Sue felt about this situation. It was almost like they were having a polite conversation. He just wasn't sure what to do next and found it hard to admit this. He didn't know how to broach the subject of sharing the bed that loomed behind them, as they looked out to the misty town. Instead, he asked Sue if she fancied a drink.

'I know it's only three o'clock but …well we can have a celebration of getting out of the rain. What do you think?' Sue pursed her lips in response, slowly tilting her head from side to side, then rolling her eyes and breaking into a smile. 'Come on, we might as well make an event of it.' He felt like he was hamming it up and that what he was saying sounded artificial somehow.

But Sue just said it sounded a great idea and he could see her relax, simultaneously becoming more aware that she had otherwise been a bit tightened-up, the same as him.

Sue told Peter to get whatever he fancied – to surprise her. But she also said she had to get something from nearby in town. When Peter reminded her most of the shops would still be shut, she just said it was the nearby pharmacy she needed to visit. He knew he looked quizzical, but she looked a little embarrassed and he didn't ask any more, realising it was just something personal.

'Sheena and Wendy pointed one out to me. It's just a couple of minutes from the hotel.'

They decided to walk down all the stairs as "an attempt to keep mountain fit" according to Peter. They separated at the bottom. Peter went off to the bar area, which was quite chic but also managing to keep a welcoming feel. It was fairly empty though. A couple of people having coffee. Another couple having pastis. It was the manager again who eventually came to serve him when he dinged the bell. The man explained that early afternoon when it was generally quiet, he tended to do everything around the place, doubling up on roles. At least, that's what Peter thought he said. The manager enquired with his eyes and then followed Peter's gaze along the array of bottles on the bar shelves.

Peter ran his eyes through the display on the chrome and mirrored shelving. He told Phillipe he was looking for whisky and was pleased when the specific words single-malt clearly meant something, and that this enquiry was, in fact, met with approval. A few bottles were identified, then clustered together on the bar counter, each then shown to Peter with a bit of a wipe and dust with a linen cloth.

There was some Glenfiddich, a rather older looking bottle of Glenmorangie, another make that Peter didn't know and what looked like an unopened bottle of Lagavulin. In addition there was a MacAllan ten year-old, just under a quarter full. There was also a Johnny Walker Black Label, which they both agreed was nice, but not the same thing. Peter started to think if he hung around here much longer, it would turn into a tasting session!

Peter went for the MacAllan, confirming yes please, it was two glasses. He was appreciative of the stylish approach when two decent sized servings of whisky were presented to him in large, heavy tumblers, also retrieved from the shelves somewhere and similarly spruced-up with a cloth. He was given a small silvered tray with a glass of ice and little jug of water put to the side of the glasses.

It was pretty expensive but Peter felt he would have paid anything at this moment, feeling shakier by the minute. As he was about to lift the tray, Philippe tilted the bottle of MacAllan to examine how much was left, and then placed it alongside the glasses. 'Pour vous, et pour mademoiselle. C'ést la maison.' he said. On the house, Peter understood. But then Phillipe put his hand on Peter's arm and added, with nods of his head, an encouraging smile and the more definite look of a man who had seen a lot of life, 'Bon courage monsieur. Bon courage.'

'Merci bien' said Peter, feeling touched. As he lifted the tray, Phillipe looked up and then pointed with his chin towards the reception area. Sue was returning, whatever chore she had needed to do, it had been done quickly.

Peter did indeed find himself wondering about courage as they went up the lift together. Sue wrapped her free arm around one of his, as he held on tightly to the surprisingly heavy tray. She said she was delighted with the whisky, that it was a very thoughtful idea and they should do a toast to Scotland and to old times.

Back in the room, to Peter it felt like they were both physically avoiding the bed as they moved around the room. Sue sorted some things with the bedside drawer, and he found the side-table and chairs by the window seemed to be designed for sitting down with the tray of drinks. Perhaps that was their actual purpose!

Sue came over to join him. Still standing, they took a glass each from the tray, looked at each other and Peter said 'To the mountains Sue. To meeting each other all that time ago and becoming friends'. He felt like he was making a point by stressing the last word. He hadn't intended that. They tilted back the glasses and Peter, unintentionally, took quite a gulp.

'Cheers to that Pete. Gosh it's all just a strong taste at first isn't it? Quite overpowering for a moment but then you can feel it going down, and then the lasting taste is just lovely.'

'No rubbish Sue. I love this malt, it always transports me to another place.'

'You're a romantic Pete. But you're right. Ooh this is nice isn't it?' She moved herself alongside and right up against him. She took another sip and turned to look out of the window again, folding her arms, relaxed, still holding the tumbler in one hand.

Peter could feel the politeness of the situation was at a risk of becoming unbearable. He thought if they had another conversation about the swirling clouds above the Town, it would be his fault. But did she feel the same? In the end he decided he had no choice but to hit the situation head-on.

Then he found himself pausing for what seemed ages. He knew he just had to move, to do something, to start a course of action that felt so hard. Mostly he didn't want to get it wrong and upset her. Would she think he was taking advantage of her? It must have only been seconds. He sighed and took an audibly deep breath and Sue half-turned to him in surprise.

He moved away from her to take another sip, then put down his glass back on the tray. He turned back to her and gently took her glass from her hand and placed it on the table too, next to his. Sue held his gaze steadily and with a look, he felt, of expectation but also nervous anticipation. He stepped towards her, put his hands on her waist and then met her face as she looked at him. They kissed and Peter knew immediately this was very different to the kiss they had recently shared in the tent.

This one was not about affectionately catching-up with each other's lives, nor consoling someone. This kiss was about desire and it transmitted all Peter needed to know and to feel assured that Sue was on the same track as him. They had both been showing a bit of trepidation about what was now underway but having started, the relief was palpable and evident to them both. He could imagine that she had been going through the same sort of thoughts and questions as himself.

So, here we are, he thought. Someone I really like, someone who makes me feel good and makes me feel normal. Someone I have been naked with once and near-naked a few times. Has it always been inevitable that this would happen one day?

It was a long, evolving series of kisses but shortly they stepped apart again and Peter simply reached over his shoulders and pulled-off his sweater and T-shirt together, quickly but neatly folding them onto to the back of the chair. He checked with his eyes first, to get permission, and then took the bottom of Sue's jumper in his hands and lifted it clear over her head. He noticed how soft the wool felt and he couldn't help putting it to his face, feeling her warmth and scent, before putting it gently on the chair, next to his. She had no tee-shirt underneath, just a floral bra of a soft fabric.

They kissed again. He felt the strength of his own desire and was surprised at how strongly he received that feeling in return from her. On parting this time, they both just started to strip-off the rest of their clothes. Peter removed his socks and jeans and Sue was down to just her underwear at the same time as him. He recalled then, being with Sue on his mountain when they were about to become naked. He remembered how stupid he had felt trying to cover his nervousness then with what now seemed inane comments. There was no hesitation this time though and both of them were naked in moments. They kissed deeply again and Peter could hardly believe how aroused he had become.

They hugged each other then as they moved awkwardly across the room to the bed, clutching each other all the way, and then eventually clumsily falling onto it, with a bit of nervous giggling from them both. They used their hands to explore each other but Peter needed to get to what he now saw as an inevitable and essential event that had been incredibly long in the gestation. Also before, he briefly worried, any doubts could alter his physical reaction. Sue had grabbed something from the bedside table and then he realised with a start what she had slipped-out to buy.

'You need to wear this Pete.' The first words that had been said. He was kneeling between her legs. An anxiety appeared in his mind. But before he had time to become more concerned about it, she simply and hurriedly rolled the condom over him, held him tightly with her hand and, without letting go of him, pulled him forward and straight towards her.

He felt her squeeze around him so tightly at first, he couldn't move, but when she relaxed a little he heard himself gasp and knew it couldn't last for long. He realised then what he wanted most of all. He just had to be, and needed to be, as deeply inside Sue as he could be, as deeply connected as it was possible to feel. To be matching the emotion with the physical feeling. She must have sensed this or maybe felt the same, or both, and she wrapped her legs tightly around him in response, pulling him in. At the end, which arrived very quickly, he could feel himself trembling, shaking almost. Sue hugged him tight and held him. Still without another word being said.

Peter found himself in a dreamlike state, on another plane and he wasn't sure how long they lay like this. Then they were on their sides and Sue was stroking his back.

'Sorry, bit out of practice.' More than a bit, he thought in his head.

'Shh Pete', she said gently.

'But I…'

'Shhh.' She put a finger to his lips and held it there until he just smiled.

He felt like he was floating and that he could almost be heading towards sleepiness. Everything had slowed down now and Peter noticed how comfortable the bed was, and then also thinking that anywhere would feel comfortable for him right now, with her alongside.

Soon though he felt Sue wanting to kiss him again and at first that happened slowly and unhurriedly as she took his hand and placed it where she wanted it to be. He lost the sense of time, the kiss started becoming more forceful and finally even urgent. He knew he was responding physically and at that same moment realised that Sue was reaching across to the bedside, repeating the same action as before. She was in control of what was happening and he at last felt completely at one with her.

This time it went on a little longer. Long enough anyway for Sue's breathing to become progressively shorter and deeper until at one moment she arched her back under him, so strongly that he felt his own body literally lifted upwards. She stayed like that some moments. As she lowered herself, she drew her legs around him again, even more tightly than before. There was no choice for him but to let himself go. Her legs were almost vice-like in their hold. He buried his head into the pillow next to hers.

The only sound then was their breathing. He realised that somehow it was now in synch. Sue still held him and he really felt as if he truly was an actual part of her.

Peter brought his head up and they kissed.

'This is lovely.' Sue spoke first.

'Yep, it is. Really lovely.' Peter found himself gazing at her and then feeling slightly embarrassed about the feeling of staring. They smiled at each other.

'You look like the cat who got the cream,' she joked.

'Well you don't exactly look unhappy do you! You have that sort of Cheshire Cat look yourself!'

'Can you feel me purring then?'

'I can actually.' He laughed, then smiled, raising his upper body, onto his arms, still looking down at her. 'Ok, you can maybe let me go now though.'

'No, I won't - actually.'

'Come on angel, I can't stay here.'

'Nope.'

Then they both laughed lightly again. They looked at each other and Peter knew at that moment what pure delight both looked like and felt like. He paused, wondering how long she was going to tease him.

'Not to move off you and be on my side next to you?'

'Nope.'

Another pause. 'Not even to get a glass of water?'

'Nope.'

'Go to the bathroom?'

'Nope. Definitely nope.'

'OK. What about getting the whisky?'

A slight hesitation and a big smile forming on her lips. 'Nope.' They both giggled.

'Not to get up?'

'Nope.'

'Go back to the tent to get some Marlboroughs?'

'Hmmm. Nice idea…nope.'

'Get dressed? Go out for dinner?'

'Nope, nope.' They were still looking straight into each other's eyes, just inches apart. Eventually he asked quietly,

'Not ever?'

Another hesitation. She put her hand behind his head and pulled him down to another kiss.

Peter then just immersed his head into the pillow beside her again. She released him then and they turned over onto their sides and went into a close hug without another word being said. As sleep started to envelop both of them, Peter started to wonder actually, just what it would be like to stay there forever.

Waking later, a good part of the afternoon had gone. Sue went to the bathroom on her own and Peter felt content, really content, to just lie there looking at the ceiling and feeling surprised and elated about what had happened. After a while, Sue came back into the bedroom, still drying herself off with some towels. Again he had a flashback to the two of them drying with a shared towel after a swim in a tiny lochan. An age away and what has changed, he asked himself? Sue broke through his reverie, encouraging him, pushing him really, to go and shower too.

Drying off together wrapped in towels, they sat in the window. Facing each other, cross-legged. The evening was approaching and at last it looked as if the weather was breaking-up. Glimpses of snow on mountains, glaciers looming out of the billowing clouds. They decided to finish the whisky and then go to dinner before they just gave into slumber from which they would wake up feeling rough as well as hungry.

'I didn't know if that was going to happen or not Sue.' He gently sloshed his whisky around the glass, watching it move around, admiring its dark amber colour, suddenly feeling a bit embarrassed to look at her.

'I think we both were a bit on edge getting here Peter. It felt a big thing coming to a hotel bed together. You felt the same didn't you?'

'Yeah, of course.'

'You know when Sheena, Wendy and I went to the loo at the bar, you know, don't you, we had a chat about this?'

'I guessed.'

'Do you know what Wendy said?' Sue saw Peter looking quizzical now. 'She said, I don't know if I have the exact words though - "Sue, you told me he's gay! What's going on?" I needed her to ask that.'

'What did you say?' Peter was now leaning forward, hanging on to every word.

'I said to her that in the tent you and I had just talked and hugged. That we had kept our pants on. Oh, and I had cried. A lot. They both knew that already.'

Peter touched her arm, 'You did.' He paused. 'And?'

'Wendy asked if we were going to a hotel together for more tears then? I told her I thought it could, potentially, be more than that. I might have just said that in my head though.'

'Did you!?' Peter was genuinely surprised. 'Really!? I didn't assume or know this would happen. Not for sure.'

'I wanted this to happen though Pete, but I was nervous about it.' Sue leant across and they kissed. 'But, you know, I think I've just taken advantage of you.'

Peter was taken aback. 'Don't be daft Sue, it doesn't feel like that to me.'

'Thanks.' Another kiss. 'God, whisky loosens the tongue more than anything doesn't it!? Look; being in the sleeping-bag with you the other night was so good. I needed that. Meeting you again reminded me of life before Colin. You brought to the surface a lot of feelings I needed to raise, that needed to get out.'

'You make it sound like throwing-up Sue. It was so sad. For me. Seeing you like that. I didn't know what to do really.'

'You didn't need to do anything. You had already done it – just being there. I felt so much better when it had all come out – when I had thrown-up, as you put it.' She smiled and paused, looked out at the town again, gathering her thoughts, so it seemed to Peter. 'Then, when we were in the Alpenstock earlier, I realised how much I had been needing and wanting a guy again. Physically. Inside me.' She turned to him. 'I really needed to be screwed Pete.' Another pause. 'Are you shocked at me?'

Peter was taken aback by the starkness of this remark. Then he shook his head, 'Of course not.' But he felt a bit unsure what he thought. Just mostly surprised at what Sue was saying really.

'I really needed to feel a guy again. To be ok with that stuff again. But after Colin…' she hesitated, then spoke very slowly. 'After Colin, it had to be someone I felt really, really, really, really, comfortable with.'

Peter still felt a bit astonished at this conversation, but now surprised and humbled at the same time.

'That moment when we were deep together that was it Pete. Being one with a man. Just where I needed you to be.'

Peter just looked at her. 'I wish it hadn't been so quick.'

'Don't be silly, it was just fine as it was.' She touched and held onto his arm, 'You know something? I don't know anyone I could have felt more comfortable with than you.'

Peter didn't know what to say, eventually thinking out loud, 'Are we going to have another kiss?' He leant over to her now, finding her lips. 'So, did you say all that to Sheena and Wendy?'

'More or less. Amongst other things.'

'God. No wonder you were there a long time. How did they react to that?'

'We had a girly hug. But they insisted I went to the pharmacist.'

'I thought it must be your time of the month or something when you went out like that.'

'Oh, did you!? You must have felt disappointed then!?' And she giggled.

'No – the opposite. Thought it might provide an excuse not to go through with it.'

He saw Sue was giving him her scrutinising look, the one that felt like she was peering around in his head. He quite liked the feeling. She nodded, just said 'I know.'

'I just didn't want to end-up disappointing you Sue.'

'Ah. We had this chat years ago Pete. You don't disappoint me.' She reached across and stroked his leg. 'Wendy said I had to get condoms. She said I had to think about…well, you know. She also talked about medical stuff coming out of America – the gay plague, sorry to use that term. Working in the lab she gets to hear stuff of course.' Sue looked very thoughtful then. 'I had told them you were having a very rarefied sex life.' She said 'none of us really understand how the virus works.'

Peter was looking at the ground now. The horror of the disease seemingly targeting gay men in The States, more uncertainty about a world he was trying to avoid.

'Sorry Sue.'

'Hey!' She moved off from sitting, knelt by him and put her arms around him. 'Do NOT feel bad about it Pete. Don't. Please don't.' She said firmly.

'I would never do anything to put you in any danger Sue. Not anything.' And he looked at her face, so close to his, in a way that felt a bit like defiance, but he hoped that it came over as just honest.

'I know.' She said. 'I know. I really feel that with you.'

'Do you remember me and you going across that incredible scree slope?'

'Exactly that Peter. I'll never forget that day. In that lovely kilt from Julie's aunt. It was the way you just cared about me – my safety.' And she gave him a kiss on the cheek.

'One important fact is though, I am not on permanent contraception. Now anyway.'

Peter furrowed his eyebrows. He wondered for a moment if she was just wanting him to feel better about it. Then he imagined life with Colin.

'Oh, right. I imagine Colin wasn't a condoms sort-of man?'

'No, you must be joking! No, of course not. I tried different Pills. Needs must… Didn't get on with any of them. And now I don't have to! Well, who knows?' She smiled at him. 'Come on you, let's settle down here a minute. I'll get the cushions. We may get the view after all.'

And indeed, the fleeting clearances of the view had now settled into a proper improvement. The valley side opposite was now pretty well exposed and they could see the Bossons tumbling down. They poured the last drops of the MacAllan.

'You know?' She said, piling the cushions around them. 'Right here and right now, I just feel good. Just a few days ago I didn't.' He was giving her his full attention, already feeling the need to just hug her. They laid back, side by side. Peter felt happy to just let Sue talk. He realised the whole afternoon and this discussion hadn't exactly been planned, but Sue was using what had happened out here, in the Alps, to straighten-out her life a bit. He didn't feel used, like she had been suggesting, he just felt so pleased with himself to have seemingly helped her – and in such an outstandingly wonderful way for him.

'Yep, I'm in a different place now. I have been on some good walks.' She continued. 'It's just great being in the Alpine sun, wearing as little as one can get away with. Definitely, I've been in a lot of sun, until the downpours anyway. Got a tan though!' She held up her hands, pretending to count-off a list of good things on her fingers. 'What else? Oh yes! - been saved by a group of knights from the imminent danger of a group of marauding French climbers.' They both laughed.

'Yeah, Dougal the Defender is what we will call him from now on.'

'I was really touched by it all Pete.' She paused again. Peter felt he wouldn't be able to hold back much longer the desire to just hug her and hug her. 'And I've cried my eyes out – a bucket load of negative thoughts washed-out in tears.' A pause. 'I've had a brilliant whisky and … I've even had it off with a nice bloke…' Peter felt humbled again. Sue gently laughed a little and he joined her. Which just about managed to stop both of them welling-up.

'…one I really care about.' She continued, looking at Peter, her eyes now going moist and his doing the same in response. They reached for each other, fell backwards into the cushions and cuddled so closely it felt to Peter like they were trying to melt into one another.

Chapter 8

The remaining days in Chamonix went quickly, with the trip for the Welsh contingent finishing sooner than for Peter and his friends. There were a couple of days of gorgeous weather after the rainstorm, a lot of walking, some climbing. A lot more eating and drinking at the Alpenstock. By the time the whole crowd had to finally part the combined group had become a semi-permanent feature of the bar and had taken-over the raised area of the brasserie most times, so much that they joked about it being a British enclave.

Sue and Peter had not spent another night together since the hotel. Peter thought this was due to the simple practicality of getting a tent together, which was awkward when everyone was around at the same time. He found himself feeling a bit coy about it and he and Sue had chatted about not wanting to be like a couple, trying to evict Sheena and take-over the tent. And he could hardly throw out his climbing partner, although Simon had offered to try and find somewhere else.

'It's OK, thanks,' Peter had told him, 'it was nice at the hotel, but we're not moving in with each other.' Simon had given him firstly a questioning look and then secondly something more sceptical.

The day soon arrived when the Welsh club's tents were being taken down and stuff was being packed into cars. Sue and Peter took a short walk together on their own, prior to her departure. They walked into Town as far as the Bar Nash and had coffees at an empty table outside but nicely tucked-away in the shade.

Neither of them had said much on the walk.

'I'm going to miss being here.' Sue spoke first, then reached for her coffee and took a sip, looking at Peter over the top of the cup.

'Me too, but mostly I'm going to miss you!'

'I know, I feel the same. I'm wanting to be cheerful, but we're both a bit subdued aren't we?'

'Guess so.' Peter produced and lit a cigarette. It wasn't exactly a crisis but definitely a time when a cigarette helped a lot. He took a deep drag before blowing out a cloud of smoke, feeling he might look like a local with the cigarettes and the coffee, sitting outside the Bar mid-morning. A look that was impossible to imagine anywhere in the UK. 'It's funny how a fag and a coffee seems so different out here to back home.'

Sue stared at him a moment, and then her face broke into a broad smile. She giggled and said, 'That's just what I have been thinking Peter!'

He furrowed his brow, taking a moment to get the joke. 'Oh, I see! Very funny. Insulting me on our last morning…!'

Sue sat up straight, lifted herself a bit, reached across the table simultaneously giving Peter a kiss and taking his cigarette at the same moment.

'And now you're stealing a drag of my cigarette!'

'I'm going to keep it actually.'

Peter lit another, pleased they were sharing a bit of teasing together. He felt another awkward conversation was hanging around and he had been planning what he wanted to say. A lighter mood helped, but it felt tricky – to him anyway. He wondered if his relationship with Sue, if that was what the friendship was becoming, was always going to be a set of such moments, strung together over time. He decided again the best thing was to just get on with it. Whatever reaction she was going to have, it would only be made worse by prolonging it. He took a deep breath and spoke quite quietly.

'Er, I was wondering…Er…Would you like to come and see me in Bristol Sue?' He paused. 'You know…for a weekend?' He thought he had nearly fluffed it and found himself blushing a bit and took another draw on the cigarette to cover it.

'Yes please.'

Peter felt he could have choked. Of course, he should have

known, Sue would have worked-out that this question would arise, anticipated it, thought about it and determined what she wanted to do. He realised he was just looking at her, feeling a bit stupefied.

'Well, is that alright? When? Let's get back into work and stuff and then do it? Give us time to get some photos developed too maybe.'

'Yeah, sure.' She said. 'I've a weekend away towards the end of September, so perhaps before then? Mid September? Say three weeks' time? Two maybe?'

'Two sounds good' confirmed Peter.

Sue leant across and kissed him on the cheek again. Looking more serious, she said, 'Are we starting an affair?'

'Don't know, you tell me.' He looked around the street and thought of the last week and half, how much it had meant to him. Just being in the sunny Alps had been great. So much walking, great weather a lot of the time. Some laughs – quite a lot of those really. But the whole thing of meeting Sue again and the sheer wonder of sleeping together; all still seemed dreamlike.

'Penny for them! Again!'

Peter just smiled at her. Stubbed out his cigarette. Took another sip of coffee.

'It's been funny. Not funny ha ha. You know what I mean. Meeting you out here I mean. Being with you, like now.'

'I just felt sorry for you Peter. You don't seem to be getting any and I was pleased to help out!' She had her elbow on the table and the hand with the cigarette propping-up her face.

'Ha ha, very funny. You're full of them this morning aren't you! So, that means you're some sort of sex philanthropist, does it?' He shook his head, laughed and she joined in.

'I told you Pete. I think I might have used you! Still am maybe. Have you thought of that?'

He paused. 'Well I'm thinking about it now and it sounds fine to me.'

Sue shook her head now. 'I don't think either of us know what we're doing Pete. But I like it and want to see you. So, thanks very much for inviting me.'

'You are now making it sound so formal.' And this time Peter leaned across to kiss her on the lips.

'Are we going to do this all morning?' They smiled together at Sue's recall of another time.

The waiter came over at Sue's signal. They paid-up then and hurried back to the campsite. It was all sorted and people had just got to the point of settling-up with the campsite guardian. There was a lot of various denominations of banknotes going between people, shaking of hands, friendly comments and some hugs. Dougal and all four of them had driven over from the other side of Chamonix to say farewell too.

Sue and Peter found they were now having the final hug of the holiday. To both of them it suddenly felt hard to leave. Sue felt a knot forming in her tummy.

'Damn, I think I'm going to cry again.' And in fact a few tears did then start to run from Sue's eyes and she pursed her lips, looking straight at Peter. Then they put their arms round each other's shoulders and held a long hug.

'Me too. You've always had that ability to make me do this Sue.'

'Hey, don't blame me for you being a softie. Goes with the territory doesn't it?' and she squeezed him hard to reassure him that she was teasing again.

'I will miss you Sue.'

'I will miss you Pete.'

They took a long look at each other, had a final kiss and then she got into Ian's car, alongside Sheena. He called-out 'Take care Arthur.' And winked at Peter and gave a friendly wave.

Peter watched them go and was surprised just how upset he felt.

Simon put an arm round his shoulder. 'Just an old friend, you said.' A pause. 'Of the very best sort though, eh?'

Peter could hardly speak. Just leaned into his friend and nodded his head, eventually just managing to say 'That's so true Simon. So true.'

Part Two

Loch Eriboll, 1984

"Today he felt he had strayed into a country in which he must find his way alone, through which no Narziss could ever guide him."
From Narziss and Goldmund, by Hermann Hesse, 1930.

Chapter 9

They pulled off to the side of the A838 road, parked the car on a bit of the old roadway in front of a derelict cottage and got out. Crossing the single track road on foot brought them to a viewpoint looking across the loch and over the small island just off the shoreline. Peter stood there, gazing outwards, hands on hips, stretching and arching his back a bit – easing his body after the long drive.

'You can see it's not technically an island – there's a bar of sand attaching it to the shore, not that visible just now. What do you think though?'

'It's great. It's also great to get out of the car again.' Said Sue, also doing a stretch by tilting her body slowly from one side to the other and back again. With each movement, her long hair falling, fanning out a bit in the breeze. 'I don't know about the little rocky island so much, but the whole loch is amazing. It's so big and so peaceful.'

It had been a long drive from Scourie where they had stopped for a comfort break and a tea. The continuous single track road had seemed very long to them both, despite enjoying the views and the breadth and depth of the scenery. Sue was wondering if she should now take over the driving for the last leg.

'Yeah, good idea if you're ok with it.' Agreed Peter, when she broached the subject. 'The concentration takes it out of you after a while. About another hour and we're there I think. Anyway – just look at this.' And he swept his arm around through a one hundred and eighty degree arc, taking in the ruined cottage and the parked car, across the hill of Ben Arnaboll, over the extent of Loch Eriboll and out to the sea in the north.

Sue came alongside him and put her arm round his waist. 'It's so wild Pete. I mean, you can hardly see the road on the other side of the loch and you wouldn't think anyone lived here. There's a little building on the island though isn't there?'

'It's an old lime kiln thing. When I was here on the field trip, one of the lecturers knew what it was. There's an outcrop of limestone – the same as we saw in the field and cliffs when we came through Durness, a little while back. That's what they used in the kiln. And Smoo Cave is the same rock. You liked the sound of that place, didn't you? The name is intriguing in itself I think. We can come back this way with the others maybe? Not tomorrow though – I mean after we've all recovered I suppose. We can come back then.'

'Hmm - I don't know, we'll see what everyone wants to do. Not everyone shares your love of geology and landscape you know!' Sue thought Peter must be tired to be rambling a bit with his words.

'If that's true, why have they decided to come then?' argued Peter.

'They just want a relaxing holiday and we, you and Sheena particularly, convinced them that coming up here would do nicely. Don't spoil it by goading them into exploring the great outdoors with you all the time!' He wasn't sure if she was actually having a go at him or attempting to josh, realising she also was just tired from concentrating on the roads.

'I know when you're teasing me you know.' He laughed, shook his head. 'If they don't come, I will have to go out in the wilds with just you then.'

'Maybe Pete – but not every day!'

After a while they drove off again, Sue in the driving seat this time. She drove pretty fast, Peter thought, but then he forced himself to just sit back and relax. He hardly ever let anyone drive him and he needed to shut up about it. As it happened, the next bit of road, which was new to him, allowed them both to see a long way ahead and it all felt more open and expansive. It stayed like that for quite a few miles. Not that there was any other traffic to be concerned about.

Sue was enjoying the drive, seemingly just happy musing to herself but after a while asked Peter how he felt about meeting-up with all the others. He didn't say anything at first, but just waved a cassette in front of Sue's face and she swatted it away. Taking this as an agreement he slotted it into the player and they were then soon accompanied on the short journey by The Pretenders.

Peter sang along vaguely to Chrissie Hynde's voice. His mind roved around from studying the scenery to just being here in this moment.

'In a way I was just thinking it would be nice if it was just you and me.' He eventually said, thinking Sue had been very patient, waiting for his response to her question.

'I knew you would be thinking that way.'

'Well, I suppose we have tonight anyway don't we? By now they will be well up the M6 and thinking of the stop near Carlisle. It's a good B&B, popular with climber types – I stayed there with Simon once on the way to the Cairngorms.'

His mind drifted a bit then, realising he must be more relaxed about Sue driving than he initially thought. He asked Sue to remind him what everyone was up to at work, again, – so he didn't make any social faux-pas, as he put it.

'OK' she said. 'Well, Julie is teaching, like me, as you know. Her school is over in Fforestfach – a tougher bit of Swansea then mine. Suits her that really. She can get stroppy as much as the kids!' she chuckled. 'Wendy is doing microbiology research in the University, same as when you met her in Chamonix.' That new department has really got going now. Ian is some sort of engineer manager in the chemical works at Baglan. Sheena's at the Leisure Centre, as you know. Gosh, it doesn't seem long since we were planning this trip does it?'.

'Yeah – that was March. Seems ages though. Just checking nothing's changed with anyone really!' He paused. 'Diane's the one we all know least. Mike I'm getting to know better at work. We get on well there.' He paused looking down at the road atlas. 'Hope we all get on ok, all together up here.'

'It will be fine. Everyone knows everyone a little bit at least, or soon will. It's going to be a bit cramped but it's cheap, and anyway, look at all this.' Sue nodded to the left and right, acknowledging the wild landscape all around them.

Peter found himself staring mostly to the right of the windscreen, at Ben Hope to the south. Then he brought himself back into concentrating after a moment of reverie brought on by the tape. 'Er – you see Sue, you like the big views as much as me. Kyle of Tongue coming into sight any minute now. Here we go in fact. When we get a sign to the left, to Talmine, take it. Obviously! I will find Sheena's notes again. Think we might be there in just a few mins actually.'

Sue's friend Sheena had a cottage in Talmine, a family place that her grandmother used to live in and in which her mother had been born. It was still her Mum's place technically, but she managed all the lettings – often to friends at a bucket price, as on this trip. It being so remote, Sheena and her Mum were just glad to have people go and use it, and air it, apparently. The other place, a couple of cottages away, was another occasional holiday let owned by a family friend. That was more expensive, but they shared all the cost between the eight of them. Although both places were small, combined they gave enough room for the group of them.

The tiny road compelled them to drive slowly, Sue concentrating as a few cottages appeared. Peter had to wrench himself to attention on what they were doing, instead of admiring the long and wide expanse of water and sand running parallel to their approach.

'This is it Sue.' He looked up at the little cottage a few feet above the road level. It was whitewashed and stone built, with a newish looking slate roof and a dark red front door. 'It says on the note, to just park on the scoop of ground on the left. This bit in fact.' He paused as Sue brought the car smoothly to a halt. 'Maybe just go forward a bit and then reverse back?'

'Yes, thank you. I do know how to park the bloody car Peter!'

'Aww Sue, we are on holiday, there's no need to shout at me!' Peter feigned hurt feelings.

'And there's no need to tell me what to do – and don't adopt that whimpering tone either!' Sue completed the manoeuvre. 'It doesn't let you off and it's not endearing.' But she looked at Peter's pretend sad face, smiled, leaned across and kissed him. 'Here's an idea I've been musing while you were talking. How about we just quickly get unpacked and go for a swim? You know, let's sort ourselves out minimally and then go down into the Kyle right away? It'll be a great way to wash off the journey. Sheena said it's really nice and it's easy to get down there; and not as cold as we might expect. I'm happy to give it a go.' Sue knew Peter would need no persuading.

'It looks fantastic.' Agreed Peter.

So, about thirty minutes later they headed out of the cottage, back along the way they had just come, to where Sheena had told them there was a track down the steep hillside and onto the beach. Even though it was pretty overcast and breezy, it felt warm enough to have changed from jeans into shorts for both of them. They had jumpers on though and Peter carried the rucksack containing towels and swimwear plus the flask of tea and sandwiches they had packed earlier in the morning back at Scourie. They saw no one, except the postman's van nipped past just as they located the track. The only company they had otherwise was that of a dozen or so rabbits in the fields. There were burrows scattered around all over.

'Those two islands just there ahead of us are called Rabbit Islands, according to the map.' Said Peter. 'But I think some must have escaped back to the mainland!' he paused, watching his footing until he got onto the sand. Sue was carefully doing the same. They walked across a bit of the wide-open beach and then decided to settle into a sheltered area at the back, by some rocks and in front of a small, low cliff. 'It's amazingly empty here and it must a be a couple of miles across, easily. Stunning! I had no idea it would be like this. What do you say we go in the water first and then come back for the sarnies?'

'Yep, I agree, but it looks like a fair distance to the water.' Sue remarked. 'Oh it doesn't matter does it. Let's get on our swim stuff and jog across?' And with that, Sue stripped off and put on her bikini while Peter slipped on his trunks, and then they set-off.

'I like that by the way Sue.' Peter found he couldn't help glancing at Sue repeatedly. 'A lot!'

'You just look where you are putting your feet and don't leer at me!'

'What!? I'm not leering at you. Oh – is it a day for telling me off then Sue?' he joked. 'If you didn't want people looking at you, maybe you shouldn't have got something skimpy, trendy and new, with tie-sides like that.' And he attempted to pull at one of the fabric knots of Sue's bikini bottoms as they ran forward. Sue just slapped his hand away.

'It's just comfortable Pete and, more importantly, makes me feel good. That's the main thing really. I feel free, light and happy in this. And I've decided I'm going to wear it whatever, come sun or rain. In a few years I might not be able to get away with it.' She sighed.

With that, they arrived at the water's edge and were surprised to encounter a line of what appeared to be greasy blobs of various sizes running parallel with the sea. Stopping to examine them, they then saw that they were in fact jellyfish. Mostly grey or black, a mix of transparent and semi-translucent lumps but one or two more looked like discs, and quite red in colour. The latter were each easily a foot or more across.

'Oh no, this looks a bit sad. Hmm - do you think they're in the water just around here too?'

'Don't know, but maybe we should try and keep an eye out. Do you think they would sting? Let's just go down a few yards and try and go in where its jelly free.' said Peter. They talked about them and wondered if they were still alive, waiting to be floated away by the tide, or in fact were stranded? They didn't know and had never before encountered anything like them.

The water was cold but they thought Sheena had been correct. It really didn't feel as bad as they had imagined it might. It was also noticeably clear, giving them the confidence to believe they would see anything floating in the water. Slowly getting in up to their waists, they noticed the sea remained like crystal. They plunged in, thrashed about a bit, swam a few strokes and then quite rapidly made their way back out. Then it was a faster run back to the rocks and their towels.

'What's this rock then?' Sue asked, drying her hair and perusing the cliff.

'Oh – are you trying to make it up for being snappy now? By asking me about rock types and pretending to be interested in geology?' Sue gave him a withering look and rolled her eyes. 'I wonder if you're teasing me again now – even if you pretend you're not. Anyway – it's Schist, if you're really interested. Look, all these wiggly bits are the rock material flowing. Well not flowing now, but was flowing, sort-of, when it formed. There's lots of mica in it – all that crumbly, silvery stuff you can see.' He rubbed a small fragment of the rock between his fingers, a cascade of shiny, fine particles fell from his hand.

As was usual, Sue could hear the enthusiasm in Peter's description. After briefly examining the rock herself, she looked southwards, down the length of the Kyle, to Ben Loyal. Sue was finding the breadth and variety of landscape to be so much more than she had been expecting. 'That mountain is really beautiful and majestic Pete – looks huge. It looked good from the car on the way across, but seeing it from here is something else. Really dominating the view like that and so spectacular. Is it schist too?'

'Ooh – maybe you are really interested?' Peter asked, receiving a look from Sue, shaking her head and raising her eyes heavenwards again. 'No, it's mostly granite apparently. It's all quite different up here to the stuff I was studying in Kinlochewe, with you.' He paused.

'I didn't have much to do with it Pete. To be fair though, I did learn a fair bit from you, Graham and Steve especially.' She turned, now facing Peter. 'I was trying to distract you most of the time, I think. But little did I know!'

'You did distract me!' Peter exclaimed, shaking his head and ignoring the allusion to Steve. He instantly cheered-up, enjoying the better mood he now perceived between them, wondering where it might lead.

'And you still do', he continued, making another half-hearted grab for one of her bikini knots, resulting in another swipe away. He sensed Sue could get annoyed with him, so he went back to the subject of Ben Loyal. 'I really want to get us all up there soon.' He said, drawing an imaginary line across the skyline ridge. 'It's quite a trek to do the whole route, which I've never done. According to the book.' He gazed down the sweeping sand and sea and up to the flanks of the mountain, trying to figure out the approach and admiring its distinctive set of summits. 'I was hoping we can do a group expedition!'

'Hmm – don't know. Ian and Sheena, yes definitely. Wendy maybe. And me!' She smiled. 'Julie would rather stay and read. Mike and Diane?' It's not a mountaineering trip we are on though is it?' Peter wasn't sure if she was asking a question or making a statement.

'I suppose not.' He agreed, taking her remark as a question. 'When we first chatted about it, way back in Chamonix last year, not everyone was initially enthusiastic, but the premise raised by Sheena and Wendy was definitely for it NOT to be a climbing trip!'

'Quite right.' Said Sue. 'Having come down here with you now, I would be happy to be here every day to be honest, as long as it's not too wet or turns freezing. I blame you for turning me into someone quite happy to be wearing little outdoors whenever I can, by the way. You and your cavorting around the Torridon hills without much on.'

'Cavorting around the hills!' Peter started to protest, 'Without much on!' He was feigning being hurt by her remarks, clutching his chest as if wounded and bending his knees.

'Stop it you fool.' Sue said, smiling at him. 'It would be a shame not to do a bit of mountain walking though, especially that one. And it's on our doorstep.'

Sue turned back towards the view. She was standing ahead of Peter on the sand, gazing at the mountain again. 'Looks really great doesn't it?'

Peter regarded her, thinking how lovely she looked and now becoming clear in his mind about what he would most like to happen next. 'It does. It certainly does.' He was aware of a slight quiver in his voice. 'Must be the best view on the whole beach.'

Sue knew very well this change in tone from Peter and turned to him slowly, looked down and received confirmation. She tutted and gave her head a very brief shake. 'I was actually referring to the mountain!'

'Yes, I know, but it's been a long drive, you have been a bit prickly with me and it would be a nice way of chilling-out, wouldn't it? For both of us?'

'Sometimes I don't think you need much of an excuse Pete, especially when in places like this. Not very practical right now though is it?'

He thought Sue's question showed she wasn't rejecting the idea outright. 'I don't know sweetheart.' He looked around the deserted sandy expanse, slowly and deliberately, then back to her. Next he looked down from her face towards his towel, spread back out on the sand, and then back again giving her what he hoped was an encouraging smile. 'There's nobody here. It's empty and beautiful – and we have the place to ourselves, don't we?'

She stepped toward him. 'Right out here, right out in the open?'

He nodded, looked again from her face to the towel and back again.

'You so love the outdoors don't you!?' She said. To which, he just shrugged and smiled, still hoping she was now warm to the idea. 'You know what though Pete?' she put her hands on his hips, now close to him, facing him. 'I think, in truth, you are as turned-on by the landscape as by me!'

Peter found the last comment running around his head as they embraced each other and kissed.

Chapter 10

They spent much of the next day getting everything ready for the arrival of the others at, so they hoped, around teatime. They obtained the key for the other cottage from a neighbour, discovered it had a big old range as the means of cooking, heating and producing hot water. It was coal-fired and took a while to get going, closely adhering to the hand-written instructions. It occupied most of one side of the downstairs – this being the kitchen part of the one room, open space. The whole of it was cosy with three different sofas in it and it seemed like if they were going to eat together, this would be the place. Sheena's cottage was smaller, especially the kitchen and eating area.

'So, how do you think it will be Sue?' Then, answering his own question, Peter continued. 'Sheena will want to be in her own house, of course, taking the other room beside ours. Doubling-up with Wendy? Mike and Diane have one of the rooms upstairs here? The other's a twin, so I guess that means Ian and Julie?'

'Maybe. But Ian might prefer to be on the bigger sofa down here. He shares climbers' huts with women and men but he might think as Julie is a big mate of mine, he'll want to give her the space to herself. You know what he's like on the chivalry front and he's quite capable of dossing anywhere.' Sue was looking around as she spoke. 'What else is there for us to do now?'

A quick examination outside revealed a barbecue. That could be a real treat, Peter thought – if they could manage to light it and keep it alight. His previous experience didn't encourage him on that front. 'There's some charcoal, and just out the front of this cottage, there's about enough space for some chairs and maybe someone sitting on the wall. That will be the best place for it – perhaps the only place. We just need a nice evening! If we make some smoke it will keep the midges off.'

'Maybe it's always breezy here Pete – seems like it so far. And we haven't been bothered much yet, have we? Perhaps that's why the settlement is here – the locals knew where to build their homes to not get eaten alive the whole summer!'

After a bit more sorting out of the cottages, they went into what they had christened The Town – an affectionate joke they had already made about Tongue, the main settlement three miles down the road and over the other side of the estuary. To be fair, they did think the place had the functions of a bigger place and it did feel quite densely built-up around the hairpin bend of the main road – certainly compared to the sparsely populated nature of the wider area. The hotel dominated the position. A little more housing stretched south down a smaller road. However, in reality it was definitely a small village. One that just happened to be the biggest place for miles and miles.

They liked the drive across the causeway to get to it, and the way that the road crossing the Kyle had the effect of actually widening the landscape. They imagined it was how bits of Canada would appear. They warmed to the feel of the village too. The small supermarket seemed to have everything they wanted and they had already got information about local delivery vans for bread, meat and fish, from the notes and details left in the cottages.

One surprise was a craft shop just on the way out of the village, heading north. An old weaver's place apparently. It had a range of souvenirs, including some woolens, T-shirts and sweatshirts, the latter with a line outline of Ben Loyal and the word Tongue underneath. Peter was really taken with these and bought one in maroon. Sue told him it was a good fit. There were also some books and maps and amongst them a stapled A4 booklet, seemingly written by an archaeologist. The owner of the shop explained this man had been doing research up here the previous two years, and produced and left a supply of booklets for local people and visitors.

There were two of them, one local to Tongue and a thicker one about the Bettyhill area.

'It's actually very interesting' she explained. 'I don't think folk knew, I didn't anyway, that the hills and shore around here have so many traces and remains of people who lived here in the Stone Age.' Peter was intrigued and bought each of these booklets too. As they were about to leave, the lady said, 'If you're minded, it's quite easy to follow his notes and a lot of the remains are hereabouts. Just near the road or the edge of the Kyle, easy to get to from the road. Also all along from here up to Bettyhill actually.'

Getting back in the car, Sue agreed with Peter that the names of places up here were enticing and that they just had to go to somewhere with a name like Bettyhill. But, thinking of their friends, they decided to leave it for another day and to go back to Talmine now, just in case people arrived earlier than expected. Plus, they had bought a lot of vegetables to make a soup for everyone – stove permitting.

As it happened, the two car loads of friends arrived at 5pm. There was a mix of handshakes and hugs then, and introductions where needed, with people acquainting and reacquainting themselves. Ian and Julie, who had each drawn the short straw and driven the last part of the car journey, both looked and sounded really shattered.

'When did road engineering come to a halt going north?' asked Ian, pretending to be angry. 'Bloody hell, about a hundred miles of twisting single-track. Mike and Diane actually fell asleep in the back. What am I? Taxi driver? I thought, it's alright for some!'

'The thing is Ian, I think you are only happy in one seat in that car, and that is the one with the steering wheel!' Said Diane, to general laughter.

'That's so like Pete too Di,' said Sue, 'these men don't like being driven by girls; that's their problem.' Peter and Ian started to protest. 'Well, that's one of them anyway!' she added.

Peter wasn't sure if she meant she was referring to just one of the men or if she meant that was just one of many problems the men had. He decided to join in the joshing. 'That's not it Sue actually. Ian and I just like looking after women and letting them just be comfortable being driven and taken to places, plus giving them a chance to do the navigating instead.'

'You mean, giving them a chance to learn how to use a map Pete' said Ian, to more groans from the five women.

Julie explained, challengingly, that she was definitely a woman and had actually liked the drive, hadn't minded Wendy and Sheena nodding off now and then. 'But,' she slowly continued, 'I can see and hear now, just how lucky it was that a car with three women in it could make its way to here at all! Over such treacherous roads and with no man to tell them what to do!' There was general laughter to that.

'Is this just setting out the battle lines for the fortnight ahead?' Asked Ian, trying not to grin.

But it had all been a cheerful start to the evening. People sorted themselves out while Sue and Peter finished the supper and got dishes ready for everyone. The two of them had bought a couple of litre-boxes of wine from Tongue and although it wasn't a brilliant taste, it went down well with everyone. By the time they had all finished eating, the mood was cheerful and everyone seemed relaxed. Peter realised he had been a bit on edge about the big gathering, as he saw it, but instead now could see that the next couple of weeks could actually be really good fun.

Chapter 11

About halfway through his second morning, and most people's first, drinking a mug of coffee outside on the wall, Peter realised that his desire to be doing stuff was not shared by everyone in the party. It is a holiday after all, he thought, and some are just going to be content to read and do little else. The weather forecast was good with a settled high across the country. Although they were on the northern flank of this, it was expected to stay pretty dry, with sunny intervals and warmish temperatures. It doesn't matter, he thought, there are things to do just locally – exploring the coast and into the interior behind the cottages, an unknown area named A-Mhoine on the map for instance, that appeared completely wild and attractive to him.

Sheena came across then and joined him. 'Sue says she fancies going to Bettyhill. She likes the name. Says you do too. I have been there once. Think there's an attractive bit of coast and the drive's quite nice. There's a hotel there for sure – they might do soup or something if we wanted to have lunch?'

Peter nodded enthusiastically. 'What do you know of these neolithic remains then, scattered around over there apparently?'

'Oh yeah, I hear you have picked up a map or something, er some sort of booklet or pamphlet? Sad to say I know nothing much about that. There is a good ruined broch of that age – you know an old round tower thing. It's a ways from here though, back towards Eriboll and down the wild road to Ben Hope.'

'So, if we do Ben Hope, we could see it?'

'Yes, think you park right by it actually, from memory. Poucher has a picture of his car by it. Are you making a list of trips out then Pete?' She smiled at him.

'Yeah, I know I have a reputation for it. There's Ben Loyal, of course' He pointed at it with his right hand and seeing his own fingers outstretched like that, for some inexplicable reason he suddenly fancied having a cigarette. He might have to cadge one off someone, but not sure who still smoked occasionally apart from him. 'Poucher's mountain guidebook describes a route over that too. Then there is your Ben Hope and the broch. I want to explore this bit of coast in front of us up there north a bit. That's three. Bettyhill as you're suggesting? That's four.' He looked thoughtful. 'I want to take Sue to the very first geological mapping area I did, just above Eriboll and then there's a trip to Durness for all of us I suppose…'

'Well, that's most of the holiday sorted!' said Sheena. 'For you anyway! Don't know about the rest of us. Shall we do the Bettyhill suggestion then, today?'

In the end Peter calculated they would get to the hotel in time for lunch, if they served it. Fingers crossed they did. They took two cars, he and Ian volunteered to drive, an act to which Sue made a show of looking weary, much to the amusement of Julie, Wendy and Sheena. Peter felt it wouldn't be long before they enrolled Diane into their cabal, as he had started to think of it.

Sue decided to go with Ian, Wendy and Sheena, so Peter set-off in his car with Mike beside him and Diane and Julie in the back seat. They were the two who knew each other the least although Peter thought it wouldn't take long to learn more as he noticed they were chatting away amiably from the off. He turned briefly towards Mike as they headed up to Tongue from the Causeway.

'Before this, what was the furthest north that you got from your Gairloch holidays then?'

Mike thought for a moment. 'Well, like I said back when we talked about this trip, I know we all went as far as Ullapool. One time anyway. I can remember the ferry coming in or going out – to the Hebrides. And we had good fish and chips on the harbourside. That's probably about it. We stayed pretty local really.'

'Like me up this way, I guess. It took longer to get anywhere back then, I was lucky with the field trips though.'

'Oh yeah – remind me again Pete, you had actually come this far north hadn't you?'

Peter slowed down for the road going round a long bend, to head east to a hamlet called Coldbackie.

'Well, we stayed in Durness. You came up here from Dingwall and Lairg yesterday, but there is an even longer route up the west. From Ullapool northwards, then east across to here. Durness is on the corner – miles over there.' He pointed out of Mike's car window with his free hand.

'There was an old RAF station there, at a place called Balnakeil. Glasgow University had one of the old accommodation huts as a rough base. This trip was to learn the basics of geological mapping on a hill called Ben Arnaboll. Obviously it wasn't some randomly chosen hill. It's actually steeped in the history of geology as a science. Anyway, Sue and I also stopped there, on the roadside anyway, coming up here the other day.'

'But did you get right over here too? Back then I mean, when you were a student?'

'There was a breakaway one day – a splinter group, led by a research student. He drove a few of us over to the base of Ben Loyal, just back there.' He pointed with his left hand over his shoulder this time. 'Think he was wanting to see granite outcrops but I'm not sure we found anything much other than some plane wreckage!'

Peter went on to explain that the wreckage had some significance. Having failed to find any useful granite outcrops, they had all gone to the pub in Tongue where they encountered the local GP having a drink. He had told them that there had been a bomber sent out from Wick in 1943, during the height of the War. It had crashed into the mountain killing all the crew, except one. Peter explained how moving it had been to hear this tale, little realising that he was about to encounter something similar on his own mapping project later that summer.

Mike had been listening thoughtfully to all this. 'I think Gairloch was caught up with the war too but don't know much about it.'

'Yeah, it definitely was Mike. Where I mapped down in Kinlochewe, the Nature Reserve Warden and a chap from Gairloch, they told us a bit about it. There had been a massive military operation going on up here around Loch Ewe. None of us knew. In fact I've never seen or read anything about it since.'

'But that was after being up here on your Durness trip?'

'Sorry, yes, to finish that story of the geology trip. From the Balnakeil place we went south to Scourie one or two days but mostly we were on dear old Ben Arnaboll. So, never to Talmine. And I had never heard of Bettyhill until yesterday.' He paused, distracted momentarily by sheep lying alongside the edge of the road. He knew they could easily just wake-up and run into the road. 'And it's all new to Di?'

Mike nodded. Peter saw in his mirror that Diane looked up from her conversation with Julie when her name was mentioned.

'Just talking about you Di!' he smiled at the rear view mirror, but Diane and Julie went straight back into the deeper conversation they had been having. He and Mike talked about work a bit and then before long they were on the last stretch of the little road north, that soon emerged onto coast leading into the settlement of Bettyhill, by a river flowing across the sandy beach. The white-painted hotel was up to the side, easily the biggest building in the visible area. And there, they were pleased to discover, soup was served. Everyone opted for a glass of beer too, then coffee to round things off.

Peter had brought the pamphlets with him and opened the one titled *What to see around Bettyhill. A guide to local history and archaeology by Kevin J O'Reilly*. The author was a lecturer at North London Poly he noticed. He spoke to everyone across the two small tables. 'This chap marks out a half-dozen places to see just beside the road going back south from here – do you fancy a look?'

Everyone consented, but most of them also expressing hope that it wasn't going to be too boggy, nor too far.

'Well, according to our friend Kevin here, the places are along the side of the road because this is where people lived – near both fresh water and the sea. Makes sense when you think about it. I don't suppose the neolithic villagers were into mountain walking too much!'

'OK Pete. You have the job. You're the guide.' said Julie. 'Just be gentle on us.'

Just then, Ian came back from a loo trip and talked about the sign in the corridor. They were all amazed to hear him recount the limited information on a plaque pinned to the wall. Apparently King Haakon The Seventh of Norway had stayed at this hotel during World War Two. Peter looked north out of the panoramic windows at the grey sea and slightly bluer sky and wondered how It must have been to look out back then wondering what was happening back in your own country maybe just 300 miles away in a straight line. Just half of the distance they had travelled from home to holiday.

More history emerged as they followed Peter's reading of the pamphlet. There were several sites to see, which necessitated short drives down the road to places to park-up, followed by short walks over tussocky moorland. One of these was a Highland clearance village originally called Achanlochy, now mostly pieces of thick walling of different heights, half buried by peat and vegetation. It had been abandoned to make way for sheep farming a century and more earlier the booklet stated. The back story sounded awful and was another revelation to them all. Even Sheena had only a vague idea of the Highland Clearances. 'Maybe if my Mum hadn't moved down south before having me, I might have known more.' She said.

In addition to this, they were amazed to be able to actually enter, and go inside, two or three old chambered cairns in different places – burial chambers from the Iron Age, almost big enough to walk into, the taller of them simply having to stoop a bit more. Peter and Ian stood outside one of these and found themselves looking across the terrain.

'You know what? Ian was literally scratching his head as he spoke. 'This tops anything down in England really, except Stonehenge itself. Just the fact that the place here is littered with history and you can walk right into it!'

Peter agreed. 'I suppose they just get so few visitors around here or we might have heard of it. It's a wonder they're preserved though. You would think the stone would have been reused over time.'

'Maybe they revered the area Pete, or maybe there is enough stone around not to have to dismantle old ruins? Your Kevin O'Reilly chap documents dozens of villages, houses, tombs. Astonishing really. Must have been a busy community – but thousands of years ago! And not just then, but continuing through time – people living here for centuries on centuries.' concluded Ian, shaking his head, almost in disbelief.

They spent more time around the area than they had expected, all of them being taken by the sense of history and continuity of life. By the time they set-off back to Talmine they were tired, in part from trying to process so many pieces of information, partly from the previous day's long drives, and then also from just settling into holiday mode. Peter thought the lunchtime beers had something to do with it too.

Julie came up to Peter as they unloaded themselves from the cars, back at the cottages. 'Thanks for that Pete – it was great. You doing the guiding reminded me of old times. You back in Kinlochewe telling us all about the geology and the mountains.'

Peter thought that was a nice memory and he smiled at Julie.

'Thank you. Er - you mean, you've remembered me for all those years, boring you to death about rocks!' he joked.

'Actually you were mostly pretty quiet then, but sometimes your exuberance came out.'

Peter felt he hadn't ever considered himself exuberant and felt surprised at the word, but before he could reflect further, Julie added.

'I'm glad we are all up here together. I love my old chum Sue – different way to you maybe, assuming you do?' Julie went on before Peter could say anything. 'You and me should have a chat while we're here.'

Peter felt she had sounded quite enigmatic but he also felt that she had made the proposal as one that he hadn't any choice in accepting.

Chapter 12

As a result of the tiredness, they all decided to just hang around for the following day and reward themselves with a day-off, as Peter called it. Wendy took herself away early, to the beach to read and be in her own world for a while – even before some of them had got up or had breakfast. She took warm clothes, some fruit, a swimming costume and, most importantly, her book. Right now she was reading The Name of the Rose. Peter had asked her about this as he knew nothing about it and thought it sounded a bit highbrow when he read the author note inside her copy. She had told him that actually it was a bit of a who-done-it story that bowled along at a pace and was really enjoyable. She also said she had read a magazine article that they were going to make it into a film.

Peter thought it looked thick enough to keep her satisfyingly absorbed for a few days. He was chuffed that Wendy had suggested he borrow it when she finished. Seeing her go off on her own provoked him into thinking he might do the same thing – but more by way of a walk. He had a check of the map and decided he would just go up the coast a bit, mainly to get a view of Rabbit Islands from the north, plus he thought he might also find some interesting rocks to examine or just see some wildlife.

Everyone else decided to go in a group down to the beach. Most of them were initially sceptical of Sue and Sheena's assurance that the sea was easily accessible and simply involved a nice walk past rabbits and across an expanse of sand They were even more doubting that it was bearable in terms of temperature for a swim. But any doubts were trumped by enthusiasm to just get out into the wild space.

Firstly Ian, and then Mike, decided to take rucksacks as the easiest way of carrying their things. Noticed by the others, they soon found themselves packing everyone else's jumpers, towels, swimwear, food, water, books and various small bottles of what they thought were lotions and potions. The five women set-off carrying very little, also leaving the two men with the job of locking-up.

'Pete had the right idea I reckon! Buggering off on his own.' said Ian. 'What about you and me then? Have we got the word mug tattooed on our foreheads?'

Mike laughed and said 'We will get our reward one day no doubt.'

'You might Mike! I'm the bloke here on my own! Honestly, five great women for company and we end-up being the beach sherpas.' He hoped Mike knew he was joking and decided to change the subject. 'What do you make of us all then? Hope we're not too cliquey. You could come across from Bristol and go on one or two of our trips sometime?' Mike gave a bit of a shrug, effectively saying maybe but not being sure.

'Pete fits in fine when he's across our way.' Ian continued. 'You ought to, you would be one of us very quickly I reckon.' He paused to adjust his rucksack, then continued. 'There's not much doing during the summer, as everyone's away – like us here. Come the autumn though. We have a trip to Ogwen for instance, just below Tryfan – mountain you might know. It's camping – you ok with that?'

Mike thought that Ian was very chatty. 'Well, camping, yes, er … if like in Greece, or Cornwall one summer – Diane and I liked. Might need some persuading about Snowdonia in October though! Di definitely wouldn't like that!' He hesitated then. 'Is this the track down the rabbit warren field do you think?'

On the path down from the road to the sand, Ian extolled the virtues of autumn and winter camping to a disbelieving Mike. He thought he might try it if Peter also went across and took him along. Then he thought that was perhaps unlikely as Peter would certainly be going with Sue. He found himself warming to the idea more though, as they soon found their way to the area of sand backed by the schistose cliff, where the women were all waiting for them. Mike thought this trip already felt like an adventure and Ian's Snowdonia suggestion might be another.

The five women were in a line, hands bunched in fists, pressed into the tops of their hips, all pretending to be fierce. 'What took you so long?' said Julie, speaking for them all and deliberately sounding disdainful. 'There's no point in us hiring porters and them not being able to keep up!'

Ian scowled at her, but then grinning. 'Well if you can find a cheaper porter – go ahead Julie! Cos so far we haven't seen a silver shilling have we Mike? And anyway…' he went on without waiting for an answer, '…it's quality you want isn't it? Not cheap service.'

'Speed is what we want Ian actually.' Julie shouted, to giggles from the others. 'Now get those packs off, so we can get ourselves sorted.' There was a brief moment when everyone sorted out their belongings. 'Now, you two boys are going to have to have a very good look at Ben Loyal.'

'Why's that then' said Mike innocently.

'Because we, us five girls that is,' Julie continued, 'but we may deign to invite you two soon as well, are going to take a shot at getting in the water shortly and have a swim. Therefore, we need to get into our cozzies. And we aren't going to wiggle about inside the towels and all that faff, when it's simply easier to just get you two blokes to look the other way!' She looked at the two men with her fists bunched on her hips, and then pointed at Ben Loyal - so they dutifully turned round.

'You're a bully Julie.' said Sue. 'Poor lads.'

'And you always were a bit soft with the boys Sue! Come on. Let's get changed.'

Neither Mike nor Ian knew much about this mountain other than Peter's comments the previous evening, but were happy to scrutinise it from a distance for a few minutes. 'Sounds like we are going to have a go at it tomorrow?'

'Is that what Pete said Mike? Fine by me. Guess we'll be joined by Sue and Sheena. Weather's good for it. I believe. If it's five, we can go in one car.' Ian paused. 'Could be warm weather even, once we get going. Might be a lot of heathery bouldering though, so maybe not ideal for shorts.' Mike felt he would be happy to go with the flow.

'OK lads.' Julie said from behind them, 'we are all kitted-up and decent now, if you can call Sue's swimming stuff decent that is, and you can turn around.'

All the women had changed, now spontaneously made a mock fashion show line-up, with hands gently resting on hips this time, turning around and giving Mike and Ian a teasing look over their shoulders with much fluttering of the eyelashes. The two of them laughed and applauded.

'I'm staying here, by the way,' said Wendy, addressing the two men. 'I'm hoping to get a bit of sun while just lying here reading. However, I'm not going to spend several minutes staring at Ben Loyal though, so if you two want to change I promise to keep looking at this book and not to peek!'

The six swimmers soon all walked in a line across the sand to the sea's edge. After a plunge for some, and a proper swim for others, people soon decided to go back to the cliff, settle down, dry off, read, chat and think about lunch. After a while, and at just the right moment, Peter came along the sand.

He nonchalantly sat down on a rock that was just protruding through the beach, on the edge of the group. Sue and Ian were nearest to him and he told them about his walk a couple of miles north from Talmine and back the same way. He said it had been mostly trackless, a few sheep around, quite boggy in places but some interesting rocks. He hadn't seen anyone else between leaving Talmine and then returning.

Sue persuaded him to change and go with her for a walk across to the water. They wore jumpers on top of their swimwear, deciding they could just leave them on a towel if they went in the sea. Peter could sense Sue wanted to talk about something.

'I've been thinking Peter.' The use of his full name immediately put him on alert and concentrating on what Sue was saying. 'I think it's being with a group of people again, on holiday, having fun. Makes me think of Chamonix!'

Peter thought she sounded cheerful and relaxed again. 'Yes, it's a year since we were there.'

'A year since we started…' Sue left the sentence unfinished.

Peter then knew for sure that Sue had wanted to be with him on her own and wondered where the discussion was going to go. They reached the edge of the water and found there was another line of jellyfish on the sand. They both speculated again if they were still alive and why they appeared to congregate in such large groups.

'The only thing is, I can't tell when the tide comes in or out Sue – these sand bars seem so extensive all the time.'

'Hmm – I hope the jellyfish manage it ok.' She took Peter's hand, continuing the walk but more slowly. 'Do you think our thing, relationship or whatever it is, goes in and out Pete? A bit like the tide?'

Peter felt uneasy. 'How do you mean?' he asked, suddenly feeling a bit unbalanced, even though Sue's tone was just normal.

Sue talked about how things had been for her since the previous summer, how much she liked Peter as a friend, as a boyfriend, and felt at ease with him and comfortable. It hadn't been overbearing, which she liked, after the marriage with Colin, and had enjoyed all the attention and affection she received from him. She wondered though what would happen next?

'Can't we just carry on as we are?'

'It's a bit tedious isn't it, driving across at weekends to Bristol?' She took a moment to look around towards Tongue, watching some quite big birds on the water's edge not far from them. 'Don't get me wrong.' She took his hand. 'It's lovely being together but don't you think we both sometimes find other things are going on, so that the weekends when we miss meeting-up, those have occurred more often?'

'I'm not seeing anyone else Sue.' Peter found himself surprisingly defensive.

'I never think that Pete.' Sue exclaimed. 'I think I would know. But. Look, the truth is … sometimes I think of you and Steve.'

Peter felt his stomach start to tighten, a bit uncomfortably. 'It was a long time ago, never to be repeated. I've told you.' It felt dismissive. He didn't like this conversation but needed to stop sounding sharp and as if he was being challenged.

'Never.' Sue stated this word flatly, not as a question. 'Hmm - I wonder though, when you're on your own, do you think about it.'

Peter wondered what, precisely, she meant, and felt a need to assert how he felt about things. 'I'm with you now and I don't want to go anywhere else. This holiday is going well, seems good fun, it's all fine isn't it?' There was uncertainty, probably insecurity too, in his voice he thought. He felt hollow when he imagined the possibility of no longer having her as his girlfriend.

Sue intuited this and said. 'I know you feel that Pete. But what happens next? For us? Do we live together properly, all the time? What does that mean for work?' She stopped now and looked Peter square on. 'What about a family?' She saw he was looking a bit sadder by the moment.

He felt his mouth had gone dry. He had never imagined being a father – was that because of the gay thing or was he just not paternal, like the gene hadn't switched-on for him? Yet? Maybe he would feel like that one day? This conversation had actually got his heart pounding, it felt a bit like being on the crux of a rock climb. He wasn't sure what the next move was.

Sue perceived all of that running through Peter's mind as she held her look at him. She didn't want to upset him but needed to be open about how she felt. Asking the questions was helpful surely? But Peter had completely clammed-up, she could see, and if anything he now looked frightened. Was that about having kids or about losing her? These thoughts made her start to feel sad and she decided to change the subject.

'Never mind Pete. As you say, we are having a good time. And you're right – it is an easy-going holiday.' She put a hand on his hip. 'I did miss you when you went off this morning. Come on, let's jog back.' And she grabbed his arm more firmly as they set-off.

Peter was pleased the conversation had been dropped but it left him feeling more than a bit unsteady. He was pleased when they re-joined everybody else and he readily tucked into the sandwiches he'd prepared. The conversation turned to the possibility of having a barbecue that evening. The VHS machine would provide the music – Wendy's tape was felt to be ideal. The three men were delegated to get the food from the supermarket, and the wine. Sheena quietly suggested that Ian, being an engineer, was just the person to stoke-up the barbecue itself and keep it going for the evening.

'It's servitude now!' Exclaimed Ian, 'that's what it is – men servants is what we are now!' Everyone just laughed.

They all felt Ian had been the right choice though when, by seven o'clock, flames were leaping out of the battered, ironmongery of the barbecue. He had positioned it up-wind a yard or two from the seating area and warned everyone it would get a bit smoky – 'but that's half the fun of it' he said. He also let people know that it would be a little while before the charcoal settled down and developed a white ashy surface which would mean, according to him, that it would then be hot enough to cook the things they had got from the supermarket. Locally made sausages being the main ingredient.

Peter and Mike had organised chairs outside, along with a couple of side tables, the plates, glasses and the cutlery. They had also set-to making some salad and putting mayonnaise, coleslaw and sweetcorn relish into bowls.

Meanwhile, the five women had gone for a stroll down to Talmine Beach, the little cove just below the houses, and when they came back just settled down outside and continued to chat, evidently in good spirits. Peter and Mike came out from the kitchen area then, changed into their best trousers and white t-shirts, each with tea-towels draped neatly over one arm.

'Would any of you ladies care for a drink?' asked Peter, feigning a posh voice.

'Thought you'd never ask.' Said Sheena, giggling at them. 'Service in this restaurant needs fixing.'

'Well, excuse me!' said Peter haughtily. 'Here we are, us blokes, been labouring away all afternoon it seems, getting supplies from the shop, getting everything ready out here. Ian has had to apply everything he knows about thermodynamics to get the barbecue ready. And what do we get!! Eh?' He turned to Mike, rolling his eyes and shaking his head. 'What we get,' he continued, 'is just criticism and poor attitude. Right! We should go on strike Mike.'

'Aww, you boys don't know you're born,' chipped-in Julie, 'being away here with five beautiful women! Ordinarily…,' She was interrupted by the other four shouting noises of agreement. '… Ordinarily we,' she swept her arm across the female friends, 'we would be the ones doing everything, so consider yourselves lucky to be given the opportunity to put things straight a bit – on behalf of all mankind.'

'Yes please' added Wendy, 'mine's a large white wine!'

By the time, Ian and Mike cooked and served the grilled meat, everyone had drunk a fair bit of wine. It had stayed fair and they had kept open the door of the cottage, so the video soundtrack could be heard. Wendy's three hour Top of the Pops recording assembly was well appreciated, more so as the evening wore on. Occasional locals went past with a cheery evening greeting exchanged and apparently unbothered by the group of young visitors having a happy time.

Peter felt he had eaten a bit too much and decided to go for a short walk to shake down the food, so he said. Sue didn't want to go with him but Julie jumped up and manoeuvred herself over the wall to follow him. Catching-up with him she produced a pack of cigarettes and offered one to Peter.

'But you don't smoke Julie.'

'Only on holiday. And only the last few years. I know, I know, I know it's stupid to start but I went out with this guy a while back and he was so cool doing it that I joined in. This will be the first one on this trip, as you've seen, and I don't feel like I'm addicted.'

'I do' said Peter, taking one and enjoying the new sensation of Julie lighting it for him with her lighter. He inhaled it deeply and liked it. 'I am trying to stop though. Back as a student, as you know, I puffed away all the time, but now I feel I am continually trying to stop. Truth is I really sometimes go for a drink or do something, specifically because I associate it with having a fag and feel I can justify it. But I don't buy them regularly at all.'

'You don't have to justify yourself to me Pete. Not for smoking anyway.' Julie looked around and saw another bit of roadside wall, around a garden. It seemed to be detached from the nearby cottage, so she suggested to Peter that they sit and smoke there a few minutes. They were pretty sure nobody would take offence.

As soon as he sat down, and after her last passing comment, Peter realised Julie was going to ask him about Sue. After all, he had seen at first hand how closely the two women supported each other and he could see now how much Julie was doing this again after Sue's debacle with Colin. He felt relaxed though and the alcohol and nicotine made him feel receptive.

Julie took a drag, blew out the smoke looking back towards the cottage and barbecue a hundred yards away. 'How do you think Sue is doing post-Colin?'

'Well, you know that we have been seeing each other a lot since the Alps last summer.' he paused to get Julie's nod and she now gave him her full attention, in such a focused way , it made him feel a bit unnerved. 'It's not every weekend, work sometimes makes it difficult to drive across to Swansea or her to me. You get to Friday evening and ploughing through the delays on the Severn Bridge doesn't always feel attractive.'

'But you obviously think she is though! Right?'

'Of course. We've liked each other a lot since Kinlochewe, as you know. I didn't ever think we would become a couple though.'

'Is that what you are?' Julie ran her hand over her forehead and down through her flowing curly locks. 'Hmm. You are affectionate friends I can see that. You have definitely helped Sue get over Colin.' She ran her hand down Peter's thigh. 'Sweet boy that you are! You know, she adores you for doing that.'

'Does she?' Peter felt like he had blurted out the question, surprised and relieved simultaneously.

Julie fixed her eyes on his, then she said quietly. 'You know she does.' A pause. 'I think she always will. You helped her feel good about herself again.'

Neither of them said anything then, They looked out to Rabbit Islands, dusk gently starting to spread across the hills and the water. Peter felt very moved. They finished the cigarettes, stubbing them out on the wall but not immediately getting up to go back. Julie changed tack a bit.

'Sue tells me you might be getting a new job. They must like you. This one sounds like you will be travelling all over the place? What will that mean for your weekend Severn Bridge ventures I wonder?'

There were quite a few thoughts running through Peter's head now. The conversation had made him think of the practicality of travelling up and down, all over really. He thought Julie was right – his firm probably did like what he did work-wise. Well, obviously they did, to promote him. He felt it was the justified reward for all the work he did though. But would it mean seeing Sue less, he realised he hadn't thought enough of the reality of that. He knew he would need to be with her more than ever, but would that happen so often? Just as he was mulling this, Julie asked another question that completely knocked him off-balance. She said it slowly, almost annunciating each word.

'Pete, why…' Julie held a gap in the question, '…why do you think you never kept in touch with Steve?'

He took a moment to react. 'Blimey Julie. It's a long time ago, I was twenty then and now twenty-seven.' He wondered about asking for a second cigarette, then thought he just wanted to get back to the group but he couldn't be impolite. He tried to dismiss the subject, feigning being light-hearted. 'I'm not a poof I suppose. Maybe he's not now either - for all I know.'

Julie didn't say anything, tilted her head to one side looking thoughtful. She just looked at him and held the silence. Peter felt there was then a telepathic discussion going on between them. He hadn't before appreciated that Julie could do this too – nearly as well as her best friend. As the moment stretched out further, Peter found himself asking the same question repeatedly in his head. It was a good one! "Why do you think you never kept in touch with Steve?" Eventually it dawned on him that the true answer was a very simple feeling, one not at all easy to admit. It was because he was scared! Very scared of what it said about him and also what it meant for the future.

This realisation felt a bit of a shock. Then he thought he might get emotional and he could feel himself trembling. Julie had been very clever, he thought, to speak with him like this. He bit into his bottom lip, not quite stopping a tear emerging. He turned to Julie and nodded his head slightly, two or three times. She leant across and gave him a hug and a peck on the cheek, then took out a tissue to dab his eyes. 'Come on, lovely old friend. Let's get back to the others, shall we?'

Dusk had brought with it a slight drop of the breeze and with that some midges had emerged it seemed. As Julie and Peter returned, everyone agreed they might be better off clearing up and going indoors. Sheena and Wendy suggested they have a disco, watching the video. There were whoops of agreement and it was clear to Peter that everyone was in the mood for a bop, and felt relieved as this mood infected him too. A mood fuelled by alcohol but also by everyone now just feeling relaxed and happy with each other.

'More wine is what we need most' said Sue, and Peter looked at her. She was not usually the one to hasten the drinking and he saw that she was a bit tiddly already. By the time they had rearranged the living space and sorted-out all the dishwashing and all had another glass of wine, it was practically dark. Julie, who had been looking out of the door for a while, turned to the room and suggested actually they could all go for a swim down in the little cove below. 'Freshen us up before a dance! Bit like having a shower before going clubbing, but northern Scottish style!'

It was the women who met the idea most enthusiastically. It was a spontaneous suggestion and it just happened to land at the right moment for people to go with it. For a couple of minutes, people were running here there and everywhere it felt, and then suddenly they were all outside Sheena's Cottage and heading off to get onto the small and rather scrappy road that led down to the tiny Talmine Bay and its even tinier harbour tucked away on its north side. It was only a five minute walk, downhill.

The one house down there didn't have any lights on and there was no dog barking. They didn't want to disturb anyone and hoped the place was unoccupied. It was located right by the turning onto the beach itself. Arriving there, they all felt like it was now their own private space. Nobody afterwards could agree who had actually first made the suggestion for a skinny dip. But it happened anyway.

Again, this idea was more readily taken up by the women than the men, but it was a case of one-in all-in, so before long there were eight little heaps of clothes on the beach and eight naked people in the water. Julie said, 'Sue has this theory that if you stay still enough in cold water it warms a little around you, don't you Sue?' Sue responded by using two hands to slosh water in Julie's direction, and then they were all doing it. After more high jinks and a bit of joshing, there was a quiet moment. Wendy noticed the phosphorescence first and pointed it out to the others. Everyone became still then, just gently sweeping their arms through the water to see the tiny arrays of sparkles it produced. Nobody could ever remember seeing it anywhere previously and it felt magical and held them all in wonder.

Getting back out, people were now quieter but the sense of happy harmony shared between them had deepened somehow. There were hugs all round as people hurriedly and casually towel-dried and half-dressed and then within a few minutes more they were back in the one cottage's warm living room. It felt very warm with the stove going and their skin cold. Someone said that as a lot of the clothes were damp why not leave them off. The cottage had three washing lines suspended across the range area and jeans were thrown over these, and some jumpers. It had somehow become an impromptu underwear disco.

Ian turned-up the volume of the telly to max and Sue and Sheena went round the room with one of the boxed wines each, red or white, pouring more into everyone's glass. Total Eclipse of the

Heart was up next. 'You should like her.' Peter shouted to Sheena, Wendy and Sue, who happened to be together at this point.

'What? Who are you talking about Peter?' Asked Wendy.

'Her!' Peter said, pointing at the telly. 'Bonnie Tyler! She's a Swansea girl. Isn't she!?' Peter hoped he had it correct, as since the days of prog rock he knew he wasn't so good on musical who's-who and what's-what.

'She sounds like she's smoked as much as you.' Sue quipped.

'Let her off.' Interrupted Julie. 'Pete's right about her. She had some sort of throat op, according to the local paper. I think she's just wonderful.'

Peter decided to try and copy the video move of the singer running down the corridor of a mansion house. There was no space to do this in the cottage really, so he ended up leaping in the air, legs apart, one arm pointing in each direction. People giggled. Sue remarked to him that she thought he was in a very good mood.

'I am Sue! I've had a lot of wine too! Isn't she gorgeous?' pointing at the telly. The video had moved on to the section where a lot of young men were also leaping around on the steps of a country house, but they were doing it very professionally.

'You sure it's Bonnie you fancy or is it those guys?' Sue whispered in his ear. Then she moved off to continue dancing.

Peter was pondering what Sue had said, because he did like the athletic men in the video but felt the whole video was arousing to some extent. He wondered if Sue was just teasing him or if there was something more to it. The wine was muddling his thinking for sure. Just then Mike sidled up to him.

'When you invited me Pete, I didn't think for one minute I would end-up dancing in just my briefs!'

'Neither did I!' Peter exclaimed, scanning around the room. 'I hope Di is alright with this? Sorry, there was never anything like this in the Alps. Nor anywhere else really.'

'She's having a good time. Look at her, hair down, literally, seems to be getting on well with Julie, Wendy – all of them really.'

'Yeah? That's good! I'd hate to think you had been brought on holiday under false pretences!'

'It's fine Pete. Just relax.'

Michael Jackson's Billie Jean was on then and everybody seemed to be trying to emulate some of those moves. Mike and Peter tried to do this from the edge of the room. This approach continued into Uptown Girl by Billy Joel. A slower one came on next, 'Wherever I lay my Hat' by Paul Young. One of the women hissed and then all five of them were name-calling the singer and the song. Mike asked Peter why. Sheena, nearby at this point, said 'It's cos it's about blokes going off and getting off here, there and everywhere and not sticking by their partners!' Then she booed at the telly again.

'Now we know!' said Mike. 'You haven't got a ciggie have you?'

'Oh God, not you too! This seems to be the holiday for people taking up smoking. You not seen the government advice on the packets either? Julie was just starting the habit too; so you're not alone.' Peter looked around the room and the wreckage assembling on the kitchen counter, spotting a black and gold packet. 'Don't worry I will get some. Don't know who's though!'

Peter then found himself standing close to Mike in the corner of the room as they lit cigarettes and leant back against the wall, crowded out by the shoved-aside furniture and by the dancing. Peter could feel Mike's thigh pressing against his own in the constrained space. He looked down at the two of them in fairly tight-fitting underwear. It flashed through Peter's mind that he thought Mike looked good like that. He was lost in this thought and then looked up at what had become the dance floor. He saw Sue dancing, surrounded by friends and being happy. Then he didn't know what to think – too much wine, too much going on in his head, all combining to crowd out coherent thinking.

Chapter 13

The morning after the night before thought Peter, emerging into a bright day, propping himself up against the door post of the cottage, mug of tea in one hand, a piece of toast spread with Marmite and peanut butter in the other. He knew that what would make him feel much better would be some good exercise. A run was a possibility later but a walk with others would be much nicer. Could he still persuade anyone to come up Ben Loyal, he wondered. It had been a rudimentary plan he had chatted about with the others, but that was before a late-night party and unexpected disco.

As it turned-out, he wasn't alone in his wish for fresh air and exercise. As people gradually emerged into daylight, it wasn't long before there was a car-load for the excursion – Ian, Sue, Mike, Sheena and himself, as had been predicted. Julie told them that she, Wendy and Diane would be just perfectly happy to have a bit more space for the day and just do nothing. These three also stated that they were feeling a bit delicate after all the wine too. Peter thought they had formed a tight little trio within the bigger group and imagined them heading off to Tongue later or maybe just another excursion down past the rabbit field.

It was only a twenty minute drive for the mountaineering group. Two miles south of Tongue, Peter parked-up by the little roadside lake, marked Lochan na Cuilce on their map. Dressed in favourite light clothes and feeling fitter than he had expected, he spread the map out on the bonnet of the car and explained the route to the others.

'OK, we start by going across this boggy field and I can see there is a bit of a track straight up into the corrie. It's a bealach really, a bit of a pass, we swing round on what is hopefully easier going ground and up to the first summit. Then along a broad ridge, hopefully, to the second peak and then a long descent and back round the flank of the mountain, along the top of the woodland bit and back to here.'

The others had been following what he said, by looking out across to the mountain itself. Ian felt this was the wrong approach as it meant a steep climb early-on that could easily necessitate scrambling and he didn't want them all to then have to find an alternative route or, worse, find they needed to back-down. He didn't want to depress Peter's enthusiasm though, so was gentle in his challenge.

'Tell you what Pete, why don't we think about taking the route you have studied, but do it the other way round? That way we would end-up coming back down towards this point quite quickly, from the final summit, but after having done the whole thing? It means a longer slog out, now, but shorter at the end?' Ian made sound it more of a question than a suggestion. 'Might be easier on our hangovers to have a gentle easing-in to the mountain?' He added.

That last point got a thumbs up from Mike and enthusiastic nods from Sue and Sheena. Peter wanted to argue but decided, when he thought a bit more, that actually the idea made sense. He just felt a bit miffed. Sue whispered to him 'You don't own the North West Highlands you know!' She said it with a smile and gave his arm a squeeze and Peter thought that she had made a fair point. He did feel a bit proprietorial about the rocks and mountains up here.

Nobody else really had a view about what to do, so they all headed off, on the route as Ian had proposed, towards the wooded western flank of the mountain. They noticed the wood was named Coille na Cuile on the map and Ian and Peter led the way, map in hand. They all commented that it was as well that there had been a dry spell of weather or it would have been very boggy. The ground steepened soon as they went up the eastern edge of the mixed and partly decaying woodland, where they encountered rough ground full of blocks of rock, boulders and thick, stalky heather.

Everyone else, like Peter, had opted for shorts to make the most of a sunny day, but they all now started to regret it as wading through the terrain meant getting scratches, knocks and bruises at times. At the top edge of the wooded area though, the almost invisible track headed south-west on a contour across steeper, but more open ground. The scattered woodland swept downwards to their right.

'What are all these trees – anyone know?' asked Sheena.

'Wendy's the biologist, she could tell us.' Suggested Ian.

'Yes, but hopefully she is using any plant knowledge right now, making a hearty veg soup for us all tonight.' Said Sheena. 'But she probably would know, to be fair.'

'They're mostly birches. Some Mountain Ash.' They all turned to Peter.

'Oooo – get you! Becoming a bit of a David Bellamy all of a sudden.' Ian said.

'It's not just rocks you know then?' asked Mike.

Peter replied, 'I was fortunate really. When I did my mapping project, there was an old woodland there too and I got to know some of the tree types then. It was, still is, a part of the old forest that cloaked the Highlands after the Ice Age. It had immense Scots Pines, plus all these types of trees too. Walked through them a number of times – I loved being there.'

'Not just walked amongst them.' Stated Sue, enigmatically to everyone but Peter. 'Come on, we haven't time for landscape lectures. My head can't take it this morning.' He looked at her and wondered if he had actually just heard a slightly sarcastic tone. She didn't return his look though and left him wondering why she was saying things like this. On this holiday particularly it felt like she was making a point at times and it worried him what might be going on in her head.

When they approached some rocky cliffs looming above them,

Ian explained they would now be turning upwards and around into a little valley leading to the bealach from which they would ascend the peaks of the mountain. The angle increased immediately and Peter realised how much of a pull it was on his calf muscles. He made a mental note to include more calf raises in his gym routine back home. Then he thought he might just have pulled his muscles a bit the night before, bopping and leaping around in their disco.

For about twenty minutes, it almost became a technical scramble, with everyone needing to use hands as well as legs to balance and clamber upwards and over the now very steep slope of boulders and rock outcrops. Around them was almost total rock exposure with scree and Peter was reminded of his student geology work, where a lot of rock exposure meant a lot of measurements, although he knew this rock was a very different type. He couldn't concentrate on that right now though as he needed to really think about where he was putting his hands and feet. Plus he now felt responsible towards Mike and the two women, even though it seemed they were just getting on with it anyway.

In the end the section of the climb felt tricky for all of them but was short-lived and they emerged from it onto easier ground, heading directly south. The route was still upwards, but less relentlessly. About a half-hour after leaving the woodland edge, they abruptly turned east and closely followed a stream upwards to a point where another lochan suddenly appeared to their left, Lochan Fhionnaich, where they took a rest.

'Oh God' said Sue, 'as if last night wasn't enough, Pete's going to suggest we all go for a swim in that!'

'Ha, ha. No, I'm not. Although it is stunning location - and pretty private right now.'

'Last night was enough for me.' Said Sheena. 'It's not the skinny-dipping that I'm thinking about right now though, just the lingering effect of all that wine!'

'I can't believe we all did that,' said Sue. 'I woke up thinking what my Mum would say if she knew I had been jumping around in the sea, naked, with a group including three men, one I hardly know!' She looked towards Mike and smiled at him. 'Then, if that's not enough, dancing around to Michael Jackson and Men At Work, in my knickers!!'

They all laughed. 'Well, we have the wine to thank for that too.' Added Sheena.

After more discussion about drinking, phosphorescence, the video tape and more, there was a need to move on. Peter and Ian had been alternating taking the lead since leaving the car, and now Ian got everyone back on their feet for the final pull up to the summit ridge.

After twenty minutes or so they were on it and more briskly walking north to the higher of the twin peaks. Once there, they took a bit of time looking at the three hundred and sixty degree vista trying to identify the things they might recognise even though the landscape was mostly new to all of them. Peter admitted his knowledge was slender too, having only previously been to the base of this hill, but he talked a bit about the prominent and neighbouring peak of Ben Hope to the west and what he thought must be the range of Foinaven to the left of it. He hoped he was right.

Closer to hand they all tried to identify the trip they had taken to Bettyhill, straight ahead of them from here, and then finally searching out Talmine and their holiday homes across the Kyle of Tongue. The extent of the sand within the Kyle surprised them and they all agreed that the walk they were doing should be rewarded by another day on the beach tomorrow. Books and fibre-pile jackets if need be, but they hoped it might be ok again for a swim again too, or even, fingers crossed, remain sunny.

Sue thought they could make out Durness, where she had

stopped with Peter on the way up. Happy to extend the time of this breather, Sheena asked where it was.

'Well it is over there' said Sue pointing. 'To the right of Ben Hope but more in the distance. It's there where the road turns the corner to come across this way if you've come up from Ullapool direction. There's a hotel there that Pete said we could go to, the Cape Wrath, - all together one day. More soup and views I think!'

'No King of Norway there though. A lot of space and a lot of history. It was the hang-out for the field trip up here that I came on.' Peter paused. 'I loved it there actually.'

'It's so remote, the hotel must have enjoyed it when two minibus loads of students and staff turned-up, even if some of you were impoverished?'

'I suppose so Sue.' replied Peter. 'Some fishermen called in I think, a couple of locals turned-up with fiddle and accordion – that was a bit of a session. That sort of thing. We were all locked in with a kitty to buy bottles of scotch.'

Peter looked around, not really wanting to feel on show but saw the other four were all looking at him, actually encouraging him to speak – maybe to yet further extend the length of their break. He decided to tell them a story and hoped it wasn't being self-indulgent.

'Well, if I'm reminiscing, there was one amazing incident. But stop me if you get bored! Have any of you seen the film Whisky Galore?' There was a mix of responses.

Peter continued, 'Well, as Mike just said, it was an old Ealing Comedy. In that film, a ship is wrecked just off-shore – over there, in the distance, I think.' He said, pointing west to the glimpse of sea. 'Think it was set on the Hebrides. Anyway, the locals salvage the cargo, which is mostly barrels of whisky! You can imagine the rest I guess. So…,'

He had been standing to admire the view but now sat down on a rocky outcrop, like everyone else. It began to feel as if he was holding an audience and he felt uncomfortably exposed like that. '…something like that happened back then. But, look, you must stop me if you're bored – these stories may mean a lot to me but you might just think Oh God why doesn't he shut up?'

'No – don't be daft, go on. Something like Whisky Galore in a hotel you said…' Ian felt he really did want to hear about this.

'Well, the minibus picked-up those of us staying in an old barracks hut just outside Durness and took us the Cape Wrath hotel each night you see. But this one day had been really cold, sleet and a bit of snow. Where the road turns down to the hotel a lorry was in a ditch. It was the brewery dray, delivering drink. The lorry and a car had tried to pass on the single-track and the truck had slid off. When we got in the pub the crew from the vehicle had been off-loading the spirits for safe keeping and they were tucking into a pint or two.'

'So, not really whisky galore then?' asked Ian.

'Ahh, you see…' explained Peter. 'Yes, all the whisky and stuff was being stashed in the hotel. But it meant all the beer was left on the back of the truck and they were delivering to a few pubs - maybe even the Tongue Hotel, I don't know, so there was quite a lot of it. When we all left the hotel and were being driven home, a couple of cars had arrived and people were helping themselves to the beer and whatever was there. The lecturer said to us "Please don't get any ideas any of you, we don't want any trouble." But when we were back in the hut it didn't feel like possible trouble. There was a big discussion, though some just went straight off to their sleeping bags. In the end, four of us set-off across the fields for two miles back to the truck.'

'With head torches?' said Ian a bit incredulously but wanting to hear more.

'Yeah, it was bloody stupid really. Cold wet, totally dark. Walls, bogs, uphill and down dale. Lashing sleet. I had the compass and was trying to be navigator. This big Welsh guy, Garym, led though. Strong bloke, but a bit crazy too.'

'Sure you're not romanticising the story Pete.' asked Sue.

'Ha ha. No I'm not actually,– it's all true! When we got to the truck it had become a feeding frenzy. Quite a few more cars and people were putting stuff into car-boots and there was a great camaraderie really.   Honour amongst thieves I suppose.   Didn't feel like it was nicking stuff though. We got some 24-can packs of MacEwans Export and Tennents Lager and then did the reverse trip back to the hut, which was much worse.'

'Well you had half a ton of booze weighing you down. You must have been desperate?' asked Ian.

'Poor, more than desperate, I think. Christ knows what time we got back in. The next day we had to drive past the spot to go to Scourie and the lorry was completely and utterly ransacked. Honestly, there was nothing left – only a couple of broken wooden pallets. "Hope none of you had anything to do with that!" said Rod, the lecturer – to complete silence from the bus.'

'I wish I'd done field trips like that. Did you really do any work too!?' said Mike, and everyone else laughed.

Peter felt himself blush. 'Yeah, I know I go on a bit but it is true. I reckon in the homes over there…' he said pointing back over his shoulder to the distant north west. '…you would still be able to find the occasional old aluminium beer keg gathering dust in a back garden or shed.'

Sue said, 'I like the story Pete. I haven't heard that one before. Plus I also like we have had a chance to get our breath back!'

They were relieved when Ian said it was pretty well all downhill from here onwards and he led them off the tops and down more open terrain and slightly easier angled ground than the ascent. Within a mile they had reached the broad Bealach Clais nan Ceap before a final slope onto the ground they had originally crossed on the way up, four hours earlier.

On this final slope though they were surprised to encounter large sheets of metal and what looked like remnants of some machinery.

'I had forgotten exactly where this was', said Peter. 'I was here a few years ago, it was a greyer and wetter day.'

'I feel I'm on rewind again.' Said Sue. 'Firstly we have ancient woodlands, then a lochan to swim in and now a crashed plane.'

Peter looked at her and felt moved for a moment at the sense of history Sue's comment had evoked in him. 'Yeah, it makes you wonder doesn't it.' He said. 'Different locations, Similar events. Both today and yesterday.'

'Geologist, tree-identifier and now philosopher!' joked Ian. 'Think you two have both good memories and maybe a lot of good things to be bothered remembering!'

Peter found he was enjoying being teased but he was feeling some broad connection between places and times though. 'There must be quite a few of these wrecks around the Highlands!'

'I wonder what happened to the crew?' asked Sheena.

'You could make a guess couldn't you!' said Ian. 'Look, this stuff is scattered, unless someone's moved anything. It obviously hit this slope at some speed. I can't imagine anyone walking away.'

This made everyone feel a bit sombre and they all quietly picked their way around the site, a bit lost in their own thoughts. Peter said to the others what he had mentioned to Mike earlier on the trip, that apparently one person had, incredibly, survived the crash. After a few more minutes, they moved off and back to the car, all a bit sombre, thinking about the inevitable demise of the air crew.

Sue came alongside Peter and took his hand. An action that moved him so much that he momentarily, and surprisingly, thought he might be upset again; an emotional occurrence that was becoming wearing. Without seeing it coming, he now realised this holiday was becoming a reappraisal of his relationship with

Sue – certainly as far as she was concerned, and it felt very up and down, catching him off-guard at times, like now. He also now had a beautiful memory recur though, of a time when he hardly knew Sue but they had shared some stories of their lives with each other, and Sue had held his hand then too. Walking off another mountain, in another place, and in another time.

Chapter 14

Things finally settled into a steady holiday rhythm then. A mix of everyone often joining in together but also doing their own thing at times too. Wendy finished Umberto Eco's book, passed it on to Peter and worked her way through a few others, Sheena took over from her and became chief cook, taking pleasure in preparing meals for everyone. Mike and Diane did a lot of strolls here and there, enjoying their time together. Sometimes they were joined by Julie.

Ian had forgotten to bring books of his own but read some of Wendy's and also took to reading all the various magazines people had accumulated - everything from Cosmo' to New Scientist. He also found himself developing an onsite project, recreating pieces of gym equipment, mostly for himself and Peter, making use of the wind-blown trees in the garden and bits of driftwood and scrap metal they found lying around. After a day or so there was an array of home-spun pieces of apparatus for pull-ups, dips, raises, inclined sit-ups and more.

Peter went up Ben Hope one day, with Ian and Mike, much to the delight of the other five who made a point of lining-up along the road to wave them off for the day, including mock tears and the waving of handkerchiefs. When not going up a mountain, Peter went for a run most days – usually down to and across the causeway and back, occasionally with Sue. She otherwise found herself feeling like she used to feel some years earlier – not too troubled by doing anything in particular, but making a good job of just being.

Collectively they did some more exploring, including the Tongue Hotel bar a couple of times, the Cape Wrath Hotel forty long miles away and more energetically around further neolithic remains and the deserted village of Scrabster. The latter helped again by Kevin O'Reilly's archaeological papers. And they went to the beach and in the sea, some of them anyway, whenever it looked settled enough.

Towards the end of the second week, Sue and Peter headed off on their own, back to where they had stopped on the way up – above Loch Eriboll. Peter had wanted to show her around Ben Arnaboll, the place where he and twenty other students had learned about geological field mapping. This time they parked the car as before but then headed off to explore the hill, with lunch and flasks in their rucksacks. Peter also carried an old blanket to sit on, although he wondered if there might be another use for it too – hoped more than wondered, he admitted to himself.

They soon found, once again, that they were the only people around. Having not been here for seven years, Peter found the actual geography didn't quite fit with his recall. Back then he had spent a few days here in sleet, snow, rain and sunshine, all in one Easter week. He had slowly mapped all the rocky cliffs and outcrops, but now it somehow had an unfamiliar feel for him. He decided they should head east on lower ground around the northern flank of the hill, beneath a steep rocky section and then turning south along the edge of a birch woodland. All the trees were drenched in lichens and mossy plant material which made them both feel they were in a primordial place. It was completely trackless.

After a short clamber up a slope and scrambling over some rocks, Sue exclaimed when they suddenly encountered a small lake. Peter didn't think this lochan had a name, not one he knew anyway. It was a couple of hundred feet across, forming a rough oval with the broad summit of Ben Arnaboll a hundred feet further up above them.

'Wow, this is a surprise! You didn't say. I like it.' Then she hesitated. 'And before you say anything, I'm not going in!'

'I know, I wasn't expecting us to.' He grinned at her, 'I don't jump into every mountain lake, you know!' And he put his arm round her waist and pulled her towards him so they could kiss. 'But it's nice you think about it, and remember it.'

'Hmm, maybe,' Sue said, 'some girls get to remember candlelit suppers, but romance with you is all mountains, rocks and freezing swims!'

'Ha, ha.' He said slowly. 'It's true though, I can picture you back then. You always look great in the outdoors.' And then after a minute or so… 'Not just outdoors. Obviously!'

Sue smiled at him and they restarted their walk around the southern tip of the lake and then on to the summit.

'It's only about seven hundred feet high, but what a view eh?' Peter went on to point out the hills, lochs and mountains that were visible in a panorama that was all around them. He explained to Sue the significance of this location for geologists, not just for the rock sequence it contained but for it being so central to the history of the science.

Sue tried to imagine Victorian geologists here, all men together of course, sometimes on horseback, nearly a century earlier. Listening to Peter talk about it so enthusiastically, she was reminded of the Kinlochewe days again and her own discoveries back then about geologists - much younger geologists. What Peter was saying she could see in her head from when they were just twenty.

'So, it's the same as you made me describe back then is it?'

Peter knew what moment she was referring to. He remembered very well when he invited Sue out on his mountain. He had been excited about the day and what might happen. He had been over-excited about the rocks though and showing her what he had been doing. The fact that she recalled him jokingly asking her to repeat back to him, amazed him. 'Go on then, do it again Sue!'

'An action replay you mean? No, I would muddle the words. It's the same though isn't it. The same rocks, gneiss and sandstone, some others, and again all muddled up so they aren't the right way up. That's it, isn't it?' Peter nodded. 'What was that word you were using when we set-out this morning Pete?'

'Unconformity. A bit clumsy isn't it, as a word? But the big discoveries back then were all related to unconformities – especially up here, and the one on my mountain. The first one named like that was over at Dunbar – something like that anyway. There was another on Arran. He placed one of his hands flat across the upright fingers of the other. That unconformity was like this, my hands being one layer of rocks horizontally lying across a vertical, upended, sequence of rocks. That's a very dramatic unconformity.' He paused, wondering if he was going on too much, but Sue was still attentive and listening. Her eyes urged him on.

'Here though, They knew the rocks were out of sequence. Rocks looking like they are in the right place at first, but sitting on top of other rocks when they shouldn't be. So that was, is, an unconformity too. They had to find an explanation. They knew they were looking at incredibly old, crystalline rocks – the gneiss, as you mentioned just now. But here, that rock is sitting unconformably, another awkward word maybe, on top of younger ones. At first, it looks as if they were part of the same sequence, but they're not.'

Sue was still looking and listening, her hands on the collar of her jumper, pulling it up her neck. He could see her mind was working hard and he suddenly recognised the mood and it struck him that she was thinking of their own relationship as much as the relationships of the rocks around them. He felt a bit unnerved then and could feel a conversation coming that he wasn't sure he wanted to have.

Sure enough, Sue proposed they have a tea here as it was such a great viewpoint. Peter spread out the old blanket and they used one of the flasks to fill two cups. Peter opened the Tupperware box with the cheese and ham sandwiches and offered one to Sue. They were mostly quiet while eating and drinking. When they finished, Peter wished he had brought some cigarettes because he could sense the next conversation would require one.

'Coming up here then, can you remember being here? Can you feel yourself here?'

'Yes, I can feel it actually. The feel of being here back then, with my student mates. But like we said, it's also different somehow. It feels a smaller area than I remember. It's a lot warmer today!' he joked. 'This was the training ground for what I then did in Kinlochewe. There wasn't a nice campsite café here though, with you and Julie in it, as you can see.'

'Aww, Jules and I distracted you from working didn't we?' She was pleased Peter was nodding. 'I loved that summer, working in the café. Julie's aunt and uncle. The students – you especially.'

'Yeah, you took a lot of my concentration Sue.' He was remembering, looking at the space below his feet.

'Ahh, but so did Steve didn't he! More than me really.'

Peter nodded and knew that they were into a conversation now that Sue had been probably been working-up to all holiday. There had been a series of comments, half-jokes, bits of conversation, some sharper tones from her than usual. Then there had been that telepathic interrogation from Julie, which he imagined would have also been discussed with Sue. He had seen her often looking thoughtful and reflective, but also so often nicely relaxed and enjoying herself. He guessed the holiday had been some sort of turning point for her. That troubled him but he knew it was something he couldn't control.

As if reading his mind, Sue said, 'This trip has been good Pete. Nicely unhurried. Peaceful. I feel I am back to my old self, like before Colin.' She leant across and kissed Peter on the cheek. 'Thank you.'

He smiled at her, hoping he wasn't looking as worried as he was feeling. 'Don't think I've done much. You look… have looked, serene though. Many times.'

'That's a nice word Pete. Yeah I feel it, I think. And you've had a good time getting back onto favourite rocks and up mountains. Plus we had a naked swim! Another favourite thing eh?' A good trip for you too I would say!'

Peter smiled and nodded, not saying anything, waiting. There was quite a long wait, both of them sitting upright, leaning on their hands, taking in the views.

'Where do we go from here though?' Sue asked, eventually.

'Well,' said Peter knowing this wasn't what she meant, 'we will head off from here that way,' nodding over his shoulder towards the watery sun peeking through the clouds, 'down to a little stream, then over a deer fence somehow, back up the valley below us and then back to the car.'

Sue looked at him and sighed. 'Don't be annoying Pete. You know exactly what I meant.'

'Of course I do. Just trying to avoid it really.'

Sue hesitated, wanting to find the right words, the right way of explaining herself really. 'With you, rocks are very helpful. You tell me things and then that fires off thoughts for me. You probably triggered this back then. So, this unconformity thing Pete. I'm trying to relate it to you.'

'Are you?' Peter was surprised but even as he spoke he could see where Sue's mind was taking her. He nodded then, very slowly, thinking.

'At school and then with Penny at University, you had girlfriends. Liked having girlfriends.' She kept looking at him while she spoke, checking and looking for little nods and signs of agreement. He was keeping his head tilted downwards, listening and concentrating. 'Then in Kinlochewe, you discovered that actually another guy, Steve, did a lot for you – physically and emotionally.'

'Until you!' Peter interrupted.

'No Pete.' She reached up and stroked the side of his face. 'No, that's not right. Not until me. After you and I had our mountain encounter, you and Steve continued – more intensely if anything. Didn't you?'

'Yeah. Well… You know that…' Peter took a big, deep breath – a distinct sigh. He could see being naked on the mountains with Sue. He could then also see himself naked in a caravan, a woodland glade and a hotel bed, with Steve. 'Yeah.' He repeated. 'But since then I have been ok again, like with you. Very much so with you.' He wasn't sure which emotion sloshing around in him was strongest right now. Fear? Irritation? Sadness, he decided, was the main feeling rising-up.

Sue brought-up her knees and propped her elbows on them, her hands cradling her face. 'What if you meet another Steve?'

'Well, I won't will I? I'm with you! Look – that's all in the past.' He was trying to keep calm, but really wanting to shout this from the rooftops. 'I'm not with you all the time, but when I don't see you, like some weekends, I'm not seeing anyone else either. I don't want to.'

Sue tutted, then sighed again. 'It is like the rocks here Pete. I'm looking at you, like now.' She turned her head to meet his eyes again. 'What am I seeing? Is it all a logical progression? Was Steve just something, inexplicable, out of sequence, an unconformable interlude?'

'Bloody hell Sue.' Said Peter, turning to face her now, impressed, annoyed, saddened, cheered and, predominantly now, a bit scared, all at the same time. 'I'm not taking you on any more geology walks! Ever!' And he ruffled her hair.

'You're right Pete. I'm trying not be too heavy.' She took a deep breath herself now. 'I like you. I like being with you. A lot.' She paused and looked at Peter and he felt humbled. 'I really like being with you. We've had a lovely holiday.' She continued, 'I need to think about my life though. Maybe it's some hormones nagging me but at twenty-seven…' She paused, taking her time with her thoughts and words.

A breeze blew across them and Sue's hair flew outwards in the draught. He suddenly just thought how gorgeous she looked. He desperately wanted to move away from the psychological to the physical. 'I think my hormones could be nudging me too.' He said, leaning into Sue, his gamut of feelings having suddenly been channelled into the simplicity of desire and an urgent need to change the subject if possible.

She pushed him away, but making light of it. 'Stop it. And don't think I hadn't understood why you wanted to bring the blanket on our walk!' And this time she playfully pinched his cheek and wobbled it a bit. 'Seriously though, for a moment, what if one day you go swimming in a mountain stream with a friend and find yourself fancying him? Because that is what actually happened, wasn't it? Or, for that matter, just having a drink in a pub?' She looked at him intensely when she then said 'You've felt that haven't you? Come on, I know you have…'

Peter didn't know what to say, wanting desperately just to get back into enjoying the holiday. Wanting to hold onto that feeling of desire too. Sue was making him feel tense and awkward now and, worse, untruthful. But mostly, he wasn't sure what he felt. He recognised what Sue was getting at, did look at other guys, in magazines at home, and in real life too. He didn't want to admit it though – not admit what Sue was getting at, not to her. And not to himself.

For a minute or two, they both sat there and said nothing. The minutes ticked on. He felt Sue had this ability to hold him in a place, quiet and unmoving yet not feeling trapped, just held. This was the second time on this trip he had found himself experiencing questioning by telepathy.

As the moment went on, Peter began scanning the far shore of Eriboll and out north to the sea. He started to feel the sadness come back and then sweep-up like a tide, his eyes welled-up, blurring his vision and then he felt embarrassed about it, thinking it was happening too often. Too many emotions were running through him, a lot of regret, a bit of relief coming from a feeling of resolve. But not feeling at all sure what resolution might mean.

Sue unwound herself next to him, seemed to relax a bit and leant backwards, the feeling of being mentally held by her dissolved for Peter and he felt their dialogue had ended too. For now. She settled her body down, leaning right back at a shallow angle to the ground, putting her weight on her forearms at her sides. Her hair fell backwards over her shoulders, a swathe of it reaching onto the ground.

Peter couldn't help looking at her intensely then, just overwhelmed with the thought of how lovely she was. He ran his eyes very slowly over the length of her form, across her body, inch by inch from her feet, up her legs, over her abdomen, then her bust and eventually up to her face. When he reached that point, after a mini eternity, he discovered she was looking at him, watching him watching her. He could see a small tear had started to run down from her right eye, which made his own do the same. He could sense it was going to soon be over between them and this made him feel he wanted to sob. Trying to hold back, a few tears ran down his cheeks. 'I want to kiss you.' He managed to say, very quietly and softly.

'I want you to!' She said quietly, as she lay back flat on the blanket and invited him into her arms, both of them now shedding tears more freely, gently and silently. The only sound was the almost imperceptible rustle of the grass and heather in the breeze.

Chapter 15

Although they all felt they had been away for ages, when the last full day of the holiday actually arrived, without exception they said the fortnight had gone too quickly. The slightly flattened mood was exacerbated by some clearing up, cleaning, putting rubbish out and packing-up their stuff. They had decided they would get up at dawn the following day and try and do the whole journey in one go, rather than stop-off at B&Bs. They felt it would give them a free Sunday at home to catch-up with themselves before the Monday morning and the inevitably bluesy return to work. The three men had a huddled and detailed discussion about places to stop on the route for refreshments and loo breaks. The women just let them get on with it.

By mid-morning, chores were completed and the weather looked like being a bit grey and mild, but settled. The eight of them marched along the road in file, to the field of rabbits and the descent to the beach for the last time. They all intended to make a day of it before coming back for Sheena's last communal stew.

As was usual, the huge sandy expanse was empty but for them. Their favourite spot beside the low cliff became the setting for a series of photographs as soon as they arrived. One after another they took turns taking photos of the other seven. They all had to stand close together in a line, in order to fit within the shot. Ian and Mike had SLR's with a few seconds delay-feature on them and managed to prop these up with a mix of boulders and clothes, to hopefully capture all eight people, comically running back fast from the camera and rapidly squeezing into the line-up. They promised to send copies to everyone else when they had them printed.

Peter made everyone do this all again when they had changed into swimwear. He insisted on these photos because he said people back home would never otherwise believe you could do this in the northernmost part of Scotland.

'I hope the goosebumps don't show-up on those snaps.' Said Julie.

'Nor me breathing in.' said Sue.

Julie frowned at her friend and rolled her eyes. 'Don't be stupid Sue. Mind you, we might all have added a couple of pounds with Sheena and Wendy's kitchen delights!'

'Ooo – I could open a business with that name!' Sheena suggested. 'Maybe take over the café at the Leisure Centre.'

Julie took the opportunity to have a little walk along the back of the beach, taking Sue with her. 'You alright pet?' she asked, taking her friend's hand in her own.

Sue nodded. 'Not too bad Jules. I will miss everyone. And miss just being here.'

Now it was Julie nodding. 'So, you had the big talk. How do you feel now about what happens when you get home?'

'I don't know Jules. Pete's pretty upset, you can see it can't you?'

'He's been an emotional bunny all round, I think, the last fortnight really. He wears his heart on his sleeve, as we know. He seems to have been quite close to tears a lot of the time – I've worried about that a bit.'

'I know,' said Sue. 'It's hurting him the thought we can't continue ignoring things.'

'You have helped him not be himself Sue, the last few months. I guess it's been a pretty amazing escape for him. Now he's terrified I think, of what he would do without you to keep him on the straight and narrow.' She turned to Sue. 'Straight being the operative word.'

They had walked southwards into the expanse of sand but then stopped and reversed their steps before they reached the water's edge. They walked very slowly, taking in the view back to the cottages where they had been staying, up and along the road. They were both mulling over the conversation.

'It's funny,' Julie continued, 'what you did originally, back in

Kinlochewe was help him to recognise himself! It's been a strange turnaround.' They walked on a few more paces, just quietly. Then Julie added. 'You know, but I'll say it again. The two of you have helped each other the last year. It's been like an unspoken pact, as I have seen it! He's adorable and sweet to you, making you feel cared for and wanted - in a nice way. He's got you over all the crap with Colin.'

'He's been a sweetheart for sure.' Sue said softly, feeling a bit emotional about the conversation.

'Yeah, but for him, having an affectionate relationship with you has stopped him having to think of other men.'

'Yeah, you have said all that Jules, I do listen. It's been very comforting with him. Very comfortable – that's the truth of it. Its nice. It's easy. But actually we are impeding each other… oh, bother – now it's me getting silly.'

'Gosh, I'm getting through the tissues on this trip,' Julie said, trying to make a little joke of it, drying Sue's eyes with a Kleenex and managing to give her a cuddle at the same time.

'Just a second Jules. I think what I just said is right. He and I – it's… I'm struggling to say it right. That bit I said about impeding each other. It's true isn't it? I feel I am a bit on hold with him, it's so easy, and I think he just blocks the gay thing. And that makes it easy for him too. I just think we can't do that ad infinitum!'

'Well, you know that's right.' Julie hugged her and stroked her hair a little. 'Come on pet, things will work out in the end, I know they will.'

When the two of them went back to the group, most people had settled down, sitting, lying, or a mix of the two. Only Peter was initially interested in a swim, so he took himself over to the edge of the water, heading up towards the sand bar going across to Rabbit Islands. He stepped out at a fast pace as he was feeling the chill in just trunks, even though he put the towel over his shoulders. He

155

thought he was on his own but when nearly near there, he realised Mike was hurrying after him.

'Hard to keep up with you. Are you going in?'

Peter looked at the water, hesitating at first then moving forward into it. 'Might just go up to my knees.'

Mike joined him and they decided it would be fun to wade through the edge like this in a great long arc down in a southerly direction, towards the causeway and back round to where the rest of the group was sitting. After a little while, they moved a bit closer to the dry sand, so it wasn't such hard work going against a depth of water. Peter thought it would be a mile or more before they turned towards the others. In front of them the whole way was the majestic prow of Ben Loyal.

'When I was a teenager coming up to Gairloch, I never did anything like this. Never seen anywhere quite like this.'

'What did you do then?' asked Peter, intrigued.

Mike told him how he used to come with his cousin and they would go out some days in his uncle's boat for them all to do a bit of fishing. He didn't remember many fish but did have strong mental images of seals in the water. He explained that he didn't remember doing much on those holidays but he recalled the feel of being there, some days reading at the cottage in the rain, others just mooching about. 'It never seemed to get that dark' he added.

Peter could see that the young Mike had experienced what he too had always felt about just being in the North West Highlands. 'It will be a bit hard going back into the office, won't it?'

Mike nodded. He thought that he didn't want to go back really. He had liked being with Diane – their first UK holiday together. He had felt closer to her but they had actually spent a fair bit of time doing different things, being separate. He thought about the office and realised one of the things he liked most about it was bumping into Peter every day, their cheery chats, by the photocopying room, at the tea trolley, going out to the pub at lunchtimes. It suddenly struck him Peter's job would remove him from that regular proximity. 'Yeah – and you will have to get into your new job. Going out to all the branches is going to keep you occupied.'

Peter talked about that a bit and how he thought he would schedule it. 'I inherit Jane – she is a great assistant I always imagine, hopefully she will keep me organised.' Then he changed the subject.

'Has Diane liked it up here?'

'Yes, she has. I think everyone has. I was just thinking it's been good for us two, but we've also each done our own thing too. Different to other holidays maybe.'

'Yes, it's special to have choices. We are lucky – just being here I mean. There's so much pain in the world right now. The miners fighting the government for their livelihoods. Europe and the Soviet Union, a hair trigger from nuclear war. It's a million miles from all that.' Peter thought about these issues, and others, which were continual preoccupations for people at the office – during the tea breaks or in the pub after work. He now realised he hadn't been thinking about such stuff for nearly two weeks.

'I will want to come back here.' Peter went on to compare it with Kinlochewe, Balnakeil and other places he had stayed. In doing so, he realised they had slowed down and that Mike was really listening to him, which he suddenly found very flattering. Then they were closely side by side and Mike said, 'Being here with you has made me feel lucky Pete. Lucky about life. It's made me feel like that.'

Peter wasn't sure how to take this remark but again he was aware it made him feel good. He looked at Mike and smiled. 'That's a really nice thing to say.'

Then somehow they had arms round each other's shoulders as they started the return leg to the others – two friends, being comradely. Neither of them said anything more but Peter felt the sense of a familiarity and fondness for Mike that he hadn't noticed before. Or, he thought, maybe just hadn't let himself notice.

Before supper and an early night, Peter found he was feeling troubled. Mostly he just wanted to stay up here. Ideally, just stay up here with Sue. He decided to do what he always did, when feeling a bit fretful, so he took himself off for a run. He went north, as he had done once previously, on a five mile round-trip, through the strung-out settlements of Melness and Strathan to the road end by some croft buildings named Dalvraid on a gate sign, where he turned round. On the return leg he went into the phone box overlooking the sheltered inlet.

He hadn't mentioned it to Sue but had decided he would book a stay near The Lakes on the way back. He knew The George Hotel in Penrith from a work trip when they had secured a big national contract. It was a nice old-fashioned place and he could already imagine having a last evening there with Sue, just the two of them, with a whisky in front of their log fire, hopefully. He had an ill-feeling, almost a foreboding, that he and Sue might not see each other for a while. Work travel was probably going to make it trickier for him but it was more than that he knew. His feeling of unease had been growing since the walk and talk on Ben Arnaboll.

In the morning, Peter thought everyone was finding it a struggle to end the holiday and set-off on their journeys. Peter, Ian and Mike were doing the driving initially, and they'd agreed to try and drive together in convoy at least as far as Aviemore, where they would all fuel-up and get a cuppa in one of the cafes. After that they would go at their own pace. Getting away like this, at just after six in the morning, meant they hoped to all be back in Bristol and Swansea by mid evening. By then, Peter hoped he and Sue would be relaxing together in Penrith.

All went to plan, everyone got home safely and in good time. Peter had his fireside whisky and enjoyed his time with just Sue. It felt romantic. It also felt nice even though they both noted how quiet it was to be without other people around them the whole time. Most of the next day's journey they listened to tapes – The Pretenders again, some folk collections, David Bowie and some Rod Stewart, all keeping them happy. Often singing along. But by the time they drove over the Heads of the Valleys Road and down to Swansea, Peter was dreading dropping-off Sue and the drive back then, on his own, to Bristol.

On the Sunday afternoon, outside the house she shared with Sheena, standing by his car, Peter felt the first spots of rain.

'Damn typical of Swansea. The first rain we have seen really for a fortnight and it has to come just as you're setting off.' Sue looked at Peter sympathetically. 'You really don't want to go do you sweetie?' She came alongside and hugged him closely in way that he imagined was utterly unique to her.

Peter couldn't speak at first. He had left Sue here quite a few times over the year since the Alps but it had never been so upsetting before. He was trying to think - it wasn't anything specifically that had been said, nothing had actually expressed finality, but just all the conversations together seemed to add-up to the same thing. The unconformity conversation loomed large in his mind. He realised just how good the holiday had felt and now he was going back to his little flat, on his own. He would just miss being with everyone. But mostly, above everything and everyone, he was going to miss being with Sue every day.

He would miss getting up every morning to make a mug of tea for them both, he would miss her being there all the time to chat with, to share shopping with and all the other little routines of life. He would miss her warm body being alongside his own every night, going off to sleep.

'I'm just a self-pitying old sod.' He said to Sue, but as he tried to look at her face, it became all blurry and he just couldn't hold back a few tears. They were running slowly down his cheeks as she put her arms around him and hugged him closely.

'You're just the same old Pete, aren't you?' She nuzzled him. 'I will miss you too Mr Soppy, but we will see each other again soon.'

But when he finally drove away, out of Killay, down through Sketty and onto the main road to get out of Swansea, all he could think was that they might not see each other soon and that whatever they had together might now be at an end. It was only two hours to get himself back home but it felt much more. Getting unpacked in his empty flat, he could never remember feeling so lonely. He knew that he needed her to be with him, all the time, to be his partner, to share his nest. But she was rejecting that possibility, he could see now so clearly.

He sat down on the old G-plan sofa his Mum had obtained for him. He usually felt content and comfortable sitting on it but that feeling wouldn't come. He poured himself a Scotch but that didn't have the usual effect either. He was fed-up, alone and, in truth, a bit disgusted with himself. He really wanted to be angry with someone but the thought of directing this towards Sue made him despair, so he turned it on himself instead. He felt he had spent a large part of the holiday in a pathetic, self-pitying mode.

Sue had been right. She had always been right. She knew the truth of it all, of him. She had more or less seen him with another man, even if it was years ago. He wanted all that to be in the past but instead it was right here. And it was here all the time. He knew it, she knew it. He put his hands on his head, cradling his forehead, his shoulders drooped and he felt shattered and fed-up. With everything. 'Why can't I just be normal?' he muttered to himself.

Part Three

Suilven and Quinag, 1985

"…we have to stumble through so much dirt and humbug before we reach home. And we have no one to guide us. Our only guide is our homesickness."

From Steppenwolf, by Hermann Hesse, 1927.

Chapter 16

'Do you know why this place has the same name as that bit by Talmine.' Mike was standing by the small road sign noticing that the little community of houses and caravans was called Strathan. 'You know the place up the road from the cottages where we stayed last year – one of your runs went up there. We did a walk there as well, to see the bay. We even saw a seal pop its head out of the water!'

'Yeah – I remember. I think there are a few of them, places called Strathan, think it's just another word for valley. I guess it's a name like that, which just distinguishes different parts of these scattered communities.' Peter hadn't noticed the sign but now Mike had mentioned it, he did recall clearly the place where they had spent their holiday with others a year earlier. He remembered running up there a few times and also recalled walking there with Sue, Mike and Diane, spotting a couple of seals in a coastal inlet.

Given what had happened with Mike and him since then, he looked back fondly on moments like that. If it hadn't been for that holiday, they wouldn't be here. There were a range of moods went with that thought. One was that they were happy and looking forward to time together. Another was that they were now a lot more stressed than back then.

A couple of hundred yards further and they were at the edge of the sea, which here came into a tiny, sheltered bay. A small fishing boat was tied-up. Peter thought it couldn't be much bigger than a rowing boat. The sort you might see in The Serpentine or at Richmond Bridge – recent discoveries from times in London. He wondered if it was the same sort of boat in which Mike had been taken fishing by his uncle in Gairloch, wondered if that was what he was thinking about too. The truth was though, that he didn't know Mike well enough to guess what was going on in his head all the time. They were still finding out about each other.

As it happened, Mike didn't comment on what he was thinking about other than to say to Peter that it looked like it would be a good day for a decent walk. This pre-breakfast stroll had perked him up and he felt energised about getting up a mountain.

Peter found he had been thinking the same thing. 'OK, yeah, so…' he waited until Mike had turned away from the bay to look at him. '…is it a day. Even THE day, that we might go up Suilven then? Or do we need to build-up to it more?'

Mike smiled and nodded a couple of times and agreed. 'Maybe we should just have a go at it?'

Peter gave him a quick hug and they half jogged their way back to the caravan site. There were only four caravans in total, so calling it a site was a bit too grand. None of the accommodation was very deluxe, but it was adequate, or their's was anyway. Comfortable enough for a week, just the two of them. And the view out was definitely spectacular, embracing the sea loch that led around to Lochinver and the wild hills above and beyond the far shore.

They had their holiday breakfast treat of porridge, cream and honey, and packed their rucksacks. Peter was thinking of how much to carry on what could be a long day, wanting to keep down the weight, but on the other hand knowing it was wild country and things could happen to anyone. He felt responsible – the slight age difference, plus Peter couldn't help feeling he just knew more about climbing and hillwalking. He could hear Sue in his head saying something about allowing other people to decide for themselves and that he shouldn't try to do everything for everyone all the time. Nonetheless, having taken them out, he then put back in a headtorch, first aid kit and emergency rations, despite the weight.

It was also an unpredictable day weather-wise, so Peter stuffed in a pair of shorts but wore his black tracksuit bottoms, tucked into thick socks, and his brand new purple Patagonia fleece top. The trip had provided a good excuse to go to the outdoor shop. Mike had his new Rohan trousers on too. 'We look like models for a Field and Trek catalogue,' said Peter, smiling. 'We could do with these bits of kit looking less shiny and new!'

'Well that could happen pretty quickly up here Pete!' Having said this Mike hoped though it wasn't going to get too muddy. He felt like going on a good hill walk, but hoped the ground underfoot wouldn't involve sliding around too much.

Peter insisted Mike looked at the route on the map together with him. It was probably the key objective for the holiday – as far as walking was concerned. Peter hoped it would also help with the less tangible objectives they had for the trip too, like trying to understand their feelings for each other and figuring out what they were going to do about it!

On the ten minute drive down the road to the starting point of the walk, they were surprised to go round a bend at one point and encounter a beautiful bay. The tide was low and exposed a fair-sized stretch of shingle and sand, backed by larger boulders. They parked up and got out, wanting to examine the view with Peter's pair of binoculars. Mike looked first. A concession from Peter that he felt happy about, given Mike was better at both spotting and naming different birds. It was the second time that day he heard Sue in his head, telling him not to be possessive with things.

'Eiders!' Mike sounded delighted. 'How good is that. There must be twenty or more – pairs. Look!' He handed the binoculars back into eagerly awaiting hands.

Peter studied the view too and felt pleased he could share Mike's thrill – the colours on the males was so distinctive – sharp black and white blocks and such a clearly green neck marking. 'Brilliant. I love that. You're right too, pretty even numbers of males and females by the look of things.'

It wasn't more than a half mile further on before they had to park up. A few cars were already there but there was plenty of room. Peter felt a bit disappointed though. He had wanted the day just for the two of them, even though he knew that was unrealistic. But he wanted it to be a special day out on a special mountain. Mike suggested that this might still happen as some of the cars might be here only for people visiting the bookshop. He actually thought very few people would be setting out on the long return trip across moorland to Suilven.

Until they arrived in Lochinver, they had never heard of Achin's Bookshop but soon discovered it had a fair bit of local and regional fame. Now here it was, an odd find in a remote location, nestling under trees. It was clearly a dwelling as well as a shop.

When they went inside, they found quite a few other people were indeed in the shop. It was a bit of a strange place, a very large central table with piles of books, maps and papers stacked-up everywhere. Around the room, shelving seemed to be weighted down with yet more books. Some old framed paintings and black and white photographs filled in gaps on the walls. It all smelled and looked a bit musty.

There was a hatch, which appeared to be where one would pay for anything. Going up to it Peter found it was also possible to get teas and some shortbread, so they did. The person serving assured them there was nothing to pay for parking – it was free so long as people came in the shop as well as doing a walk. This conversation reminded Peter how far they had to go and he soon had to drag Mike away from the books, but only by promising they could call in again when they return. This became their goal then, for the remainder of the day.

The path up the mountain started literally outside the back door of the bookshop. Through a gate, although there was also a stile alongside, one of those with a panel that could be lifted to allow through dogs. However, the gate seemed easier and quicker.

'You OK?' Peter checked with Mike, starting to get his head around the fact it could be several hours before they returned here.

'Yep – I'm good to go. Let's get on with it I suppose.'

'Right, you could sound a bit more enthusiastic! Good steady pace then. Alpine pace! You know, steady sort of walking that you feel you could sustain all day if needed.'

Mike hoped it wouldn't be needed quite like that, but was already familiar with Peter's walking style on long or steep days, and this was possibly both. Mike thought Peter looked the part – taking it seriously but also looking relaxed, his climbers' rucksack looking nicely packed and sitting solidly on his hips.

The first mile appeared to be an estate road, firm and gravelly underfoot, but after that became a narrower, but well-defined footpath. They steadily gained height walking along the side of a steep valley, all the time looking down at the River Kirkaig to their right. After a half-hour's walking there was a little rocky viewpoint above a waterfall, although it was partly obscured by woodland. Soon after this, the upward trend eased and the walk opened-up onto moorland and a large body of water. This was Fionn Loch, according to the map. Above the loch, looking north was their objective, the mountain called Suilven. The view immediately brought them to an abrupt halt.

From Lochinver and also from the various roads through Assynt, Suilven's distinctive profile had been easy to spot and had reinforced their desire to climb it. However, in those views although the mountain had looked steep, it had also appeared fairly benign. Now up close, and at a distance straight ahead of not much more than a mile, the mountain looked truly enormous and, if anything, a bit unassailable.

Mike articulated some of this and Peter agreed, saying 'Well, I don't actually know anyone else who's been up it, so we haven't much to go on personally, other than guide books. But that's more to do with distance from home than because of notoriety. We just don't know many who've been this far north, on these mountains.'

'Are you sure it's not rock climbing?' asked Mike, feeling daunted by the amount of rock and scree along the length and depth of the mountain.

'It's not technical, no – not a climb or too hard a scramble. I mean, it's not supposed to be like the Cuillins or Liathach.' Peter named a couple of places he and Mike had also discussed. Peter had been on the former and had an aborted attempt at the latter. 'The route goes straight up from this moor, as we can see, up that steep slope, to the saddle, the low bit, between the west and east peaks. It does look a bit vertical and intimidating though, I agree.'

'It looks impossible.' Mike declared, sounding more than a bit doubtful. They just stared at it for a while. Peter thought of the aerial image he had carried in his head for ten years, since A-levels, a shot of Suilven in a stratigraphy book by a female geologist called Dorothy Rayner, he remembered. He had been drawn to this place for so long and now he was actually here it felt a bit surreal.

'Keep going?' asked Peter, shaking off the memories and his own doubts at the same time. And with that they set-off again, seemingly in the wrong direction, heading what at first felt away from their target, but with no choice in order to circumnavigate the loch. The map showed clearly that the path went left, westwards, at this point, then right around the considerable expanse of water, before heading up to Suilven itself.

The track was tedious, often wet and they were beset by midges whenever the breeze dropped sufficiently, which wasn't that often, but often enough to necessitate stopping and applying a liberal amount of midge repellent. After a while, the path did head back down the other shore of the loch where it became even wetter and boggier in places. Peter remarked that it was as well that it hadn't rained too much recently and that he also wished and hoped the wind kept up. Mike was disappointed with the mud, but noticed the way ahead now looked drier.

As they moved away from the loch, up the side of the river Alltan Fearna, running down from the base of Suilven, Peter found his geology mode switching on. It was the effect of the landscape at this point - the rolling gneiss moorland of the five miles from the bookshop, plus the enormous bulk of sandstone mountain right in front of their eyes. In addition, at this point in particular they were encountering large blocks of rock seemingly perched on the moor. They had the appearance of just being dropped there.

'These are erratics aren't they?' asked Mike.

'I guess so.' Can't think what else could account for them. It's like a scattering of giant stones.' He stopped walking, the better to take in what he was seeing. 'There's quite a lot of stuff at the base of the mountain that has probably come off the top. That's a bit scary to think about – look at the size of some of them! They look enormous even from a mile away. But, yes, these blocks out here in the open, must have been left here by retreating glaciers.' They went up to one of them, much higher than them, dark maroon in places, other bits dark grey, almost black. It was obviously not part of the hard, crystalline, grey rock on which it sat.

As was often the case for Peter, the awareness of being on incredibly ancient rocks made him reflective. He was aware that the shallow slope they were walking up was where the softer sandstone had been eroded and weathered off the harder surface of the gneiss underneath. The age gap between the rocks was nearly two billion years – half the age of the Earth. What he found most incredible though was that this slope was literally the original landscape surface on which the sand had flowed.

He shared this with Mike, who was initially doubtful. 'No, honestly it is. Look over there.' Peter walked a few yards to touch a sandstone block. 'This bed hasn't been eroded yet. Essentially this block is the solidified sand and grit that poured off an ancient mountain range nine hundred million years ago. Think of an image of, say, Death Valley. So, right here…' Peter knelt down and touched where the sandy rock adhered to the hard gneiss surface. 'This contact point is a tiny part of the original landscape of all that time ago.'

Mike found his enthusiasm touching. 'This is home ground for you though isn't it?'

'Yes' confirmed Peter. 'My mapping area is actually a hundred miles from here by road. Much less as the crow flies. It's the same geology though. Incredible – the extent of that landscape. Nowhere else in Britain like it really – just the continuity of this hard gneiss and this gorgeous sandstone on top. From Durness to Skye and beyond. It's amazing both of us have actually spent part of our lives on it.'

'You sound like you're in love with it!'

Peter wondered if he was being gently mocked. 'Ha ha, well maybe I am! It's my favourite rocks for sure. The Torridonian Sandstone especially.' Peter stepped towards Mike. 'And maybe its not the only thing I'm feeling fond about out here.' He said, his voice softer. He went to give a hug, but Mike backed away.

'Ahh – don't do that! You're always turning away and looking over your shoulder.'

'Can't help it.'

They did then kiss, but more briefly than Peter would have preferred. 'There's nobody can see us out here you know!'

Mike said nothing and they went on across the rolling moorland leading steadily upwards to the foot of the sandstone cliffs of the mountain. The next stage made their route so far, up to this point, look easy. The path ahead rose vertiginously almost in a straight line.

'In the Alps' said Peter. 'This path would be a zig zag.' The both looked skywards. The route looked a bit like a shallow trench cut vertically into the rock slope. Worried they might both lose their nerve if they studied it for too long, Peter strode forward and started up the climb. Sooner than he wanted or hoped, he found himself having to use his hands, more for a sense of security than physical necessity. He hoped Mike would feel alright about it and wondered if it was better he led, as he was doing, or following behind Mike to give him encouragement. Anyway, after a couple of hundred feet it became impossible to turn round or easily get past each other and the easiest thing was to simply continue, to plough on.

It was eight hundred feet, Peter had calculated, from the flat gneiss moorland to the saddle between the two peaks of Suilven. He knew he had hurried the last hundred feet, where the path had steepened still further. He had felt it just best to get it over with as soon as possible. It was a relief for both of them, when they arrived on the rounded, grassy slope and stopped for a breather. They agreed to keep going rather than stop longer, and to have lunch on the top of the big western summit of Caisteal Liath, even if it would be blowy up there. Neither of them wanted to think of the descent back the way they had just come.

The path from there to the summit peak was clear, if narrow, rocky and at times unnerving. Even though it was scary in places, the evident fact that many others had done the same thing was reassuring to them both. After another half-hour of clambering, they eventually sat in the shelter of the summit cairn to have cheese and ham rolls with mayonnaise, hurriedly made by Mike before they left. Peter thought they tasted great but he was wishing he had remembered to put in extra water. Sun had been intermittent and the breeze kept the temperature lowish especially up here, but the exertion was making him thirsty and he wondered if they could eke out their dwindling supply.

Mike noticed Peter was relentlessly looking around at the

landscape. It was spectacular enough but he assumed to Peter, the study of geology added another tier of interest and excitement. He had to say something, to exclaim what he was thinking.

'That was pretty hard work Pete, getting here. And a bit frightening at times, but bloody hell – the view is amazing. In all directions. So many mountains, so much rock. Then, over there – that view to Lochinver and out to sea. God – it's stunning. I really feel on top of the world – as a viewpoint I mean.'

'Yeah, me too. Maybe on top of the world in other senses too. The last few months have been uphill too, haven't they? Up here though, right now, I just feel great – liberated!'

Conscious of time, they moved on soon from the lunch spot, intending to drop down to the low bit again and then up the rocks beyond onto the eastern peak of Suilven, not as high, but sharper and more exposed. Stepping down blocks of weathered sandstone with a thousand foot drop below their feet, demanded concentration – a necessarily prolonged mental state, at times punctuated by moments of sheer terror.

However, they were soon back at the midway point and decided to have a go at the trickier peak now right opposite them. Relatively easy going at first, the way at one point soon became a tiny, narrow track above a precipice and they decided to retreat. "Discretion being the better part of valour" came into Peter's mind. The final part up to Meall Meadhonach would have to wait for another time, when they were feeling more proficient or less knackered. Or both. Peter was also worried about keeping enough psychological and physical well-being intact for the descent back onto the moorland, looking a long way below, down a vertiginous slope.

Despite these anxieties, the descent went steadily and smoothly. They both found it easiest to just keep going and not spend any time thinking about it. Just placing one foot in front of the other, over and over until it ended.

Nearly three hours after first leaving the loch, they arrived back at the erratic boulders and the point towards the loch's eastern tip and the mouth of the little Alltan Fearna again. At this moment Peter thought they were still nearly five miles from the car and with no water left at all now, so they took draughts of water from the stream. It was quite fast flowing, rocky and Peter hoped there wasn't a dead sheep or deer in it somewhere just upstream and out of view. To add to the weariness they now felt, it was getting warmer too. Peter suggested they make an effort to keep cooler, to cut down the thirst.

Even though it meant a lot of faff with his boots, Peter decided to change into shorts. They felt flimsy in this environment but also very comfortable. Mike just rolled his eyes when Peter made a joke out of this change of clothing by doing a form of slow striptease.

'Come on, we haven't time to mess about you like that. Let's just get on with it.'

Neither of them knew for sure, but guessed the bookshop might close at five-thirty. By speeding up they just made it by that time and managed to buy a large bottle of Irn Bru each as the best substitute for water. The shop assistant said they didn't need to have worried and that they more or less stayed open until dusk. Mike and Peter thought this was amazing given that dusk would still not be apparent for some hours.

It was a wearisome relief to get back in the car for the short drive back past the bay with the eiders and on to the caravans. Getting ready for showers, they were talking, unpacking, undressing and trying to keep things tidy in the limited space – all at the same time. They did feel perked up now by the sugar-rich energy of the fizzy drink and the reviving mugs of tea they had made as soon as they got in.

They found themselves re-running the day, feeling distinctly buzzy and elated. One of the best ever mountain days for either of them they agreed, long, arduous, frightening at times, but dry weather and not too many midges in the end. Most of all they talked about the views. Both on the approach to Suilven itself, but mostly from the top out to sea. They thought they had been able to see right across to the Hebrides, south to the mountains above Ullapool, and then north and south to more distant and unknown ones stretching away to the horizon. Torridon could be made-out, Peter was sure. Nearer at hand was the bulk of Ben More Assynt and Conival, with more and more peaks spreading up northwards.

'I've wanted to do that mountain since I was at school.' Said Peter, rucksack now emptied and taking-off his T-shirt, thinking of the meaning of the day for him. 'I've had that image in my head all that time. It's felt like a pilgrimage going up there today. Everything we just said about it … feels almost unbelievable to have done it at last.' Then he wanted to say something, quietly but emphatically, 'Lovely to have done it with you Mike!'

Peter leaned back against the kitchen units, now just almost totally undressed, ready for a shower. Mike had just got to the same point. They looked steadily at each other. 'What?' asked Mike, although he knew what Peter's look meant and could also immediately feel the excitement of the day translating into something else.

'Now you've summarised the brilliant day we had, I thought we could maybe top it off? You know… how about we have a shower?' He looked at Mike, feeling heady about the day and about the situation potentially developing right now. 'Together I mean.'

'It's a pretty tight space for two isn't it?' asked Mike, raising the question but increasingly liking the idea too.

'Yes! It is! It will be very cramped I imagine.' Said Peter. 'But after all those vistas and that wide-open scenery… doesn't some really close confinement sound an attractive alternative right now?'

Chapter 17

The following morning marked the start of the third full-day of their holiday and they found themselves lounging around looking out at fine drizzle. The locals had a word for it but Peter couldn't recall what it was. Two words he seemed to remember when he thought a bit more – one called something like smur and one that sounded like dreek. He wasn't sure if they meant the same thing or something different. It was fairly warm but they dare not open the door or windows because currently the air was very still and midges had come out in full force. Mike was in jeans and a light-blue polo shirt. Peter wasn't sure how the day would pan-out, clothes-wise, so had currently opted for wearing only a black T-shirt with the name of the prog rock band, Caravan, emblazoned across it. It had been in his wardrobe since University but he had dug it out, thinking it appropriate for the trip.

'Do you think we will be here all day?'

'It changes quickly up here, so I hope not Mike. We can nip into Lochinver at lunchtime if we can't get out anywhere else. What do you think?'

'I don't really want to be cooped up here, although it's nice being with you. The cramped conditions of the caravan can occasionally have some merit.'

'As we found out.' Said Peter, smiling at the thought of the shower cubicle.

'OK - we could just read and relax.' Saying this, Mike realised how much he wanted this for the two of them and was also aware how concerned he was for Peter, who didn't seem to realise how tense he was at times. 'I'm liking this holiday Pete. It feels a long way from home and work. And everything else. We need to make the most of it. The last few months…'

'I know. It's a bit unreal isn't it? Lots of it is unreal.' Peter sat down on the two-seater sofa and leant against the arm rest, propping his head up with his arm, hand pressed into his cheek. 'Yesterday for instance. Going up Suilven. Suilven! My cousin had been cycling up here donkey's years ago and he showed me his old one-inch maps from the time. I was bewitched by those groupings of intense contours - like Suilven, but also Canisp, Quinag. And then that picture in my stratigraphy book. Can hardly believe I've now actually done it at last.'

Mike pondered all that, before replying. 'It was special for me too. When we came out of that river valley, seeing the wall of rock face-on like that, I didn't think we would do it. I wouldn't have done without you.'

Peter smiled. 'Do you mean, me with my amazing mountaineering experience or just following me up that mountainside feeling besotted the whole way?' he joked.

'Don't kid yourself Pete!' Mike left the single armchair and went over and sat close up against Peter. 'Coming back here yesterday was special too. It's been great in that way. It feels different to your flat and I like that we can just hop in and out of bed. Or the shower!'

'I don't want to think about going back.' Mike then said, changing the subject somewhat. 'Do you think we can make it feel like this all the time, back in the flat? Or do we try and get somewhere else? Can we even get a place together?'

'Stop Mike. Stop now – if we start going into all this, it will just freak us out. We just need to like it – as you said. Make the most of it.' Peter hoped he had used the right tone. He knew he was as concerned as Mike about the future, but was hoping the holiday would make things happen somehow – that it would help them in some way.

Mike felt he could see what Peter was thinking then. There was something that had happened before they came away and he suddenly realised that this contemplative but relaxed discussion might be the right time. He hesitated a bit then said 'Why don't you share Sue's letter with me then. If it feels like the right moment?'

Peter considered this. The recent letters between him and Sue felt like a very big thing and he had been putting off doing this, sharing with Mike, until it felt right for him. He wasn't sure though that there would ever be an ideal time, instead always only time for prevarication. So, after a minute or two he went for a quick rummage in his kit bag and came back with some sheets of paper and an envelope. Mike looked at him curiously.

'This is Sue's letter' he said, waving the envelope. 'But I sneaked a photocopy of the one I sent to her – on the office photocopier when no one was looking. Each page takes a while and I was worried all the time someone would come in and read a bit of it. I'd be thrown out of the Company!' He held onto the paperwork as he sat down again, wondering, thinking. Then he shrugged, 'Here you are then. Maybe read mine first, it will make more sense that way round.'

'You sure you don't mind?'

'Mike, the last few months – we have shared loads haven't we? Yes. I mean no. I mean no, I don't mind. I want you to have a read. Go on, I will make us another tea in a minute.'

'Maybe put some more clothes on?'

'No, I'm comfortable like this actually. Anyway, concentrate on the letters! Please.'

Mike sat back on the sofa and then wriggled himself around so he was almost leaning back on it. He propped his back up with cushions, and then started to read. He thought Peter's handwriting was a bit hard to read at times – it had the feel of being rushed. There were a lot of exclamation marks and some underlining of words. He commented on the hurried look of it to Peter, who rolled his eyes and told him it wasn't so much rushed as just a case of not being able to stop once he got in the flow. Plus, what Mike was looking at was the last of very many attempts.

Mike sighed a bit, gave Peter's thigh a rub and read on.

Dear Sue

How are you? I know this will be a surprise to you but I thought a letter might be nice? Hoped it would be nice anyway. How's the new curriculum going? Are the sixth formers still arguing about politics with you? Do you still let them? You must be encouraging them I think.

Anyway, that's not what I am writing about really. I have stuff to tell you! Things to say to you and there's too much to do on the phone and in some ways its easier for me to write than speak. I can be sure of getting it right on paper I think, but maybe I'm also just a bit scared of telling you some things. Plus, our phone calls have dwindled, haven't they? I'm a bit scared there too – that if I ring you, something might have happened in your life.

Anyway, now something's happened to me!

I'm at my flat and it feels like I'm in a Hollywood movie right this minute. I can't remember what it's called but I think I've watched it with you from the video hire shop down here. It's Humphrey Bogart and he's trying to write a letter, keeps getting stuck, screws up the paper and tosses it in the bin and buries his head in his hands. The bin is getting very full. Like that, I have had quite a few attempts at this…

Bogart also reaches for a whisky bottle and lights a cigarette. I have a fag on the go right now, while writing this. No whisky bottle though. The ash tray is more full than it has been for a long time.

I can't believe I have only seen you a couple of times since New Year.

My job has been a bit mad, I know, and you said you were busy too. But, even so. I have missed you sweetheart. I think, know actually, that since last summer you have felt it best we put some distance between us – more than just a hundred miles of the M4!

The last few times I have come away from your place, or you left mine, I had a bad feeling about us – you and me. Since the holiday in Sutherland I feel we have drifted from each other and obviously I know why, because you told me. Not in so many words, because you are never unkind like that. I can't ever imagine you being like that actually. But a distance grew again between us, like a few years ago but this time it has been more painful for me because I have become so very fond of you. Last time in Bristol it felt like being with a good friend but you have come to mean so much more to me. Whenever I have seen you at your place I feel empty coming away, sad – and the same when you come over here and then have to leave again.

That's not right either, but I'm not going to cross-out bits or start yet again, this will have to do and I hope it makes sense.

So, what to say? I have always been fond of you. Since Kinlochewe – eight years ago now. I was very fond of you there. Came away feeling fond of you – the loveliest woman I have ever known. Then, later you were married to Colin for a while. But somehow we met in Chamonix and you became my proper girlfriend, which I have loved. In fact, I found it pretty intoxicating. So, its been hard to stop the intoxication, to stop wanting you in my life the whole time. Harder than giving up smoking and I'm making a crappy enough job of that!

The biggest thing you have done of course, is to stop me feeling I'm a poof! A word we have jokingly used with each other from time to time. It's the only word, of the many you hear, that sounds reasonable. And when I'm with you I don't have to think about any of those other words and names. And I only know the truth of this as I write it now. You have always been ahead of me with thinking Sue and I can see that this is why the distance, as I call it, has occurred. Isn't that so?

Well, you have been right all along. I still can't say 'I am a Ho…... ual' Or the Q word that all the trash newspapers use. You see Sue, I can't even write the bloody words!

Sorry – this letter is rubbish – could do better. That might be the sort of thing you say to your pupils. 'John – you must write better, write that out one hundred times!'

Well, here goes, for my umpteenth version. But I am going to post this one – the one you are reading. Hopefully you are reading it still and haven't already got bored or dismissed it as drivel!

Three months ago Mike came round to my flat. It was late March. You know that since Talmine, he and I have become increasingly close friends. Really close friends – like we have always been friends. I started to find we had a lot in common, both in work and outside. So; deep breath for this bit Sue.

We went to the local pub and had a chat about life, the universe and everything - as Douglas Adams would say. Mike asked me a lot about you. He told me a lot about Diane. Not so dissimilar stories really. It was really easy to talk to him. When I was talking about Kinlochewe I couldn't say 'and Steve and I got off with each other' but I did talk about the naked swims in the river and lochans. It was like he wanted me to say more. I couldn't admit to having had a gay sexual relationship. Every time I tried to change the subject he brought it back round to Steve. He knew!!

Then with him and Diane, he talked about how it was just assumed by everyone that they would be heading for settling down and getting married. He's been thinking of getting a job near her, and maybe living together all the time.

Then we had a couple more pints and then back to my flat. There was no way Mike could have driven back to his place, so I said he could sleep on the couch. He's done it before, as you know.

But that's not what happened this time!

We had a whisky. It's like in Hollywood, again, stuff happens when you have a whisky sometimes. We were standing together in the kitchen, talking about music or something. I had put on a tape – hits of 84 thing, George Michael, Frankie Goes to Hollywood and stuff. We started dancing, holding each others shoulders and then you can guess. Somehow we ended up in bed together. Sorry. Is that a shock?

Sue – I hope you are still reading this. Please keep reading. It's a confession I think. Obviously it is. I hope I have the courage to post this. You are the only person to know this. If I hadn't told you about Steve all those years ago, I couldn't do this now. It is a bit of déjà vu. For you too?

Neither of us have done much else 'like that'. He hadn't had the intensity of my Steve experience with anyone else. One-offs really and not much. But it's been 'like that' for us again.

But it is not just physical. I think I would have told you even if that's all it was. All!? Gosh! But this feels more than that now.

He's cancelled weekends in London. I think Diane realises a serious glitch has occurred in her life and now Mike and I don't know what to do. You see, I think we are quickly falling for each other Sue, emotionally. That's what we have said. That feeling of deeply connected friendship has morphed into something else.

A couple of weeks ago, we were in a wine bar and I told him that I really, really, really liked him. He said he felt the same. I said I thought we could maybe live together one day! Too much wine?

He and Diane need to talk. I need to talk to you. He is also scared but knows he has to do something. So, the start of 'something' is this letter. He doesn't know about this though. I have been going bonkers on my own, feeling like my head's going to burst. I wanted to see you and tell you but maybe this is better. Is it cowardly to write like this? You are more cerebral than me, maybe this works better for you.

I've probably written enough though. Except to tell you, Mike and I have booked a holiday together! In a couple of weeks' time we are going up to Lochinver, equidistant between Talmine and Kinlochewe, roughly. That wasn't the reason for choosing it though. Maybe it was though!? Hadn't thought of that until this moment!

We have a caravan. When I spoke with the owner on the phone I said it was me and my mate – that we were coming for climbing and birdwatching. He seemed ok with that and I didn't get a hint he thought anything odd about it. Two blokes in their late (ish) twenties on holiday together in a small caravan. It has one small bedroom and two sofas that make a bed – you know the sort of thing. Hope it will be ok.

Obviously, it's not good with Diane really, but Mike has said to her that he wanted to do something different before moving to London – just to clear his head and he thought I was a good mate to do that with. It's so unlike him though, she must be wondering what's going on. As you saw last summer, she's not daft!

He feels awful about it but we needed to get away from work, and Bristol and be together – to see how we really feel. About each other. About what that means. For him to think of Diane and what to do maybe. To see if it works for us I suppose. I'm a bit scared really.

I'm hoping a break in the lovely mountains of Sutherland and Wester Ross will give me a reset.

You always knew this would happen, didn't you? But last time I came out to you, you hadn't been my girlfriend like you have been this time. I'm wondering if you're still reading, wondering what you're thinking. I have been stressed out thinking of your reaction. I have the hope, maybe naively though, that this is what you wanted? For the good of both of us? Does it help you in some way? I have revisited our Ben Arnaboll talk so many times – that whole holiday really. When you imagined this would happen, did you feel it would be the right thing for you too?

Sorry again I couldn't phone and say all this. Sorry Sue. Sorry for everything that I have messed-up for you. Please can you write back? And can we meet – please?

I have the envelope written and with a stamp on it and I'm going to stop here, although there's loads to say to you. I intend to go straight out with it now, before I lose my nerve.

Lots of love.

Pete xxxx

Mike finished reading the photocopied sheet and put it down on the coffee table. 'Oh Pete.' No other words came but he held out his arms and Peter leant into them. Then they hugged.

'What do you think?' Peter felt he was gazing at Mike and knew he was biting his lower lip.

'I think it feels like the start of something and I don't know where it will lead' Mike said, running his hand through his hair. 'It feels like a runaway vehicle! But it's not too late to stop. Not sure what's best.'

'Well I had told you roughly what I had written, hadn't I? And I don't think we can stop now.'

'Yes, but reading the words is different. It somehow crystallises it. It has all felt unreal but this brings it into reality – someone else now knows!' he paused. 'I'm amazed you posted it.'

'I was then in knots until the reply – as you know. My round-Britain work tour, as I've kept calling it, helped take my mind off things though. I could never allow myself to be in the car without the radio or a cassette though. And I've drunk a bit more. Oh – and smoked a bit more. Again. You know.'

Mike waited, letting Peter deal with what was happening – not wanting to rush anything.

'So, anyway, this is Sue's letter – waiting for me a few days ago, when I got back from that conference I had to attend. I couldn't open it at first. It's been hard keeping it until now to show you. I feel in a different place, away here. Here with you. Very special place.' They kissed each other.

Mike could feel Peter was literally trembling, when he at last picked-up Sue's letter, took it out of the slit-open envelope and read, noticing immediately Sue's steadier-looking hand. He relaxed when he saw Sue's opening salutation and imagined how relieved Peter must have felt too when he saw that too.

Dearest, lovely Pete.

How hard it must have been for you to write that letter to me. It made me cry and I can imagine you reading this now and you are already starting to do the same, before you read anything else.

Well, my old softie, sweetheart, part of me wants to say 'I told you so', but that's not me really. Your letter was a surprise of course, but there was an inevitability about it too – something I always expected to hear about has now actually happened. It's a shock, in that I wasn't expecting it right now! But it's not a shock in another way, as I had always felt this would happen to you eventually, one day.

Mike is a lovely guy, I think, particularly from what I saw of him last summer on that holiday. There was something about him made me think of Steve and also of you with Steve. I read somewhere that gay people have this ability to spot one another? It's referred to as gaydar, apparently, like radar. Is that true? Could you discern something? Was there a hint? Maybe I should ask Wendy if there's any research. I doubt there's anything about men fancying men but I wonder if something biochemical is transmitted between brains of people when they fall for someone?

But, don't worry! I can hear you panicking. I won't mention this to Wendy, nor anyone else just yet. Julie wouldn't be surprised and I think all the friends would be ok with you about it. I don't know though – it's a bit untested. They will be concerned for me I suppose. I will need to chat with Julie soon actually – hope you understand that. This is a big thing for me too.

But, I don't know about your work colleagues – both of you will have to be very careful there I think.

When you mentioned Diane, it made me realise that the two of you truly are serious about what's happened – that you are already thinking of living together. If you haven't seen it like that yet, you need to know that this is what I understood from what you said. And I know you Pete.

You two are going to have to think about all this, who do you tell? You have come out to one person – me! Maybe that's the easiest because you did this to me once before! If I hadn't seduced you into helping me with my own life, back in Chamonix, you might have done it sooner…

We will never know.

Or do you want to try and keep it a secret? If so, for how long? It's clear from what you said that the feelings between you are strong – stronger maybe than Mike and Diane have had for each other and stronger maybe than you and I? But maybe that's unfair about how I have experienced you caring about me, looking after me and being so there for me all the time. So, maybe it's just that you and Mike feel right together in a different way – that you couldn't ever feel completely right about with me Pete, because I am not a man. That's why your letter was hard to write, wasn't it?

Not seeing you much since New Year wasn't deliberate, but I know I haven't done anything to keep us together – to keep our 'thing' going. I have needed space and your letter shows me that this has been right for both of us.

Like I said in the Alps Peter, I have maybe used you a bit? You turned up at the right time and I used you then I'm sure – you were the right man at the right time.

And it has been lovely for me! After Colin, you have been a constant friend, who has cared for me so much and made me feel good all the time. And you have made me feel wanted in a nice way, which has been great too. But all the time we have been together, I have never been able to dispel from my mind what happened in Kinlochewe. You know this and have always known it, without us having to spell it out. I think you always hoped it would just go away - but it clearly hasn't, has it?

And I have been your sanctuary, haven't I? Your safe harbour where you have been able to tie yourself up safely. Without having to go out into unknown choppy waters? Unconsciously we have leaned on each other. Maybe 'used' is too harsh – we have done it with great respect for each other – I know you feel that for me Pete and I will never, ever, stop respecting you.

But you have set sail from that safe harbour now I think and you will maybe have to go through some turbulent seas. You will have to lean on each other a lot!

But you can lean on me too Pete. It makes me feel very special that you could write to me like this. That I would be the first person in your life to know this.

When you get back from Scotland, let's meet and have a longer talk. Get the whisky and ciggies stored-up now eh? Oh – and the tissues too I should think.

Peter – just have a lovely holiday with Mike. Think a lot. Think of everything you've got. (There's a song there somewhere).

Take care my lovely, lovely friend.

Love, as always.

SUE xxxxxx

Peter had been re-reading the letter over Mike's shoulder, seeing it afresh through Mike's eyes. Now he felt quite overwhelmed, grabbed the cigarette packet off the table, hurriedly pulled on his tracksuit bottoms, shoved his feet into trainers and went outside.

Mike looked at him through the caravan window. He was now out there in the fine drizzle, looking across the loch, clearly lost in his thoughts, probably tearful, slowly and steadily puffing on the cigarette.

The letters were very moving, thought Mike. But another, newer feeling was building too. There was a sense of relief for him. As Sue had suggested, it was like he and Peter had set-off on a journey and there was no going back. He felt sad for Peter and Sue though, as a couple. The love and care they had for each other shone through. He had seen them together, spent time with them of course, but the words they had said to each other in writing, revealed the depth of their relationship.

Now he felt like a bit of an interloper. Worse than that, he felt he was actively helping to break-up a love affair. And yet, again as Sue had indicated, for all they felt for each other it just was never going to be completely right! The H word, the Q word. And then, after all this, Mike started to feel daunted. Struck by how much was going to have to happen – firstly to be sure they wanted to be together, and then how to make it happen.

After a while, he went out to join Peter, taking their two cagoules off the back of the door.

'Here Pete – you will be wet already, but it might help.'

Peter was unable to speak for some while, and they both stood their looking at the rain, feeling bedraggled and swotting the worst of the midges. Eventually, the damp gloom started to take on a more peaceful feel. They both felt it. Maybe there had been a subtle change in the weather or maybe just standing there quietly, just being, had moved them on in some way.

'Let's take the car and drive somewhere.' Pete eventually said, sounding snuffly. 'Don't worry about me Mike, I'm fine. Well, I'm not really… but you know what I mean.' He gave his nose a good blow. He stood up straight then, put his arm across Mike's shoulders and said, 'I was just thinking, how about we go to where it all began.'

'Where all what began?'

'Not far down the road – a place called Knockan Crag. We drove past it on the way here, but no time to stop. I mentioned it but you probably glazed over. Anyway, all geologists bow down to it respectfully.' Peter said enigmatically. 'It's not just rocks though. There's a good view.' Peter looked at the rain, his mouth twisted at the corner. 'Maybe anyway.'

Mike didn't know what to make of it but was just pleased Peter seemed to be coming round from something. It looked as if a weight might have started to lift off him and he seemed to be brightening-up. Now the weather just needed to do the same.

Chapter 18

In fact, the weather did improve, as they drove east, past Loch Assynt, down past Inchnadamph and a bit further south to Knockan Crag. Peter had remembered this place as a wet, rather unremarkable spot several years previously and was surprised to find a car park area had been built and a signboard gave information about the significance of the cliff. Evidently there was a circuitous track one could now follow, where previously there had been a mixture of scraps of paths in and around the rocks created by either sheep or geology students.

Mike thought it looked like a weathered cliff of rocks like much else of the landscape hereabouts. He was sure he would be told more anyway, but it felt polite to ask…

'Go on then Pete. Tell me why this place is important.' He hoped he had adopted a genuine tone.

'If you're going to be sarcastic or take the piss, you can forget it!' said Peter, but smiling. He continued. 'OK, short version. Back in the late nineteenth century this whole area of Scotland,' He flung his arms wide, to north and south, 'was pretty much the last bit of Britain to be understood geologically. Partly cos it was remote from everywhere else but partly because it didn't make sense. Plus just getting around here was really tough. They apparently mapped on horseback, staying at places like the Inchnadamph Hotel we just passed back there a bit. But there were only tracks, not roads, a lot of wet moorland, big mountains, sheep and not much else. And not many people.' He concluded. 'Most of those had been kicked-off! You might remember the story of The Clearances, up in Sutherland last summer?'

'Anyway, this crag was like a mini version of the whole of the North West Highlands. They eventually realised that the rocks at the top, which should be the youngest in a sequence going upwards, were actually the oldest, so it seemed upside down, and even more than that, they eventually figured out that this could only be made to happen if whole slabs of the British Isles had been thrust over the top of other bits. It coincided with geology findings coming out of the Alps.'

'The Alps don't look like this though, do they?' Mike commented, partly as a question and partly as a statement.

'No, they are much younger. Much more recent. And still shiny and with beautiful peaks and glaciers.' Peter's mind flashed back to Chamonix for a moment. And a strong image of Sue arose too - on a sunny walk by Loch Blanc, her sunglasses reflecting snow and ice, hair shining, just looking beautiful in the sunshine. He sighed before continuing his story.

'But, they then realised that mountains, like the Alps, must have risen up and been eroded back to the sea many times in Earth's history. That's taken for granted now in Uni but back then, they were the first people to figure it out.'

'And they got that from this cliff?' Mike knew he sounded doubtful.

'Yes! They really did – and from the whole area. Right up to Loch Eriboll where we were last year. They did a lot of hard, detailed work and eventually came up with two plus two equals four. Their colleagues were incredulous but now this place is known throughout the world. By geologists anyway!' and he laughed a little.

Then he sighed again. This time so heavily, Mike looked up in surprise.

'I took Sue to the Loch Eriboll bit last year.' He said. 'I explained the same sort of thing to her.'

Mike knew they would need to talk about it – probably a lot more than once! It had been good that they had both implicitly agreed to drop the subject on the car journey, preferring instead to talk about Suilven again, the other hills they might do, and a reflection or two on the shower.

'I thought Sue's letter was very gracious Pete. You had gone out for a smoke but I felt incredibly touched by her words. Moved. That she would just accept you and me – just like that. Straight-off, no question.'

'You and me.' Repeated Peter, making eye contact with Mike. 'Those are the key words aren't they? Sue has instantly leapt to the idea, to the suggestion, that we are, or could be, a couple.'

'It wasn't just what Sue said. I was also really moved by what you wrote to her. You more or less said you loved me and I can't get over that. I can't get my head round that.'

Peter looked at Mike, at his slightly wavy hair, his boyish face, the gentle smile he now had. 'I think I might do.' He said very quietly.

Mike felt a bit giddy – partly from what Peter had just said but also from the whole morning. The last few hours had felt to him like going up and down through a series of emotions – truly a rollercoaster. He felt Peter had spent the time since breakfast, oscillating between smiles and tears and Mike now wanted him to get onto a more cheerful plane – perhaps this walk could be that shift.

After a long hug, they continued up the steep northern edge of the escarpment and along the top where they stopped to look over the peaks arrayed before them. They found a reasonably dry slab of protruding rock to sit on. The base of the cloud now just clipping the top of the tallest peaks. Peter knew the names of most of them but Suilven, looking splendid to the right of their vista, was the only one they had ascended so far. When Mike asked about this, Peter explained, 'sadly, field trips didn't allow time to go up mountains just for the sake of it.'

'So, it's Suilven and then the ones we did up there somewhere,' Mike pointed vaguely northwards, 'Ben Hope and Ben Loyal and then others further south?'

'Well south, you have An Teallach – a beautiful but tricky mountain walk I believe, then you soon get round to Torridon.' Peter paused, looking south. 'So, apart from those in the far north you just mentioned, and Torridon, it's just Suilven I've been up. But all these others? We can do them together can't we?'

Mike told Peter that when he spoke of Torridon, it was always a bit reverential. Almost as if it was a holy place.

'I don't know about that Mike!' 'Not holy, not for me anyway. But spiritual, that's different.' A pause. 'I had a friend from college, haven't seen him much since the last Alps trip but he used to say I was reverential about Torridon. That same word. Simon – I've probably mentioned him.'

'Yeah – I know of him. Are you still in touch?'

'Sadly, not so much.' said Peter. 'He's got involved with a woman he met at a work event. He never showed much interest in women previously - but now they're getting married. He knew of Sue and last time I was in touch, he was obviously thinking Sue and I might be heading towards marriage too.'

'Is he someone you could come out to?'

'God knows Mike! Actually, Simon was pretty sensitive to others – oh, I don't know! We don't know how people will react do we? I can't help imagining people will just drop me as a friend. Drop us.'

Now it was Mike's turn to pause and they were both quiet for a few minutes. 'So, if we are becoming "us" now…I don't know. Maybe we think of who to tell next? It has been one person so far, but that's been ok. We can't rush it.' He wanted to say more, but could see and feel Peter tightening up. He and the two of them didn't need to rush. He and Peter should just try and relax instead – that would do more good right now.

Mike wondered how to get back to a point where Peter wasn't over-thinking stuff. He looked at Peter and became immediately aware of his physicality, tensed-up, but also lean-bodied, looking like he's suited to the outdoors, part of it almost. Mike thought he knew what he could do to shift the uncertainty and the unsettled mood.

'I think there will be more trips coming this way for us, don't you? We could come up here again?' Asked Mike, affecting a bit of coyness in his voice. He was thinking that he might try and settle Peter with some distraction – of a physical variety.

Peter immediately picked-up on the change of tone and its possible implication. 'Maybe Mike. Think so, don't you?' He moved himself a bit closer.

'And when you went to that mountain above Loch Eriboll with Sue then, that you were telling me about just now, was that spiritual for you too?'

Peter thought of that time, realised what suggestion was being offered from Mike and liked it. He simultaneously became aware that they were the only people in the whole area. He looked down to the car park a couple of hundred feet below and noticed theirs was still the only car. Without either of them saying anything, they stood-up, moved together, off the path several yards and then round a bluff and into to a tucked-away curve of cliff, completely hidden from the tiny track they had been following.

'Yes, it was spiritual actually.' Answered Peter eventually. 'I think it was probably the start of a long conversation that maybe just ended with those letters.' Peter realised the truth of that but also wanted to concentrate on playing along a bit with Mike.

Mike paused, looking straight at Peter, wanting to help him, to be nice to him. Wanting him to think of something else. Wanting him. He tried to imagine Peter and Sue back at that moment, on Ben Arnaboll, making love in the wilds. 'Purely spiritual? Or also, maybe, a bit physical?'

Peter now felt himself being turned-on by the clear change in mood. They were teasing each other. He felt a swiftly passing physical memory of Sue. As always, the intense emotions that had been running around all morning also made him feel full of pent-up energy. In other circumstances, a run would suffice to dissipate it, but right now Mike was offering an alternative outlet.

'Sue is a mix of both those things – to me anyway. You can guess what happened up there that day, I'm sure.'

Peter moved so that he could hug Mike but also feel the front of his jeans. He discovered Mike was very aroused and he felt himself responding in kind. Mike was returning the same gesture and then had his hands inside Peter's tracksuit bottoms, which he gently pulled down to the ground. He had crouched down to do this and was now kneeling in front of Peter as he also slid down his underpants.

'Think you really need this Pete,' said Mike. And then the conversation ended for a while. For a time they were both lost in their own world, off-loading the emotion of the last few hours. Timely interaction in a timeless landscape. Only the wind to disturb them.

On the return to the car, the path proved to be very steep and they had to do a wide arc to the south to find a gentler gradient. Peter felt he didn't care right now, whatever they did was fine. He felt light-headed and almost a bit like he was drunk. In fact, he felt very light in other ways too, as if some weight had been lifted.

Mike noticed this too and thought that maybe both of them were feeling the same thing. He made a joke about it to Peter. 'Feeling happier now, are we? So a cliff-top blow-job was all you needed eh?'

'Yeah, it was great. Not just me though. I returned the favour and I have since noticed you have been more gazelle-like coming down here too.' He stopped for a moment and looked around. 'Yeah – that was a good thing to do Mike – helped me a lot. Both of us.'

Mike smiled, nodding. 'Nice bit of fun wasn't it! Do you think your Victorian geologists did anything like that on this cliff then?'

he asked, a bit mischievously.

Peter laughed at that idea at first, then he thought about that situation a bit more. Men together in the wilds for weeks and months on end. 'Oh, I can't believe for one minute we're the first.'

Mike found himself thinking about Peter's remark. 'That's actually a really good thing to say Pete. I think I spent the best part of this morning thinking how isolated you and I are. Being together I mean. As a couple?' He realised he was using this word for the first time to describe themselves. 'Just for a moment though you've made me think we're not so strange after all. We won't be the only guys to make-out a bit up here, we are not the first guys to do stuff like that on this cliff… nor are we the first to feel like we do about each other.'

Peter smiled at that and for the first time in the last few weeks felt a growing sense of confidence they could work it out. That was what he wanted to do anyway. He knew that for sure.

CHAPTER 19

Encouraged by the letter-reading and the discussions they'd had as a result, they decided to do only one more big car driving day before they eventually had to go home again. Hopefully, they would then get a couple more of the local Assynt and Coigach peaks tucked under their belts. But Peter had managed to persuade Mike that today they should return all the way up to the north coast and specifically to Durness and Balnakeil.

Mike knew this was another special place for Peter and felt that their trip to the Cape Wrath Hotel the previous year had not given anyone the chance to explore it fully. Peter always wanted to reconnect with things and Mike was very happy to go along with it. He was happy, full stop. The previous day had been a good one for them both – a bit thrown around like being at a fair, but with the end-result of eventually feeling much calmer. At least for the moment. So, he sat back in the car, listened to Fleetwood Mac and let Peter drive to the far north.

In fact, the first place they encountered when they eventually stopped, had this epithet. The Far North Pottery was what it said over the door. The studio occupied one of the huts in the Craft Village at Balnakeil. The genial proprietor was also the person who created and made the extensive range of pots and other items aligned on the wall outside and across every shelf inside. She talked with them and asked them about where they were from and what had brought two young men to this place. It didn't feel like an interrogation but Peter had the feeling she knew the truth. She was Swedish, she told them, but now settled here. Peter felt sure she had tuned-in to them.

Looking around, between the potter's wheel and the kiln area Peter was taken by the cauldron-like casserole pots and spontaneously decided to buy one. 'It's the colours Mike' he explained. 'She has an eye for the landscape and I love the way she captures the sense of sky and moorland. '

'So we will have a little bit of the North West Highlands in our kitchen all the time then?'

Peter looked around then, to make sure they were not being overheard. Then he looked back at Mike quizzically, but allowing his face to then soften into a broad smile. 'What's all this "we" and "our kitchen" then?'

There was a moment of surprise from Mike and then they both laughed. 'Is that how it happens then, do you think?' Asked Mike. 'Is this how a couple forms?'

'You'd think there would be easier ways than travelling seven hundred miles from home to an old RAF station to do it though!' replied Peter.

They both smiled and laughed a bit. Mike added 'We'll be wanting to go to Habitat together next!' Then added. 'At least it would be nearer.'

They walked around the village and Peter explained how just a few years earlier it had been more clearly an old air force station, with the concrete buildings then all being in various states of repair. He and his fellow geology students had stayed in one of the better blocks – owned by Glasgow University as a base for students on field trips of any purpose. Peter explained it was very primitive but had been very cheap – the main consideration for him back then.

Peter eventually found what he thought was the right building and mentioned various goings-on back then, including the Whisky Galore incident. Mike looked south from the hut to the rough terrain in the direction of the Cape Wrath Hotel, although that was hidden from view. He thought that Peter and his mates had been very determined, or very drunk, to set-off across that land at midnight, in the middle of a hailstorm!

After the village, they made their way down to the bay, somewhere

Peter could hardly recall, just beyond the ruined church. 'I think we didn't have time to explore locally back then. It was up and out for the fieldwork, then back for dinner and then the pub. Oh, and we all fitted in having a shower when we could. There was only one for a dozen of us, mixed, and it was tepid at best.'

And it had been a pity not to have seen this view back then, thought Peter, as he and Mike arrived at the sandy edge of the arc of beach leading from a rambling old estate house, northwards.

'Wow' exclaimed Mike.

They had not been aware that the sun was so strong, but the view before them was bathed in sunlight, producing sharp, distinct colours of blue, white, green, sand and cream. Peter looked behind to check and discovered the sun was high in the south although the sky in that direction had a fair bit of high cloud. In front of them though, there were just some scattered, white fluffy bits of cloud, floating above the coast. It felt like the edge of the world.

The sea was a rich royal blue, except where it broke against the sand, almost the entire mile-long line all in one go, cresting in clean, bright whiteness. The sand dunes to their right merged with small green, tussocky hillocks. At the end of the beach was a distinct, small rocky cliff, jagged black and shades of grey against the other colours.

'I guess you want to walk to that, don't you?'

Peter blew out a big gust of air, shook his head a bit. 'All of it actually Mike. The whole beach and around. Can't remember this. It's so beautiful though, I've a vague memory now of seeing it in a storm and getting soaked, just walking. A couple of the women students wanted to check-out the church back there. I think that happened anyway. It's hazy.'

'Well, it's not hazy here. What do we do now? What does the map say?'

Peter unfolded the map and they learned that the beach in front of them was part of Balnakeil Bay, and the second part, another beach, was out of view – beyond the dark cliff outcrop. The area west, to their left was indicated as a low cliff-line, heading back around to the Kyle of Durness and the Hotel.

'The whole little peninsula is called Fharaid Head. Seems to be about a couple of miles to the end of it, about five miles round-trip back to the car, with a bit of exploring. I'm carrying a bit of water, some trail mix; what do you think?'

Mike needed no further encouragement. He set-off but Peter wasn't immediately alongside. He turned to see what was happening. Peter was rolling up the legs of his jeans. Mike thought that looked like a great idea and within a few minutes they were both wading their way through the edge of the surf heading up the beach.

Groups of ringed plovers and sandpipers were always running just ahead of them, always keeping just ahead of the sea as it swashed in and out. They passed maybe a dozen people in all, sat on the sand here and there, spread out along the sandy bay. There was a young family group at the craft village end, then a couple with two young kids, another a more middle-aged pairing. They all exchanged short greetings.

Just before the cliff, Mike spotted what at first seemed like a fishing buoy, but it submerged and reappeared and they soon realised it was the head of a seal, about twenty yards offshore. They watched for a while and were amazed to feel that the seal was checking them out as much as they were doing to it. It felt very special to them both to be inspected in this way.

'So, what's this cliff then? Asked Mike when they reached it. 'It's all very hard and rough.'

'Hmm, well there's a lot of very dark rock and I think that may be a dyke. But there's some schist or gneiss. Not sure – it's a bit weathered by sea spray.'

Mike knew all these geological names by now and thought

Peter sounded relaxed and happy even if he wasn't immediately identifying the rock types. He could see there was another cliff outcrop a further half-mile ahead now, and in between mostly large sand dunes backing the beach. He suggested to Peter they walk up the beach and then head-up to the top of that cliff to walk around the headland.

'We should have brought swim-stuff.' Replied Peter looking out across the surf. He thought of the people they had passed and others who had possibly been arriving back by the church who had a couple of dogs. 'We're not completely alone. Some others will be up here soon maybe.'

Mike didn't immediately understand what Peter had meant. 'Oh… I see. You had thought maybe we could just strip-off?'

'Yeah, never mind. Tell you what though, I'm taking off my jeans at least, so I can wade better.' Peter folded them and put them in his sack and walked into the water just above his knees, his red T-shirt partially covering his white briefs.

'Sue warned me that you like exposing yourself - to the elements.'

'She's one to talk!'

'Really? Not sure I want to know that story. I'll just keep on the sand, it must be freezing.'

'I can't tell Mike, everything from my thighs down has gone numb! I might need some hard rubbing to thaw me out when we get to the next cliff.'

'Yeah, sure!' said Mike with a guffaw. 'If it's too risky to chance a skinny-dip, then it is most certainly too risky to do anything like that.'

Peter didn't mind. He felt in his element. The sea was very cold but walking in it felt sublime to him. It made him feel as if he was a million miles from work, from home, the flat, Sue, Diane, - from reality.

Half an hour later, with Peter restored back into his jeans, they reached the end of the headland. They had been surprised to see some sort of military installation here as they approached. There was a fence around some buildings, mostly partially hidden, but not really any information other than the stated requirement to keep out of MoD property. They knew that the Cape Wrath headland itself, ten miles to the west, was used for bombing target practice and made an assumption this was something to do with it too.

They agreed to stick to the edge of the headland and head down the eastern side, which looked as if it was higher cliffs, and then work their way back round to the car and the Craft Village. They encountered a small lake, surrounded by boggy ground. Mike quickly had his binoculars up. He was always the better one at bird identification but Peter knew first, this time, what it was they were looking at. 'It's a Golden Plover.' He said.

'Yes, it is. How did you know that one so quickly?'

'Back on my mapping area, one of those followed me up some of the path many days. A mate of mine said it was trying to keep me away from its nest. Graham. He was a bit like you actually.'

'Was he?'

'Only in a good way. He was mad about birdlife and knew a lot. I think we all underestimated him really.' Peter paused, thinking back. 'He was thoughtful, more than I appreciated at the time, and nice, and kind.' Another pause. 'Also like you.'

Mike turned to him and, as always, then looked around, checking if anyone could see them, then gave Peter a hug and kissed him. One wasn't enough for Peter and they then found they kissed a few times, taking their time. Whenever Mike tried to look over his shoulder, Peter playfully pulled his head back round.

Shortly after that spot they came onto the highest part of the eastern side of Fharaid Head. They sat down a couple of feet back from the sheer cliff edge. Lots of birds were flying about. Mike was quickly excited and checking with the binoculars, declared that the cliff was a puffin colony. Once they got their eyes into the birds' behaviour they realised that there were dozens, if not hundreds, of them and their nest burrows were in the top edge of the cliff and on other parts of the ground to the side which would be difficult for anything but a bird to visit.

Neither of them had seen anything like it previously and after a while Peter produced a field notebook and they spent a bit of time recounting the various birds and other wildlife they had seen so far. Looking at the total and thinking about it, they agreed it had been a very special place to visit.

'I've loved it here Mike.'

'Me too.'

They were half-lying on the ground which felt warm and dry, just looking eastwards, at the cliffs, the sea, the sky, the wild and enormous landscape before them.

'So, are we looking towards the previous holiday then, when we look right across there?' Mike asked.

Peter thought the question could have two meanings and realised he had been on a bit of a reverie. 'Well firstly, yes there's this line of cliffs to our immediate right, and a couple of bays we can see and that's Durness village running along the top – a very strung-out community really isn't it? Just odd houses and buildings here and there. Then that expanse of water, straight ahead, is the mouth of Loch Eriboll. Talmine is quite a few miles beyond the far shore of the loch.

Mike asked what the hills were, above the Loch.

'We drove past them, all of us, all the gang, last year. I talked about it yesterday, at Knockan. That's where I went walking up there with Sue – that's Ben Arnaboll. We talked about it yesterday. I had also been there as a student. Wanted to show her. It's an important place.'

'For you, you mean?'

'No, I mean, yeah. For me. It's an important place for me – a precursor to Kinlochewe and Meall a Ghiubhais.'

Mike knew this Gaelic name by now – the correct name for Peter's mountain. 'Do you have a hierarchy of important places then?'

Peter smiled at the question, realising he was being teased but also feeling Mike had touched on something important too. 'I have never thought about it like that but maybe I do have a set of places of significance'. Various places and memories flashed though his mind. 'But the Arnaboll hill is also really, really important in geological history – in the history of the subject I mean. That's partly why we were brought such a long way to do fieldwork I suppose!'

'And did Sue like it.' Mike asked.

Peter could sense that Mike had realised that the walk the previous year had been important in some way. 'She did. We had a nice day.'

'You told me yesterday that it was a lot more than just a walk.'

'Yes, it was.' He looked at Mike to check this conversation was going OK. 'Yes, there was definitely nobody else about that day!' He thought of that day, how it had gone, the conversation that he had with Sue. Being in each other's arms.

'That's when Sue brought our thing to an end though. That sounds brutal, but it wasn't like that. A better way of putting it would be to say she got both of us to realise … well, you know.' He hesitated. 'It was there though. Over there.' He pointed out to the distant hills. 'By the time we drove back to Swansea, I knew we would be going our separate ways. Just took a while to happen.'

Mike put his arm round Peter's shoulders and then hugged him more fully. 'Let's not get upset today, eh?'

'I'm not really Mike.' But he wiped away a tiny tear that had leaked out anyway. 'Honestly, it's fine. The thing is …almost the next day, I walked on the beach, the Kyle of Tongue beach, with you! And I felt a bit close to you then too – that was an early inkling.'

'I remember feeling the same thing Pete. We'd all spent a fortnight together. We had all got so close, you felt like a good mate.' Now it was Mike's turn to look lost in thought. 'I didn't know we would end-up like this though.'

'No, nor me.'

The discussion had the potential to become heavy but neither of them wanted to do that, so they changed the subject and soon set-off back. In the car back down to Lochinver, they were both quiet. Relaxed sitting next to each other. Reflective more than subdued. They had both felt they'd had a great day out. But more than that they had visited a place they had never seen before, and it was beautiful, and full of wildlife and they had loved it.

'And I loved being there with you.' Mike said very gently, quietly, brushing his hand across Peter's thigh.

The way Mike said this, caught the mood of both of them. Peter was so moved that he had to find a place to pull-over safely before he couldn't properly see where he was driving.

'I was getting blurry then Mike.' He said, dabbing his eyes with a handkerchief.

'Me too.' Came the reply.

Chapter 20

Peter had been outside a while, thinking about the cuckoo that he had just seen on the telegraph post, making the eponymous call that had lured him from the caravan, where he had left Mike tucked-up in bed. He was also thinking about that and the time together that the two of them had enjoyed up here. Mostly enjoyed, but intruded upon by worries around Diane, concerns about telling people, fears about people finding out or being told. Thinking about a lot of things.

It wasn't the best of days but the next was probably going to be wetter and then they would have to drive home. He needed to get out or risk a day of bluesy thoughts. He turned round and headed back in.

Mike was up now and making a cup of tea, wearing a black Ramones T-shirt and fleecy, striped pyjama bottoms. Peter thought he looked cute like that and hesitated about suggesting a walk, for the chance of maybe going back to bed. He knew what would be better for him in the long run and decided head over heart, or at least head over the part of him that had been distracting his thinking.

'OK' he said, giving Mike a big smile. 'Good news! It really is quite blowy, as we could hear in bed. Bad news, cloudy and quite low. Might lift, might not. Last day for a walk though if the forecast's right. Think we should get out.'

'Yep. Agreed. I've started doing the flasks while you've been outside. Don't really want to do something too demanding though, or too long.' Mike hoped Peter would listen and properly hear this request.

'Right. Er. Well, how about Quinag? Don't know if it's pronounced how it's spelt. Good thing is, the track I know about, it starts nearly a thousand feet up, by where we park the car hopefully. There's a lot to the whole mountain but we don't have to do it all -

can just do a single summit, up and back. That's if we can see where we're going up there! Be back here by early afternoon.'

'Sounds good, but I'm holding you to that Pete!'

'No worries. You can hold anything you like.' To which, Mike grinned and rolled his eyes.

Despite the attraction of staying in the caravan instead – a thought that had now arisen now for both of them, they managed to keep focused on getting out.

'And I'm going to hold you to something when we get back'. Peter said in the doorway, giving Mike a swift hug and a kiss.

'I didn't promise anything did I?'

'I read your mind.'

Just a half-hour later, they were parking up slightly off the road. There was one other car there, another Vauxhall Astra like Peter's, only red, but no sign of anyone. The hill slope above them to the east steepened abruptly as it disappeared into cloud. Facing west, their objective, they could see bulky mountainside rising into cliffs to their right and to their left a shelving slope that appeared to be a solid wet rock rising more gently. The multiple peaks of the mountain that were marked on the map, were nowhere to be seen in reality. Instead the cloud looked greyer, heavier and thicker the further up they looked.

'That solid slope is all quartzite', Peter said 'and I remember now we stopped here on the trip up to Durness back on my field trip. In fact I can remember something about being on the way to the ferry – just over the hill.'

'Yes, you told me all about the Kylesku Ferry yesterday Pete – you don't need to again!'

'Oh!' Peter felt a bit put down. 'Sorry if I go on about stuff back then.'

'It's alright.' Said Mike. 'I didn't mean it like that. I just want us to get on and not get cold or get put off.'

Peter agreed with this sentiment and they soon got going. They decided to take a middle way that looked like easier going, on the map and on the ground, straight in towards the main corrie of Quinag, then turning up the south slope of Sail Garbh – the highest of the peaks but looking like it was also the most easily accessible.

'We will know if we are there, because there's a trig point.'

'Hardly reassuring, putting it like that!' said Mike, a bit reluctantly.

'Well, it's about eighteen hundred feet of ascent, six miles in total, for the round trip I mean.' He looked upwards at the formidable sandstone bulk in front of him. 'It wouldn't look so daunting in sunlight.'

As soon as they started walking they encountered bog – wetter than they had experienced elsewhere on the holiday and they wondered if this mountain somehow got more than its fair share of rain. There was a hint of a path at times but they found themselves wandering repeatedly to the sides, to avoid boggy ground, at times almost losing sight of each other as the drizzle descended on them.

They had a huddle, talked about giving up and then decided to try a bit further. As they hoped, the rainy cloud blew over and they were able to see up to about the two thousand foot level and the gap between the peaks appeared directly ahead and above them.

'We aim for that col, but we'll head off to the right, north, before we get that far. Hopefully.'

'Do you think it will clear some more?' asked Mike.

'Did you pack your shorts?' joked Peter.

'No, but I bet you did!'

'Of course! Always do…' After a mile or so, which took more time than they had expected, the rudimentary track became a bit clearer and before long a little lake loomed ahead.

'Lochan Bealach Cornaidh.' announced Peter. 'I'm pretty confident about those first two words. We start going up more from here.'

Their line took them on a rising traverse across a mix of turf and scree and then they made short zig-zags up a blank, steep slope, hoping they were following a natural line up but with not much evidence to make them happier or more confident. Peter used a compass to keep them pretty much heading north. About a half-mile from leaving the side of the lochan, the ground suddenly broadened and they thought they must have emerged on to the ridge that led back to their right, eastwards to the summit they wanted. While they sat on rocks to have some tea and fruit cake, the cloud base suddenly passed over them and they could see their objective quite clearly, the trig point evident and seemingly just a couple of hundred hundred yards away at most.

To their left, the other peaks of Quinag remained hidden but ahead of them they had a vista encompassing, lochs, the sea, the new Kylesku bridge, moorlands, hundreds of lochans and a line of mountains heading inland and northwards. Or so it seemed. There was no time for being sure what they had seen before the cloud enveloped them again, now darker but no wetter. The increased gloom unnerved them a bit.

'Shall we just go back down while we know where we are?' suggested Mike.

They had a discussion about it and decided to make a pair of identifiable mini cairns just where they had been sitting, and then headed off. They followed a compass bearing but assumed that as long as they didn't lose height, they couldn't miss the summit cairn and trig point. Peter had estimated just four or five minutes would be needed, but as they walked he added a bit for the bouldery nature of the ground. But after ten minutes or so, they both became sure they were now heading downhill.

'Damn.' Said Peter. 'Don't know where we are now. 'Sod it!'

'Have we walked past the summit then? Must have done?'

'Yeah, must have done. Going up is good, going down at all is bad. We don't want to go too far east or north or we will soon be on cliffs. Right, we need to head back the path we just followed'.

Looking at the compass though, for some reason he found himself getting muddled about making a one hundred and eighty degree direction change and accounting for the magnetic deviation. He hoped as long as they stayed level or upwards they would be ok. In the gloomy cloud enveloping them, everything felt and looked the same and it was hard to tell for sure if it was gently up or gently down.

'Trouble is' said Peter, 'something that is gently down around here suddenly becomes bloody steep in no time.' He paused. 'Sorry Mike, I think we are a bit lost.' He was trying to disguise his anxiety.

'This is nuts! On the map we can only now be a few hundred yards from where we had tea and made the cairns. What do we do?' Mike realised he was getting a bit panicked now.

'Let us just…' Peter wasn't sure. 'Let's just walk slowly back the way we've come. I've messed up the compass somehow but we know its broadly west then broadly south. If we go too far west, we will soon know about it. But carrying on east would definitely have been dangerous.'

They found themselves walking slowly but deliberately. Mike was hoping they would somehow see the twin cairns they made. Peter was hoping they would just stay level, but knowing the ground would have to drop down, to get back to the spot where they had tea and cake. He was trying to figure out how much drop in height was therefore safe, before becoming off-course and heading for cliffs. There were now some distinct larger boulders around them that he didn't remember from going the other way just a few minutes earlier.

And then suddenly there was another sudden lifting of the cloud base and there was the summit just fifty feet from them to their right.

'Thank God for that!' said Mike as they both quickly crossed the ground and hugged the concrete pillar of the trig point. 'Look, I can make out where we stopped now, just along there, can't quite see the cairns though'.

'Think that's right though. OK, now let's do this right. Look there's a big boulder, maybe half our size, a hundred yards off, we need to fix that in our view, and memory, as our next step - before the cloud comes again. From there we should see and soon hit the cairns.' Peter also rapidly tried to take a compass bearing to the obvious point for descending back to the lochan. He still felt a bit disorientated but hoped that he had it right.

A few minutes later in fact, having successfully passed the large boulder, they did arrive at the two cairns they had constructed. The cloud was lower again but lighter now and the more luminous quality made them feel better as they started the zig-zag descent down, both of them chatted all the way, nervous energy expending itself in small talk. When they were again above the small lake and looking ahead to where they could see the two tiny cars parked a couple of miles ahead at the most, they gave each other a hug.

'Bloody hell Mike. That was crazy. Happened to me once like that before, on Snowdon. I was on my own then. Not quite so scary with you there.' He touched Mike's arm. 'Crazy though' he repeated. 'I had the real sense of being lost then. It should have been easy going and then suddenly it wasn't! How quickly you can go from feeling safe to feeling lost.'

They both tried to shrug it off, but the experience of feeling disorientated stuck with them both. They found they were quiet on the way to the car, not having much to say. But this belied the torrent of thoughts running through Peter's mind.

Feeling lost in a place where danger wasn't too far away had left him with a very unsettled feeling. He was surprised at how strongly he had been feeling protective for Mike, responsible even. It brought to the fore the underlying disquiet he had about what they were doing, how they might live together. Could they really do that? Who could they safely tell? Who could they trust? What were they going to do about Diane? He looked at Mike's back, a few yards ahead of him on the last half-mile to the car. Simultaneously he found himself feeling both fraternal and paternal. Was this what being a partner felt like?

At the car, they quickly changed out of wet boots and cagoules, jumped-in and headed off. Quite quickly they encountered a large number of sheep scattered alongside and on the road. They had to be slow and concentrate hard. There were lambs and these had the habit of darting in front of the car if they suddenly found themselves separated from their mum. By the time they reached the junction with the Lochinver road, they found the concentration had tired them further, but the antics had cheered them up too. Peter was glad it wasn't too much further to drive home.

'Hopefully there won't be any sheep on this section of road. They were funny weren't they? I don't know about you though but I'm feeling pretty cream-crackered now, think I was quite keyed-up on Quinag.'

'I'm the same.' replied Mike. 'And I was definitely keyed-up, as you put it. I was getting pretty spooked up there Pete, to be honest.' He reached across and stroked Peter's leg briefly. 'I feel like nodding-off. Could do with a lie-down for an hour when we get back.'

Peter thought about that. Thought that a nap would be good but yet again, something else might arise that could be more impactful on the stress he was feeling. 'Now, that sounds a really great idea.'

Mike picked-up on the change in Peter's voice. 'I didn't mean what you're thinking!'

But as soon as they were parking the car by the caravan, they both knew they wanted each other. More precisely they wanted the physical release of the nervous energy that was sloshing around in both of them.

As soon as they were through the door of the caravan, rucksacks were cast aside and they had each other in a tight embrace, kissing hard, each using one hand to feel the arousal in the other. They stepped apart briefly, to take off their jeans and sweatshirts. Peter moved towards Mike now in just his underpants. Then, right at that exact moment, there were a couple of knocks on the door. Just as Mike had leant back against a cupboard to take Peter in his arms again.

'Sod it.' Whispered Pete. 'Quick – you duck out of view and I'll answer it.'

'You can't answer it like that!'

Peter put back on his top and went to open the door.

'Pete! Look at you!.' Mike indicated the stretched fabric of Peter's briefs.

With no time to do anything else, Peter just put his hand over himself and opened the door, just as another knock came.

'Oh! Hello'. It was the site owner, tweed jacket, wellies, piece of paper in one hand, authoritative, resonating brogue – but not unfriendly. He looked Peter up and down and Peter hoped his rapidly deflating state was not that obvious. 'Sorry to disturb you but I saw you were just back and wanted to give you the notes about leaving on Saturday. Thought you might be busy and wasn't sure when you might go back down south, so just wanted to get this to you now. '

'Yes. Er – thanks.' Said Peter. 'Sorry, I was just getting out of my wet things.'

'So I see.' Said the man. Peter wondered if the man's tone hinted at anything else, maybe knowing what was going on, finding himself blushing at the thought. 'Have you been out on the tops then?'

Peter didn't want a conversation but didn't want to be impolite either and desperately wanted to dissuade the man's mind from thinking what he and Mike had just been doing. So, he said a few things about Quinag.

'Aye.' Replied the owner. 'You did well. The cloud can get stuck up there for days. You wouldn't be the first to get a wee bit lost. Well. Good luck to you and your friend for your return.' And with that he was gone. Peter closed the door, wondering again if the last remark inferred any hint at him and Mike being anything other than good friends.

Mike emerged from the shower room where he had quickly hidden himself. 'Do you think he's on to us?'

'No I don't.'

'Your hard-on could have been a clue though Pete! Maybe he didn't notice … or maybe he just thought you were thinking of something else.' Said Mike, feeling nervous, laughing a little.

Peter looked at him, wanting to cast-off the frustrating thoughts of the owner seeing him like that but also wanting to get back to that moment they had been having. Not to worry about being discovered and not to fret about being lost and disorientated. 'I don't know Mike. But I know what I'm thinking of now though!' And they reached for each other.

CHAPTER 21

They decided that the last day would be best if they got all the practical stuff done as quickly as possible, so they could relax and try and enjoy the rest of the time left. They cleaned-up the place, which didn't take long, packed most of their things, Mike prepared a chilli and rice for later. Peter checked the oil and water in the car.

It had been raining while they did all these tasks but seemed to be slowing down by the time they had sorted-out everything that was needed to do. They decided to drive back to the Inverkirkaig bookshop and get a cup of tea and some shortbread, have a browse and maybe buy a book or two. Or a map, thought Peter.

A little while later and now with the rain blown through, they stopped at the little beach, hoping to see Eiders again, which they did. They walked slowly along the short stretch of shore. Mike looked outwards, partly along the waves but mostly further out to sea, watching the birds. Peter had his head down a lot of the time, examining the variety of pebbles on the beach.

At the western headland of the beach, they sat down and decided to try and just enjoy the moment. Mike thought they might see a seal, coming close in the water to be inquisitive about them. 'I must have seen them in Gairloch when I was a kid,' he said, 'But I don't really remember. That's been a great discovery of this trip.'

Peter thought that was a nice thing to say and he suggested they explore that theme a bit more. Mike thought Peter should go first, having suggested the idea.

'Ok, well like you I think it has been amazing seeing the wildlife. The red deer on the mountain days, the birds here and everywhere. The red-throated diver we think we saw on that lochan near Suilven. Thought and hoped we might have seen an eagle, but never mind.'

'Yeah, that would have been the topping on the cake though if it had happened.' Interjected Mike. 'the rocks?'

'Hmmm. The rocks!' Peter smiled. 'They have been great. I just feel familiar with them really – sort of like old friends! I guess that sounds weird. I just like the gneiss and especially the Torridonian Sandstone. The black dykes we have seen. All of those and more are in the pebbles along the shore here you know!' And he showed Mike the collection of pebbles that had been bulging his pockets. Geological specimens, he wanted to think.

'What about you?', he asked.

'I liked the birds obviously. Like you with the rocks, I feel some sort of affinity with things up here – like the Eiders!' and he laughed. 'The bird life has been great. I loved Fharaid Head for that. Not just for that though.' He looked at Peter. 'Safe to give you a kiss?'

'Moments like that are another thing I will remember. Moments like this. We came away to spend time together and it's been good hasn't it?'

'Wonderful.' Said Mike, 'That day by Balnakeil will stay with me forever.'

'Me too.' Now it was his turn to sigh. 'Apart from the owner calling by yesterday, I have felt free up here with you Pete. That's been really lovely.'

'Well, we haven't held hands in public have we? So I imagine people think we're just two friends here to look at the wildlife, the scenery and go up Quinag and Suilven. Same as anyone else.'

'We gave each other a blow-job on a nature trail Pete!'

'Well, just off the path actually Mike! We were completely hidden.' He paused. 'That's another thing though isn't it? We have had lots of time for each other in that sort of way. That's been great.' And he put his arm round Mike's shoulders and gave him a hug.

'Is that because we are new and excited by each other or is it that two guys do more of that sort of thing?'

Peter pondered that a moment. 'I don't know. Some people out there. In the real world I mean – they think people like us are not only vile and despicable but also at it like rabbits. But I don't think we, you and me anyway, are any different to any other couple new with each other.'

'You noticed how that word, couple, has crept into our language Pete?' The comment made both of them think. 'How do we feel about going back?'

'Back to reality you mean?' said Peter.

They were both quiet a while then, just watching the surf gently rolling in, the group of Eiders bobbing up and down on the other side of the bay from them.

'I suppose it's what's next, isn't it?' he continued. 'Do we move in together? Do you come to my flat?' Then he shook his head. 'Before that, you have to decide whether to continue job seeking. Do you move up to London?'

'I suppose if I don't get a job or it feels too hard to get one, that gives me the excuse to stay. I could move in with you to save cash. Might work as a cover story?' Mike knew he didn't exactly sound convinced.

'I suppose it's like you're saying there really.' Said Peter. 'What we are really saying is, do we live together. As a couple. That word again. Can we do that? And if we do, who do we need to tell? I can't tell people at work. I don't know how to tell Mum but feel I would want to. We can't hide it from everyone or we'll have no one to talk to apart from each other. I can't just pretend. But the biggest thing of course, is telling Diane.'

'What if I don't? Could we see each other when we can? Maybe do holidays like this again. Spend weekends together? Carry on as normal?'

'It feels a bit easier for me Mike. perhaps, now I've told Sue. That's my, or our, first coming-out isn't it? Like in the gay switchboard booklet I got. They have a suggested cascade of telling.'

'I don't know if I can do it Peter.' Mike said, suddenly putting his head in his heads, not crying but looking anxious. Peter cuddled him, thinking he didn't care right now if anyone saw them or not. 'What about you Pete. How will you be if we stop this?'

'I can't Mike. It was awful writing to Sue, screwed-up my tummy. Thought I was going to be sick.' He paused and looked out to sea, arm still round Mike and gently stroking the back of his head. 'I don't want anyone else. It's not about being a queer as they call us. I'm not that interested in other guys. I know I like the magazines and those new VHS tapes, but I don't actually want anyone else. I don't fantasise about that as a reality. I like being with you. I've told Sue, want to live with you ... because I think I probably love you!' And now he had to bury his head in his hands.

Mike consoled him with a hug and after a bit said, 'Well this is a rubbish end to the holiday if we don't change the subject. Come on, let's shake this off or we'll be really miserable.' And with that. He jumped up, literally shook himself and pulled-up Peter from his seated position. 'Brisk walk back to the car, quickly back to the site. I'm going to walk into the village and get a bottle of wine. You're going for a run. I want you to!' Mike looked at Peter, both of them balancing a bit on the rocky edge of the beach. 'You just told me you love me.' He put his arms out and took Peter's hands in his own. 'I feel the same Pete. I think I love you too. And you're a man. It feels insane.'

They slowly jogged back to the car. Peter felt unsettled again and yet happy too. He was struggling to know what to think. He and Mike had just professed love to each other but the reality of what that meant as a way of life felt too big for him to comprehend properly. He felt Mike was right and that a run would be good, now it had stopped raining, might even be mild enough for shorts, which would make it even better. It would be physically calming. But he needed to get some of the emotions out of his head too, and realised in a flash who might help.

'Mike, can we just carry on to the harbour together? In the car I mean. If it's alright with you I think I want to see if I can telephone Sue.'

That was a surprise for Mike but thinking about it he could see that it might be helpful for both of them. After the short drive back, they parked up in the little harbour car park. Mike said he would go and look around, get the wine from the shop maybe. 'There's lot of gulls but there might be something else to see too. About ten mins?'

Peter nodded and went across to the phone box, pleased he had a weight of change in his pocket and hoping Sue would be in. Probably just got home from school he considered. Maybe tired. One hand on the phone and the other on the dial, he hesitated, then carried on, hoping Sue would be ok with it.

In fact, all the way down in Swansea, Sue was just returning to home after work. She had a bag of exercise books and school paraphernalia over one shoulder, which she was pushing out of the way, trying to get through the door, while in her other hand was a supermarket carrier bag with some things she had picked-up at lunchtime. The phone had started ringing at just the wrong moment but she was keen to answer as it felt an odd time to call and she thought it might be important.

The phone rang six, seven, then eight times. Twelfth ring, thinking the caller was probably about to give-in, Sue picked-up and gave the number. She knew she sounded a bit rushed and formal, but hoped she didn't sound hot and bothered, which was what she was experiencing.

'Sue, it's Pete. Phoning from Lochinver!'

A short pause. Sue felt a range of emotions – pleased to get a chance to speak with Peter after the letter he sent, but also a bit annoyed she might not be receptive or in the right frame of mind. It also occurred to her very quickly though, that there was never going to be a perfect time to have this conversation. *'Pete! I've just got in from school, just need to put down my bags. How are you?'*

She knew this would throw Peter a bit and he would already be fretting that he was disturbing her, yet the call would feel so important to him. She could feel his need to speak already and she wanted to do it too, she now realised.

'OK, look is this a bad time… I can call…'

'Don't be silly Pete. It's fine. Gosh – phoning me from Sutherland. It sounds a really clear line actually. Like you're next door!'

'That's nice.'

Sue wondered if he would have prepared this or just gone straight into it. She thought he would have mulled it a lot but then hesitated about when and how to do it. She waited. *'Thanks for your letter,'* he said eventually.

'I wondered if you might call sometime. Thought it might be after you got back. Is everything ok?' Sue's mind ran through possible scenarios, but hoped it was none of these.

'Yes – nothing dramatic has happened. Just wanted to speak with you. Needed to really.'

Pause. *'Ok, that's good then. So, nothing more's happened…just what you said in your letter?'*

'Yes, sorry. Sue…' Sue could hear already the potential for Peter to be upset on the call, when she heard him take a deep breath - he would be wanting to control his feelings. *'Your letter was so sweet. Is that really how you feel?'* Another pause. Peter didn't give her time to speak. *'Look, don't worry about it if you've just got in from school. Sorry, I was just thinking of me. My stuff. It's selfish.'*

'Shh Pete, don't worry about that. Please don't.' She got the call back on track. *'Is that how I really feel?'* Sue repeated Peter's question and paused again. *'Look, when I was with you in Kinlochewe, I knew how fond I was of you – even then. I'm still fond of you…'*

'Yes.' Interrupted Peter. *'But back then you discovered I had been*

sleeping with Steve and now I have confessed to you I have been sleeping with Mike.'

Another hesitation from Sue. She thought he was trying to tell her he had been unfaithful. That's how he was framing it. *'I don't think you are ever going to be the sleeping-around type. As soon as I started reading your letter, I thought "Oh! Peter has found his nest mate" - and you have, haven't you?'*

Peter felt very moved by that but was distracted by having to put more money in the phone slot. *'I don't know. Gosh, it feels a really big thing to imagine that already. It's only been a short while...'*

'Well it is! A big thing, I mean. Or you wouldn't have written.'

'But I have let you down Sue.' There was a long gap. *'Hello, you still there…'*

'You rescued me!' Sue wanted to sound calm, concerned for Peter and trying to summarise what the relationship with Peter had been for her. *'After Colin you were… you have been, lovely to me, but... '*

'We haven't seen each other for a bit though'

Sue then spoke both more softly and more slowly. *'Look, let me speak a minute! You helped me get over Colin but you know I have always thought that what has happened would happen. You stabilised me but one outcome of that was I saw I wanted a nest mate too. I need the same thing Pete. If it was with you though…I mean, I have thought about this a lot, the possibility of you and me.'* Another gap. *'I know I would always be wondering if you were going to fly off sometime with another male bird. Not on a flight of fancy, nothing like a one-night stand. It seemed inevitable, and maybe essential, you get another man as a partner.'*

That felt emotional to her and she guessed Peter would be just biting his lip now. *'I'm sorry Sue.'*

'Peter!' she was surprised at her own abruptness, but just for a moment. Then she continued, more softly again. *'Don't apologise. Please. You can't keep saying sorry. I will be alright. But will you? Has*

being up there helped? What are you going to do? Sorry. Oops, me apologising now – too many questions!'

'I will run out of money soon actually. Just wanted to speak with you – to listen to you.' She could hear Peter sound a bit choked. *'I think Mike and I might want to share a place together. A nest, using your words. The practicality is a nightmare.'*

'Let's meet up soon when you're back' said Sue. *'We can have a proper chat.'*

'Would you really do that? I thought you might be done with me for a while?' At a distance of several hundred miles, Sue could feel Peter's emotion and she experienced a sense of sadness herself. She realised now that she was losing something of someone who had been really important to her. Not completely, but a loss all the same, and in a way it was her own fault. She could have easily held on to him. But then, one day this would have happened – with or without her encouragement, she thought. The letter she had sent Peter was to help him feel ok, but it didn't make her feel ok – it was as if she had just thrown away something unique and valuable.

'That would be so nice right now.' Peter continued. He felt he had been thrown a lifeline. Sue wouldn't then drop out of his life. She would still be there.

For her own sake, she wanted to see Peter too. His letter had been a shock but it had been one she had seen in her mind – a story long foretold. She felt her own tears spring forward. She wished he was nearer, that she could have one of his hugs. *'Oh sweetie, I can hear how you are and you've got me going now. Let me get a tissue.'* Sue rooted around in her bag, thinking that Peter's money would run-out and hoping she had a few more minutes. She blew her nose and continued, *'Look, you're not on your own. We know each other.'* To Peter these words just felt so true. *'You know, if something happens, if it helps…'* This was too difficult, Sue started to wish Peter hadn't called, jumped to practicalities to help them move on a little. *'Tell*

Mike I would speak to Diane. Not to tell her about you two! That's his job! But after Mike has told her. I could speak to her if he liked. More to the point, if Di likes.'

'You're an angel Sue.'

'Don't know about that.' Pips interrupted again.

'Final bit of cash Sue, sorry.'

'Peter, stop it! If you apologise again, I will hang-up. Listen!' Sue was trying to think what to say next, maybe they could meet in a week or two. Maybe they needed to. Yes, they did need to! She needed to sort her own thoughts too. What did this all really and truly mean for her? More practicalities.

'This is for me. Do you mind if say something to Julie… and maybe to Ian?'

As soon as she said it, she imagined she had just hit Peter in the stomach. He would want her to speak with Julie. He wouldn't have thought of her speaking with Ian, even though he knew they were all drinking chums at Club evenings.

'Ian?'

'He asked me out for dinner a week or two ago. I went.' A longer pause. 'Nothing else happened Pete – he just said, "I haven't seen Arthur about very much and thought you were seeming lonely for a knight."'

Peter couldn't help laughing at that. He imagined the date, could hear Ian saying something like that – affectionate joking. 'He's fancied you for a very long time Sue.'

'Well, I was feeling a bit down, looking ahead at life. I always felt you and I wouldn't always be beside each other on the journey, but your news made me fed up with my own company, and even Sheena's. I guess I wanted an evening with a man.'

There was a silence before Peter replied, 'Damn it!, I feel a bit jealous now Sue! Stupid isn't it! And totally unfair…'

'It's not stupid, sweetie. And yes, I do know he is interested. He's also very perceptive.'

'Like you then!'

'Pete – the pips will go any moment. Just know Pete, I am here for you. Keep your spirits up. It will all work out in the end I think.' A pause. 'I will meet you soon and I will be there if you need me.' Another pause. 'I know you will do the same for me. In fact, this call's made me realise we need to think about some things together.' At that moment Sue was aware of the deep connection she felt with Peter, and it felt such a two-way thing. 'I sometimes think there's an umbilical cord between us…' The pips went. A rushed goodbye, and the call ended.

Peter fell back against the glass and metal door of the phone box. His head tilted forward, a few tears dripped on to his shirt. Her "Umbilical cord" phrase bouncing round his brain like a pinball. He got out his handkerchief, dried his eyes and blew his nose. Back at the car, fifty yards away, Mike was leaning against it, looking anxious, watching him return. Bottle of wine in one hand, by his side.

Peter touched Mike's arm, sighing deeply.

'How are you feeling?' Mike knew he didn't really need to ask.

'Think I might feel a bit better soon Mike. Maybe. Despite these tears. It was good to call. But I hope she feels the same.' He realised he was worried about that, still feeling it was all too self-absorbing. 'She said this really beautiful thing though, right at the end of the call.'

Mike thought he was still struggling to connect words with feelings, just stayed quiet as they both just leaned on the car. After a while Peter said, 'Come on, let's get back and get that down our necks.'

'You're not having any until you've done your run!' said Mike jokily adopting a stern tone.

'OK. But I might not need the run to feel better.' And Peter genuinely felt his mood lifting. 'Sue thinks we are going to be ok

Mike. She said that.' And they hugged on the quayside, noticing a couple of people walking past but, for once, maybe for the first time, neither of them caring. 'I just really hope she is too.' He added.

A long way away, Sue was unloading her school work and the shopping. She ran through the conversation again and re-read Peter's letter in her head. She had put the kettle on and had decided to call Julie as soon as she had a mug of tea in her hand. It felt reassuring on one level to have had the realisation that Peter would likely be a friend for life, that she would have this affectionate bond with him for ever. That knowledge felt comforting and also astonishing.

On another level though she felt a bit alone. For the first time since Colin, she now had to decide how her life was to be, on her own. There was a mix of feelings sloshing around in her mind – some anxieties, a bit of fearfulness, but then suddenly, also a sense of freedom. A reaction that surprised her. Mostly, she started to realise she had choices. Then it dawned on her that, in fact, she had already been making them!

Part Four

Beinn Eighe, 1986

"The body roams the mountain – and the spirit is set free."
Anon.

Chapter 22

Mike was sitting on a rock, just off the side of the road, at the back of the pebbly beach, looking thoughtful while gently scanning the view with his eyes, straining to see further. Peter was thinking how cute he looked, as he put down the two mugs of tea, wriggling them into the small stones, making sure they wouldn't fall over. He stayed standing for a moment, looking across the water to Shieldaig Island, binoculars then trained straight ahead.

'Can you see much?' asked Mike.

'Not really. The trees, obviously, there's some birds on the water but not sure what they are. Too far off to be certain.'

'You'll be pleased to know there's been a couple of Oyster Catchers flitting back and forth, along the shore here.' Mike hoped Peter would be pleased.

'Yeah, I heard them from the house. It feels like one of the sounds of this part of the world, for me anyway. I can see a couple of them out there now you mention it.' Mike strained to see too. 'It's been nice being here hasn't it?' Peter added.

'Just coming straight out of the house and sitting here by the loch is wonderful Pete.' They drank their tea and chatted about the few days they'd had here so far, mostly with good weather and fairly midge free. Neither of them had stayed in this village before but they had come to like it. They liked the feel of the place, the way the single row of houses, of which their holiday cottage was one, curved around the bay, bordering this sheltered part of the sea loch.

The local shop and pub seemed friendly and they felt everyone believed they were just two mates doing some walking and bird-watching, which, after all, was true on one level. They had explored Applecross via the long coastal road and had also been up the Bealach na Ba switchback road, to walk a couple of easy summits from the top of the pass.

The one day of less certain weather had been when they had chosen to drive north, into the Torridon mountains, and attempted Beinn Damph. It had been a good walk until the rain showers became more persistent and the cloud base dropped. Now they were about to head in that direction again.

'Still feel ok about today?' asked Mike.

'I do actually. Didn't sleep brilliantly, but think it will be good. What about you though?' It was worrying about Mike that had kept him awake.

Mike didn't answer at first. It had been on his mind since getting-up of course. It felt like another thing that had to be done. There were too many of these, he felt, for the last year and more, and this one was a big one. 'I wish we didn't have to do it, to be honest.'

Peter felt his shoulders slump. He knew how Mike felt. Sue was the first person they had come out to really. She was the first person who knew that the two of them were in a relationship and she had been supportive, helpful and considerate. But meeting her with Ian felt like something different. Ian knew about them of course, and according to Sue had been surprised but had no animosity or any other negative feelings towards them. He just didn't know any other gay men. But Mike felt awkward – about meeting these two friends together for the first time, with Peter beside him, as a couple.

And this was true both ways, Peter thought. He was feeling a bit strange about meeting Sue with Ian beside her, being her boyfriend or partner. He had a mixture of feelings about that but hoped the get-together would be good for them all in some way.

'It will be fine Mike, and we don't have to do it exactly; surely we are choosing to do it?' Peter at last replied. 'They are friends. They are on our side.' Then after a couple of minutes more, sipping tea and watching the gentle lapping of the water along the shoreline. 'Come on then, we just need to get on with it.' As they crossed back across the road, Peter wished he could just hold Mike's hand.

It was a thirty minute drive to the car park beneath Liathach in the glen leading northwards from Torridon to Kinlochewe. It was really a gravelly layby, set into a small hillock with boulders scattered around it. It was set back from the road edge and could accommodate a half-dozen cars. They had stopped here for a moment. Peter wondered if they were just hesitant about the forthcoming reunion but he did also want to show Mike some things from here.

'This is where we are coming back to soon Mike. Our walk starts from here. But, look. Over to our right you can see down on that little flood plain, that's where the mountaineering hut is and, beyond that, the drumlin field I have talked about. Endlessly, probably!'

Mike agreed the view was spectacular, but the drive was going against the grain for him and he remained largely silent. After a few minutes, Peter drove on. It was another five miles of single-track road to Kinlochewe, but they only met two other vehicles, one car that they gave way to and one van that gave way to them. Driving into the little village, Peter slowed and pointed out the campsite to Mike and indicated where he had stayed in his tent, years previously. 'Don't worry,' he said, quickly taking his hand off the steering wheel to nudge Mike, 'I'm not going to go on about it all day.'

Mike thought that was good and he also knew he was being sullen and felt bad about it. Part of this day was about Peter's memories being brought to life. He had talked so much about this place and the fieldwork, that it was actually interesting to see it in the flesh. His initial reaction was that everything seemed very small and contained – the human things anyway, the camping area, the small collection of houses and buildings, the hotel. On the other hand, the landscape seemed very large scale. It distracted him from feeling negative about the imminent rendezvous.

In the small car park opposite the hotel, Sue and Ian were already waiting for them, standing beside their car, map unfolded on the bonnet. Peter parked alongside and took a deep breath before getting out, giving a squeeze to Mike's hand at the same time. He noticed Mike was much slower than him and, for a second, thought he really was going to stay in the vehicle. Then they were suddenly all together. There was a moment's hesitation before they stepped forward towards each other. Peter hugged Sue, Mike did the same but more briefly. At first it was handshakes with Ian but these quickly moved on to very brief hugs. Peter caught himself thinking about how he needed to keep it masculine, which felt odd to him.

'Well, this is a nice surprise! Not really a surprise, but you know what I mean.' Ian spoke first.

'It just seemed an idea, an opportunity really. You two heading up to Sutherland and us two already up here.' Peter thought they were making polite conversation. 'Thanks for coming across…'

Sue interrupted him. 'Don't worry Pete. It's not far down the road from Gairloch – as you know. It was a quick drive and the B&B did us an early breakfast. Has it taken you two long to come up from Shieldaig?'

"You two" thought Peter. It struck him the casual and friendly way Sue was speaking, putting him at ease but also making him feel a bit compartmentalised. Familiar friendship being managed a bit differently. 'No, not really. We've all made a quick start, so I guess the roads are especially quiet.' For a moment it was like they were just neighbours having a chat and Peter thought maybe it was a case of nobody being sure what banality to say next.

He decided to make sure the air was clear straightaway, mostly thinking about Mike. This needs to start and finish on an even keel, he considered to himself. So, he decided to acknowledge the new reality head on.

'Well this is a bit different to when we were all last together, isn't it!?'

Sue smiled at him. In that moment she was reminded how fond she was of him. Now here he was trying to make an extraordinary meeting feel just the opposite, simply trying to make it all feel like an everyday occurrence. 'In a way Pete, yes, of course. In another way it's just four friends meeting up.'

Nods from everyone to that, Peter noticed. In his head though, he thought 'That's true Sue, but last time we four were together in one place, I was sleeping with you as my girlfriend! Mike was a in a deep relationship with Diane, and now he's sharing a bed with me. Ian wasn't sleeping with anyone but now he is with you!' But, he thought everyone was probably conscious of the same things, so he said nothing more and neither did anyone else.

'Well,' said Ian. 'We will have plenty of time to chat on the walk but we should get on with it I guess?' His thought was that dealing with the immediate practicality would stop them, particularly Sue and Peter, over-thinking what was going on.

After a brief chat, they all decided to use Ian and Sue's car to go back down the road to the Liathach car park. The plan being for the four of them to then walk the length of the Beinn Eighe ridge from down there and returning to here in Kinlochewe. Then they would all drive back down the road again in Peter and Mike's car, to reconnect Sue and Ian with theirs. After that, they could each return to their accommodation, albeit in different directions. Sue and Ian to their B&B in Gairloch, and Mike and Peter would go on from there, back to the cottage in Shieldaig. They had all chipped into the discussion about this and all agreed it was six of one and a half-dozen of the other, whichever way round they did it.

When they came to set-off, Sue jumped into the driving seat and quickly steered out of the car park, up to the T-junction and back onto the single-track road heading south. There had been a minute where nobody spoke, and the silence felt obvious.

'Don't say anything.' Said Ian. 'I know what you're thinking!

"oh look - Sue and he have only been together a few months and he's a reformed character already"!' All of them chuckled a bit and this broke the ice on what had been a strangely tense start to the car journey.

'I am amazed actually Ian.' Said Peter, 'thought you were like me, reluctant to let anyone else get in the driving seat. Let alone a girl!' he joked, pleased they were now having a light-hearted chat.

Sue abruptly slowed down the car, bringing it to a halt in a passing place. She feigned reaching across to open a car door. 'You can get out now if you like Pete!' The tone was sharp but her smile betrayed her true feelings.

Peter held up his hands in a gesture of surrender that she could see in the rear-view mirror. 'Only joking.'

'He won't tell you, you two, but he doesn't like the single-track roads really,' continued Sue. 'So you can imagine I am going to get a lot of driving on this trip up to Sutherland.'

'And what she won't tell you...' said Ian, '...she's not going to say anything about who got the driving job for several hundred miles up the M6 and A9, while she had a read and a snooze!'

Peter noticed most how at ease they were with each other. How much of a couple they had become so quickly. He felt a bit jealous, partly of them both together, and partly of Ian now occupying a place in Sue's life that he had so enjoyed for a while. He wondered if he and Mike appeared close like that to them. He thought probably not. In fact, in most circumstances, they actively went out of their way to avoid being seen as a couple. He thought it would be a while before that changed.

In the fifteen minute drive, Mike said very little. Now that the day was underway, he didn't feel quite so bad about it. There didn't seem to be any awkwardness from Ian, and Sue seemed genuinely warm and friendly. He thought Peter was over-compensating though by being pretty garrulous about the scenery, the geology, the formation of the landscape. He had also got Ian and Sue to say some things about the rest of their holiday. It had been a bit of a confusing three-way conversation about people and places though, so in the end Ian did a summary.

Ian was half-turned around in the front passenger seat, talking over the back rest. 'So, it helps me actually to go over it like this. So, yeah, when we leave Gairloch tomorrow, we will head east, back the way we came, up Glen Docherty. That the right name?' he got nods from Peter. 'Back towards Inverness, up to Dingwall, then Lairg and on up to Tongue. We meet Sheena and Dougal at the cottage you know so well. For a few days anyway. Then we're coming down the long way. You two inspired us to go to Assynt and have a crack at Suilven! But any of those peaks would do. Just the two of us.'

Those words! "Just the two of us". Peter again felt a bit of a lurch. He wasn't sure if it was in his head or in his stomach. He found himself blurting out a question, directing it to Sue. 'So, is it working out with Sheena and Dougal then?'

'It's early days but they seem to be getting on. Think it's made her feel more Scottish.'

Peter chuckled. 'I can imagine that! Dougal wears his nationality proudly on his sleeve.'

'It's not so much Scotland, as Peyton Place,' said Ian wryly, 'those trips to the Alps and Talmine have triggered a merry go round of relationships if you ask me!' There were nods and laughter from them all to that statement.

'Not bad.' Said Mike suddenly, changing the subject. The first time he had spoken since leaving Kinlochewe. 'Here's the car park coming up on the right already. It's only just gone past nine now, so we have a good lot of time, don't we? Well done Sue,' he added, hoping it wasn't sounding patronising.

'Thanks Mike, it was a pleasure. And thanks all of you actually, for managing to restrain yourselves from offering me advice along

the way! And don't spoil it now either, while I park. Especially you.'
She said, using her free hand to tap Peter's leg.

This walk had been Peter's suggestion – he hoped it would be a
nice thing for them all to do. He and Mike had it on their target list
for their holiday and the other two had been happy to divert from
their trip further north. Sue and Peter had talked about it on the
phone. They both saw it as a way of keeping connected at the early
stage of new relationships for both of them, bringing the four of
them into a fold under new circumstances. It had been left unsaid
that for both Sue and Pete, they did want to make this work – to be
able to all be friends together. They'd acknowledged though that it
was potentially awkward for all of them.

Peter outlined to them the intended route once again after they
had all got their boots on and rucksacks ready. Ian was familiar
with most of it but it was fresh ground for the other two. He was
originally planning to go through it in some detail, but in the end
kept it brief.

'Right, so we head-off northwards at first, then west for a bit,
then back on ourselves and into a big corrie. We scramble up the
back corner of that and then we're on the Beinn Eighe ridge itself.
It is five miles to that point, steadily uphill the whole way I'm afraid.
On the ridge there's a fair bit more of up and down but nothing
like the height gain of the first bit of the walk. But we are exposed
up there in places. There's another scramble towards the end of
the ridge and then we drop down to Kinlochewe. Ten, eleven
miles or a bit more, all in. We should be in the car park again by
four-thirty and after the car shuttle, we should each be back in our
accommodation around six to six-thirty, probably pretty knackered,
but hopefully happy. All ok?' Even as he said all this, Peter felt he
had probably been over-ambitious.

As if reading his mind, Ian came alongside as they got going on
the long and steady uphill path. 'What's the escape routes then

Pete?'

'Oh, I think the weather will be ok Ian – forecast is settled.'

'Sure, but I was really thinking of people. Not anyone in particular, just might be quite long for all of us?'

'Hmmm. I know what you mean. Plus I was thinking more now about the scramble elements. Getting up out of Coire Mhic Fhearchair, or however you pronounce it, is probably ok. It is short and blocky. After that, the last bit of the ridge though is a bit airy.'

'And that's when we'll all be at our tiredest. I don't know – long time since I was up here.' pondered Ian.

'Me too.' Said Peter. 'I had it clear in my head, but it's nine years ago. I might have been more reckless then!'

'Doubt that Pete! I was thinking, while we've been talking, once we go up the first scramble, there's three summits we can do from there. I mean, we could pick one, then reverse the whole route if we wanted to – back to the car park here? Has to be an option?'

Sue and Mike looked-on a bit bemused. 'Do we all get a vote?' asked Sue.

They decided to keep it in mind that they didn't have to do the whole thing if they didn't want to, and Peter was grateful that it now felt like shared leadership. Another thing Peter realised he needed to enjoy, was not so much the walk itself but the company. He wanted them all to get on but he also wanted, needed, a one-to-one chat with Sue. Maybe a tweak to the walk would enable this to happen.

By the time they had gone the first couple of miles or so, they were already stripping off layers and were soon down to T-shirts, everyone feeling warm with the exertion. Ian suggested a short break. They had been looking ahead or to the ground right in front of them, but turning round now, they were amazed to see the corries of Liathach itself, so close behind them. They spent a bit of time studying the extent of rock cliffs, scree and boulders. It looked pretty intimidating to all of them.

'And the ridge walk of that mountain goes across the crest of all that does it?' Asked Sue, sounding a bit incredulous.

'Yeah,' said Ian and Peter simultaneously. 'Never done it though.' Peter continued. 'Have you Ian?'

'I got up to the start, which is an exhausting slope, as we saw from back there, by the car. My mates and I had misjudged it though – cloud was pretty thick and I think we all got a bit spooked. So, we scrambled back down and left it for another day.'

'But that's definitely harder than this though is it? Harder than what we are going to do today?' Asked Mike, thinking that the ridge along the serrated top of that mountain looked scary enough from down here on solid ground.

Peter and Ian exchanged a quick glance.

'Yeah, Pete and I have both done today's route – and lived to tell the tale. Liathach seems like a step up – in more ways than one.'

'Thanks Ian – that's sort of reassuring. I think.' Said Mike, sounding unconvinced.

Sue came alongside him and said, 'Thanks for asking that Mike. I was thinking the exact same thing! Think I will walk along with you here at the back, if you don't mind?'

Mike didn't mind, as far as the walking was concerned. He was definitely pleased to have Sue alongside for a while. He just hoped there wasn't going to be any awkward conversation. He was now walking alongside someone who was, until fifteen months ago, the lover of Peter. With her so close to him, it was hard to accept he now occupied that same position.

After another two hours, they had completed the long, northward stage of the walk from the car park and had embarked on the rising easterly traverse round into the main corrie on the north side of Beinn Eighe. Sue had stepped up her pace and came alongside Peter.

'So, what are we looking at Peter. There's so much rock up here. Amazing landscape isn't it? Precipitous rocky slopes everywhere.'

'Well, you are going to see something truly vertical in a few minutes. The backwall of the Corrie we are heading into is one of the biggest mountain cliffs in Britain. But over there…' He pointed over to his left and ahead, '…that's my mountain! So, all this watery landscape between the mountains – that all leads up towards the quartzite plateau, where I spent so many days!' He smiled, then frowned.

'Some of the days were happy Pete! I was on a couple of them!'

Peter was thinking of that right now. 'Nine years ago Sue. But feels like yesterday when I look across there.'

'It was an important summer for you. For me too. You don't always know what's happening at the time do you – I mean, you don't know that a particular time is going to be significant when you're living through it. It's only later you can see that.'

Ian and Mike had walked past them and got ahead, but they stopped now, Ian shouted back. 'I bet you two are reminiscing. Come on, you need to keep up, we can have a break in the corrie. By the lake I thought Pete, what do you reckon?'

'Should be fine – ten minutes probably, we'll be there. And its not my fault by the way…your girlfriend was asking me a question!' And he wanted to get back to that discussion he had just started, as soon as he could.

'You just said "your girlfriend" to Ian! Does it feel funny to say that?' asked Sue.

'Yes, completely.' Peter walked on a few more steps, he and Sue being on a track just wide enough for single-file. He turned to her. 'But it helps me to say things like that. You were my girlfriend but now I have a boyfriend; as do you.' He was trying to sound positive, but was conscious it sounded both a bit melancholy and also a bit weird.

'Pete – you were a very special boyfriend. I will never have another like you!'

'That's a sweet thing to say Sue, but surely you shouldn't be considering the possibility of boyfriends beyond Ian, should you?'

'No, but…' Sue started to explain but Peter interrupted her.

'Not only that matter, but you shouldn't be saying you will never have another boyfriend like me. It doesn't sound fair on Ian. That's not right.' He hoped he didn't sound like he was telling her off, he didn't mean it to sound like a criticism.

They had both stopped on the path now, almost level with each other, a couple of feet apart, the landscape enveloping them. It was also good to take a breather.

Sue said, 'Ian feels good. After Colin, and after you, at the moment things with Ian feel stable, and I like that.' She saw Peter looked crestfallen. 'Peter…' She moved forward and put her hands on his arms '…that's not meant to be a put-down. You know that long-term …' she hunted for a word. '…stability, with you, for me, always felt elusive when I looked ahead, precarious even. It's not anything you ever did sweetie, it's what you might have done sometime. In fact, what you have done - with Mike.'

Peter was looking at the ground, thinking about what she was saying. Thinking hard.

Sue waited for him to say something, but nothing came out, so she continued. 'So, I'm not considering other boyfriends. Maybe I won't ever need to. You were, still are, very special, but Ian is not going to go off with another man and that's one very big difference.

Peter thought this was a re-stating of what he already knew and the reality of life with another man, with Mike, sank a bit further into his heart and mind and felt just a little bit more right. He decided to make a joke of it, aware they needed to catch-up with the other two.

'So, it's just by being unquestioningly heterosexual that Ian is your boyfriend now then!?'

Sue was pleased he was now teasing her and played along. 'Ha, ha, yes, that's all it is!'

They walked on and after a couple of hundred yards, the path went round a sharp turn and up a steep bit of ground and at the top Ian and Mike were waiting for them, folded arms, shaking their heads.

'If you two are going to carry on gassing with each other all day, we're not going to get up this mountain.' Said Ian. 'Come on – I reckon the lake is just up a little bit further, hidden from view, but you can see the top of the back cliff already'.

Once they arrived at the lake edge, they all offloaded their rucksacks, and sat down on some boulders. There was plenty of choice and they found some fairly level surfaces quite quickly. Peter produced two flasks and offered tea to everyone.

'Bloody hell', said Ian, 'Sue did the same thing this morning. Just one flask she packed though. I can see why you two got on!'

'Yes, that was it Ian. Right from the start I seduced Peter with tea, somewhere just the other side of this mountain.' Sue joked, pointing vaguely in the direction of Kinlochewe. 'What about you Mike – did he try that with you too?' Sue asked.

'It wasn't tea, no, it was whisky with me.' Said Mike, smiling, and he looked at Peter, wanting to give him a hug but just feeling a bit uncomfortable in front of Ian and Sue.

'Ahh yes, whisky,' said Sue, 'Another crucial part of Pete's armoury.' And she gave Peter a knowing look.

Over some shortbread biscuits and the tea, they looked across the lake, to the cliffs of the headwall of the corrie, now fully exposed to them in their widescreen glory. Even though two of them had seen this view before, the scale and grandeur of it captivated the attention of all four of them. Ian pointed out some of the key climbing routes he knew about but also pointing out he hadn't yet attempted any of them. He described the horizontal traverse line that went right across the middle of the cliff, originally undertaken by Chris Bonnington and considered to be very hard and very serious.

'What I'm thinking' said Mike, 'is that just getting this far, to this tea spot, is pretty tiring, but then doing a thousand foot rock climb…well, I guess you would have to camp, but then you have to lug all that tent stuff here too!' He shook his head, trying to imagine the extent of the effort and resources needed for climbers on those routes.

'Don't worry - we're not camping and we're not climbing.' Said Sue, emphatically. She picked-up on what sounded like a concern from Mike though, and she felt it struck a chord with something she felt too.

'You're right Mike, it was tiring getting here.' She looked at Peter, and more quickly at Ian, not wanting to pour any cold water on the plan for the day. 'Hmm – I'm just starting to wonder … on the map, there seems to be a fair bit of distance and a lot of contours between here and Kinlochewe!'

Ian came over and put an arm round her shoulder. They had a short talk together while Peter chatted with Mike.

Eventually, Ian spoke first, 'I don't know, what do you say Pete – it's your planned day?'

'Yes, it is a long way to Kinlochewe, and yes, it was a long way up to this point. As we all seem to be having an honest moment here, then yes I can feel the effort involved just getting here. Look, the view in this Corrie is magnificent but we need to get up onto the ridge at least.'

He hesitated a moment, thinking of the map and of what he remembered, 'There's three options really – once we make the ridge level, we can do the whole thing as planned. Or, we can drop down to the south, from nearer the central peak – brings us down to the road, a mile from the car. Thirdly, we reverse the route up, this route we have just taken to here, – which isn't a cop-out as the landscape will appear very different on the descent to the ascent, and we will have more time to soak it up.'

'Fourth,' said Ian, 'We could turn round here.'

Peter held his arms a little from his body, upturned palms – asking the question.

'Well, it will feel more of a success if we get up something. So, can we go up the next bit and then see how it goes?' Asked Mike.

'Suits me too – good idea.' Said Sue.

'OK – let's get on then.' Suggested Ian.

'Er – just before we do, for those of you who are interested', said Peter, changing the subject, 'that is a pretty amazing piece of geology right there too. Right in front of us. It's worth taking it on board a moment. The whole cliff is in two huge, thick layers, as you can see. The lighter coloured, upper half, is quartzite and its sitting on the Torridonian Sandstone underneath. You can see the layers of strata in both those rock units. The quartzite is about five hundred million years old and the sandstone nine hundred million.'

'That's hard to imagine – to get your head round the dates.' Said Ian, still studying the cliff.

'So, that's another unconformity is it? asked Sue.

Peter turned to her, thinking of the significance of Sue discovering that word a couple of years earlier. 'I told you I wasn't going to keep explaining geological terms to you Sue, because you end-up using them against me!'

Sue laughed out loud, but Ian and Mike both just looked a bit baffled. It occurred to Peter that his throwaway remark might mean both he and Sue would have to give explanations later.

'Anyway,' Peter continued, a little hesitatingly at first, 'no, it's not an unconformity. Not like the other one anyway. In this case, the quartzite was laid down on top of the sandstone, which at that time was the sea floor. So, it's more of a sedimentary sequence, but with a vast age gap.'

'Right,' said Ian. 'that's all very interesting and I might like to know more about that sometime.' He looked at Sue and gave her a smile. 'But right now, if you follow the cliff round to my left, towards the north, you can see the cliff breaks up and then becomes scree across this slope above us, which is … what's the name Pete?'

'Ruadh-Stac Mhor', or big red hill I think is the translation. It's one of the summits of Beinn Eighe, a thousand feet above us from here. The whole mountain is like a mini range in itself and this is the biggest peak.' He swept an arm across the view. 'So, you were saying Ian.'

'Yeah, so where the cliff is breaking up in that corner, that's where we are heading. Don't panic, it's actually pretty blocky when you get there and you need to use your hands, but it is nothing like a proper climb – easy really, exhilarating though.'

And that's how it proved to be, for all of them. There was a bit of a laborious trek across the boulder field above the lake, gradually gaining height, and then ascending the blocks of quartzite in the corner for a few hundred feet, before emerging onto the top, then at last being on the ridge network of Beinn Eighe itself.

They stood and looked around, all feeling a bit awe-struck by the scale and beauty of the mountain landscape now revealed to them. After the surprisingly long, and times awkward, ascent from the car park to this point, it felt like they had all at last emerged into a different world.

Chapter 23

Mike thought the last two hundred feet of scrambling had been one of the scariest things he had ever done. Ian had led the way, with Sue tucked in closely behind him. Peter had been the backmarker, behind Mike, which had felt safe and reassuring. As he emerged onto the flat ground of the top, he was aware of his heart beating fast. Exhilarating it had been, for sure, as Ian had promised, but also unnerving too. It had felt very vertical but mercifully he had been spared having to look down the extent of the drop, but instead focusing on the rocks in front of his eyes – searching where to put his feet and hands on rock outcrops which felt stable and secure.

But it felt strange now to be on what felt like a bit of a plateau. After the scramble, the ground felt surprisingly flat and solid, and at first sight the ground under his feet seemed part of an horizon encompassing the various peaks of Beinn Eighe. Initially it felt like a place of security versus the imposing cliffs and vertiginous scree slopes that were all around, both on this mountain and on the nearby mountains of Liathach, Beinn Dearg, Beinn a Chearchaill and Meall a Ghiubhais, as Peter had just identified for them all.

Getting his eye into the landscape though, Mike realised that the position was far from secure. Sure, there were some easy, familiar-looking types of slopes to the north and west, but a much more dramatic and narrow ridge leading up to a pyramidal peak, which was east – the direction he knew they had to go. Beyond that there seemed to be a high jumble of rocks, cliffs and scree.

'Er – what do we do from here then?' he asked, hoping he didn't sound as bewildered as he was feeling.

'That's my question too!' said Sue, coming alongside him, both of them now looking along the ridge which allegedly led to Kinlochewe, finding a bond in their shared uncertainty.

'Right, where you are looking, is towards the obvious peak – it's called…' Peter looked at the map to check, 'Spidean Coire nan Clach. That's pronouncing, sort-of, as it's spelt, but that's probably wrong! Anyway, it's a ridge to there, not a scramble but it is exposed, as you can see. From that peak east is some more ridge, a bit of scrambling and a descent to the village, Kinlochewe.'

'The highest peak though,' said Ian, is this direction. He waved his arm to the side, to the north. 'That's pretty easy from what I remember – you can see it's straightforward ground from here. That's to Ruadh Stac Mhor – and that pronunciation is probably crap too. That's the mountain we spoke about while having tea, that was above us when we were back down by the lake.'

'What's behind us?' asked Sue. They all turned round, now looking more westwards.

'You can see pretty much, it's over this broad ridge and then a bit rockier and more defined up to Sail Mhor, which is a tad lower than the Spidean peak.' Explained Peter. 'I know, it sounds, and actually is, a bit complicated! Not as obvious as you might imagine from the view off the road or from Kinlochewe.' He saw Sue looking at him. Something he had said, or something about the mountain had triggered one of Sue's looks – the ones that feel like silent and gentle mind interrogation.

Sue suggested a few minutes for more tea, or water. There evolved a discussion and much to Peter's initial disappointment, the idea of continuing to Kinlochewe over the ridge, including peaks not yet discussed, was clearly going to fall by the wayside. Apart from the discouraging feeling, he was annoyed with himself for over-estimating what would feel good for all of them.

Sue had read his mind. 'Don't worry Pete – all these Torridon mountains feel special. The landscape looks big enough from the road and from what I saw from your mapping area back then. But it is truly huge once you're right in its midst. I know you wanted to give us a good trip, but I would feel I had been on a very special day, even if we just turned round right now.'

Peter thought that was nice of Sue and her comments did make him feel better. He could see Mike had been nodding along – clearly on the same side.

Sue continued, 'Ian was telling me though, that to see across to your mountain, we ought to go to the highest point of the whole thing, that one he just mentioned – Roove Stac More, is how I'm pronouncing it.' Sue indicated the ground ahead of them rising up quite quickly over boulders and scree.

Ian nodded. 'Look, the thing is, none of it's going to go away Peter, not in our lifetime anyway. We will be back again. Meanwhile, I'm thinking …what about you and me, Mike? How about we go along west, to Sail More as I pronounce it,' he joked, 'It's easy ground, gives a fantastic view into Liathach and down the glen to more rock and scree. Afterwards, we can go back down the way we just came up. Don't worry I'll go first and test all the blocks. Then we meet you two…' He turned to Peter and Sue who were now side by side, '…down by the lake, just above the start of the descent. After you have done Ruadh Stac Mhor.'

Peter wondered how and when this had been decided. Thinking about it, it must have been Ian and Sue's chat, just before he banged on about geology. And maybe they'd chatted coming up the scramble, when he was concentrating on the route, and on Mike's progress. Now he went alongside Mike and asked quietly if he was ok with the plans.

Mike's primary concern was getting back down safely. 'I feel pretty confident with Ian leading though and I guess it will soon be over. I just don't fancy the rest of the ridge, to Kinlochewe, sorry.'

'Don't worry.' Peter wanted to hug him and kiss him, but felt a bit awkward again in front of Sue and Ian. So gave just a brief arm round his shoulders instead. He really wanted Mike to be happy that he was going off with Sue for a short time, and he wanted to be sure that this wasn't preoccupying Mike's thoughts.

After a few minutes and the tea, they broke up to go in their different directions. They all agreed they should be back together by the lake again, after an hour and a half or so, leaving them a further couple of hours to then walk back downhill to the car.

Ian and Mike set off side by side along the grassy start to the ridge going west. It suddenly felt a bit odd to both of them to be on their own. Ian chose to address the mood early on, rather than let it fester, also perceiving it would likely be feeling more awkward for Mike than for him.

'It's the first time I have been with you on a mountain, since Ben Hope and Ben Loyal a couple of years back.'

'Yeah – they were a couple of really good days out.' Mike cast his mind back. 'That was a great holiday Ian. We all just got on so well didn't we? Can't imagine doing all those things in a group again ever – feels unbelievable now really.'

'We've all had to adapt to some changes since then haven't we! But, I don't know Mike, I could see myself doing all that another time – would be fun one day. In fact, I might suggest it to Sheena for another time. I don't know Dougal that well but the time I was with him in Chamonix, I thought he was a good bloke. Don't see him dipping in the bay though, or bopping around to Top of the Pops!' Ian paused. 'What about you two – maybe we could do it again before we get too old or anything else happens?'

Mike wasn't exactly sure what Ian meant by the last part. He also felt embarrassed and knew straightaway that he looked like that too. 'Don't know. It would … it would feel a bit weird after last time.'

'Yeah, of course. Sorry.'

'No, don't… don't be sorry. It's just, you know, I was with Diane then and …' he was going to comment on Peter and Sue, but wasn't sure if Ian minded that being mentioned or not.

'Yeah, I know! And Sue was with Pete!' Ian chuckled. 'It's all a bit mad, isn't it. I would feel more odd about it if Pete was with another woman to be honest. Not sure that would work for me, to come out on a walk like this, so soon. I would feel uncomfortable about that. But with you two – well, it's completely different, isn't it? Anyway, we're all adults. Stuff happens.'

'I'm chuffed now that you two met-up with us today. I wasn't sure first thing this morning. My nerves were jangling.'

'Chuffed?' asked Ian, stressing the word, which seemed odd to him.

'I didn't take it for granted Ian. That we could all be friends like this. You know – that you and Sue would accept Pete and I as friends. You've made it feel normal.'

Ian pondered that for a moment. He realised that actually he was here with Mike and Peter and it did feel normal. He had also thought it might feel odd being with two blokes who slept together, but it had just felt like being with friends. He then realised it might not be so acceptable to everyone.

'You haven't lost any friends, I hope?' Said Ian, feeling a bit concerned. They had been walking ever more slowly, and now stopped a moment.

'No, I don't think so. Well, the thing is there's not that many know really. We've been cautious who we tell.'

'The rubbish in the newspapers is off-putting I guess – all that stuff about gay plague and pretty dismissive language.'

'It is partly that Ian, but it's the small casual comments that get to you most.' They started walking slowly again as Mike's mind wandered through numerous examples, not sure that he could say them to Ian without feeling stupid himself, but deciding to be open. 'For instance, Jill, a nice woman, sort-of friend, in a pub, talking about travelling somewhere exotic and getting holiday vaccinations. She said something about Hepatitis B. Nobody had heard of it nor knew anything about it really. She just said "it's the disease homosexuals get". It was the way she said it, a slightly disgusted tone, so unlike her. That sort of stuff crops-up all the time.'

Ian nodded, looking serious. 'Pub chat recently about AIDS – friend down the Club said "they should put them all on a ship, tow it out and sink it". Another guy said "who?". The first bloke said, "queers! Sink all the queers and you get rid of the problem". I asked him if he knew any. He said no, not likely – or some such thing. I told him you can't go around saying things like that. He did shut up, but I guess that's what he thinks. So…' He again brought them to a halt and put his hands on Mike's shoulders, looked him in the face. '…I've heard that stuff and can only imagine how it feels to you and Pete when you hear it.'

Mike felt moved by that. 'It's often so casual Ian. 'Effing queers – it's something you hear a lot. I never used to notice it. But I do now…'

Ian squeezed his shoulders a bit harder. 'You're just two guys, getting on with life. It's just the way you are. There's a lot of idiots around, don't know what they're saying.' He shook his head. Their hold broke then and they started to look around. Mountains, valleys, cliff faces, rocky ridges, scree – all of it, everywhere.

Conversation stopped altogether as they slowly walked on and noticed more the opening-up of the enormous view down to their left, west. Beinn Dearg 's buttressed bulk rising up so vertically from the water-laden ground below, beyond that the pinnacles of Beinn Alligin, and to the south the corries of Liathach. So much dark red and brown rock, so much white and grey scree, so much blue water in the lochans and streams below. Both of them felt awestruck.

'Wow - I wouldn't have wanted to miss this.' Said Mike, to nods of agreement from Ian. They just drank in the view for several minutes, just mumbling superlatives to themselves and each other, brief comments on the scale of the vista before them.

Then they continued walking on to the end peak, now orienting their view in a different direction. Heading this way, the view was dominated by Beinn a Chearchail to the north and a few hundred feet lower than them. Its summit appeared to be a flattish platform of rock. They both thought it would provide a good view of the whole Torridon range. Much nearer to hand though, and dominating the field of view looking east, was the bulky, boulder-strewn mass of Ruadh Stac Mor – the hight point of the Beinn Eighe summits.

'Look there Mike – just about in the skyline, you can see a couple of people walking along. A mile away, as the crow flies. Must be Sue and Pete. We haven't seen anyone else all day, so it must be them. They're making good progress.' He and Mike then waved both their arms back and forth above their heads, in the hope of being seen.

'They probably can't see us. Probably concentrating on looking where they're going.' Said Mike.

'They will be too busy nattering Mike, that's what I think!' To which they both laughed.

Mike realised he was feeling relaxed. The part of the mountain where Peter and Sue were walking, looked safer ground than where he was right now with Ian. It just felt so weird to him though, to think Pete was over there with his old girlfriend and here he was, with that woman's new boyfriend. And he himself was also the new boyfriend of Peter.

'If I could just stay on this mountain with you and Sue I feel everything would work out.' He looked at Ian, hoping for corroboration. 'And with Pete of course.'

Ian could see what Mike was thinking. 'You two should come and see us. Or we will come and see you. Not on a mountain, just at home. Go to a restaurant for a meal together. See a film. Make a nice time of it. Maybe get the projector and slides out – relive Talmine and other trips.' He paused. 'Have to be careful with that though! Wouldn't want to bore us all, clicking through hundreds of slides. Might be more fun just being down the pub.'

The sheer normality of what Ian had proposed moved Mike so much, he felt a bit choked. All he could say was 'that would be great Ian. Do you mean it.'

Ian thought he understood what Mike was feeling . 'Course I mean it! Assuming Sue and I make a go of it, which we seem to be doing well enough so far, you two would always be welcome. Any time Mike.' Ian held eye contact with Mike, wanting to convey the sincerity of his words. 'Come on though – we need to start heading back down.'

It was easy reversing the route along the ridge and then flatter ground again, until they reached the steep, rocky gully going back down the corner of the Coire Mhic Fhearchair corrie. The lake was clearly visible a long way below and to Mike it felt like they were about to step down a vertical cleft in the huge rocky cliff. More likely fall-down, was what he really felt. Ian tried to be reassuring.

'Something like this Mike – it looks really steep, but it feels more straightforward once you're in it. I will descend first, and I will take it real slow. There's no rush. There's some scree, which we want to keep off. Stick to the rocks and turf instead. Right, first bit, put your hands down on this block and your feet on the next one down, there's room for us both initially.' And, with that, Ian started the descent. Mike knew he had to just quickly follow before he lost his nerve, thinking that there was really no choice anyway.

He felt it would probably be ok, as long as Ian stayed just a step of two in front and didn't rush. Mike felt, and mostly hoped, the rock climbing experience of Ian would give them the ability to find a way down safely. He realised it would be the same for Pete, with Sue, when it was their turn to be here. Soon, he wished – and hoped.

After a few minutes, Mike realised he was actually enjoying it.

There was a rhythm to using hands, easing feet down, then stepping across from one side of the gully to the other, repeating the moves. At first, the lake seemed as far away as ever, but then, at some point, Mike looked up and realised he must have been concentrating very hard at the matter in hand, because they were suddenly down a fair bit lower and he could make out details of the thin track alongside the lake and could see where they had stopped for tea and Pete's geology lecture. Almost immediately, one of Mike's feet slipped forward on some loose chippings. He clenched his hands round the rocks he had been half-holding. 'I must just concentrate' he said to himself.

And then, before he knew it, Ian was standing before him on the edge of the boulder field, with the thin path descending ahead of him at an easy angle. 'We will be at the Lake in another ten mins or so. Well done.'

Mike did feel pleased with himself and a huge sense of relief washed over him, simultaneously make him feel quite tired. He allowed himself to think of Peter again then, missing him.

Chapter 24

At the moment when Ian and Mike were approaching the descent route, Peter and Sue were on the summit of Ruadh Stac Mor, sitting on a solid slab of quartzite jutting out of the ground at just an ideal height for a seat. The summit cairn was behind them, shielding them from most of the breeze coming from that direction. Mostly they were looking towards the north-east and the southern slopes of Meall a Ghiubhais.

'So, where we are looking Pete – did you go right round there? From the summit down those cliffs?' It's just such a lot of rock.'

'It is. I went straight up the nose of the summit there, just once. It was very hairy, but once I had started, there was no reversing it. There were some very steep sections I recall. I gave up trying to make any sense of the geology, it became a case of making sure I didn't fall-off.' His mind drifted more deeply into those days. 'You were there though Sue.' He pointed with his finger. 'Where those huge waves of whitish rock end – from there, right across the slope. That was our scree walk. You and your kilt.' He smiled at her. 'Looking lovely. It was a mile or two of following a horizontal line, through and across all that scree and down to the quartzite plateau. You loved it. We both did.'

'That was just after our tea and bikkies with Mr MacKenzie and the man from Gairloch. I asked them about the wartime activity up here. Still think about that. It was astonishing to learn wasn't it?'

'Yep – just after we had all decided about the possible bit of plane wreckage I had discovered. I should have said earlier, by the way, – the plane that I speculated about, back on my field work, the wreckage of that is somewhere down in the Corrie, where we are going back down. Where Ian and Mike will be heading around now.'

Sue checked her memory. 'So, over there on Meall a Ghiubhais, you found that fused metal on the little cliff – by the faultline you discovered too.' She paused, getting an encouraging smile and nod from Peter. 'Those two, and you, all decided in the end that it could have been some molten metal from the plane that crashed into the corrie of this mountain – just over there?' She pointed westwards into the vast back wall of the corrie opposite.

'Yep – that's pretty much it Sue. Then you used that faultline discovery to interrogate me about Steve!'

'I did NOT interrogate you Pete.' Sue shouted, but laughter mixed-in too. 'You needed to confess I think, to be honest with yourself – that's the best way of putting it.'

'Yeah – you brought it out of me…' Peter sighed, recalling the moment. 'You and I had some extraordinary moments didn't we? Over there on that scree slope, surrounded by all this mountain architecture. Right there at one time. Then soon after, cramped together inside the canvas walls of my little tent!'

'Hmm, I'm thinking of women friends who have had deep and meaningful conversations – usually in pubs or the kitchen! With you, locations are much more al fresco.' She teased.

A minute or two passed then while they ate some snacks and just soaked-up the view. Sue changed the subject.

'It was sweet of Ian to go back down with Mike. One of the things I like about him is the way he takes everything in his stride.'

'One of the things?' enquired Peter. 'Do you already have a list?'

'Awww, come on Pete. You can't be jealous!'

'I'm not!' he protested, knowing this wasn't completely true.

'Think you are a bit,' said Sue, smiling and receiving a smile back. Then she spoke more seriously. 'But you can't be. You have Mike now. He's right for you, in a way I could never have been.' She waited to get a nod of agreement. 'In a way, WE could never have been.' She clarified.

'Yeah, I know, I know. I'm just getting used to it I suppose.

Being with you today has helped. You know – just being good friends together. And it really is lovely Sue that you are a good friend…more than that…'

'I always will be Pete.' Sue leaned over and kissed him on the cheek.

'Thank you sweetie.' He leant over and kissed her on the cheek too. 'I'm still just glad you haven't been revolted.'

'Revolted?' Sue thought she knew what he meant, but couldn't imagine having that feeling herself.

'Yes, come on. You know. Some people feel visceral about it don't they? They're disgusted by the thought of two men together, doing stuff. I'm just pleased you have never said "Yuk - you disgust me you poof, go away and don't come near me" or something similar.'

'I would never, ever, say anything like that.' Said Sue emphatically.

'And you never have. That's what I mean really, you have always accepted me. Down there on my mountain and in Kinlochewe.' He swept his hand across part of their field of view to the east. 'Then you accepted me as a boyfriend. As a lover even.' He looked straight at her, diving into her eyes, smiling, thinking, remembering. 'And you're still accepting me, even when I left you for someone else, for another – another man even!'

Sue laughed quietly. 'It's nice to be good humoured about it Peter. Just to be clear though, I don't think it's a case of you leaving me for another man.' Sue emphasised the you and me.

'Don't you?' asked Peter quietly.

'No, I think it was a shared decision. Hmm – not a decision perhaps. More a dawning realisation – we both came to. Don't you think? It's working out too, isn't it?'

'Are you and Ian going to be happy?'

'Are you and Mike!?' The questions hung in the air a little. 'None of us know, do we?' 'I thought I was going to be happy with Colin. I really liked, and still like, you and your company. I like Ian a lot and he makes me happy. I don't know Peter. In the long term, I mean.' Sue found herself surfacing feelings she hadn't yet examined critically, just being at ease sharing her thoughts with him, but also realising just how emotional it all felt to be here talking like this.

Peter wondered what was coming next, but he thought it must be important, being heralded by the long form of his name.

'I don't know what will happen next.' Continued Sue. 'I have been feeling broody at times…'

'Really!' Peter was shocked. 'I … I, I didn't know!'

'Well I'm not pregnant! In case you suddenly think that. But I might be one day. Ian seems like he would be right in that way.'

Peter felt slightly stunned – something he just hadn't considered much. 'Yeah, I have never been paternal. Sorry…'

'Peter! Don't you start your apologetic refrain again. You don't need to do that. Ever, please.'

There was a long pause in the conversation. Both of them, in different ways, were thinking about maternity. They both shuffled along the rock, until one side of each of their bodies was pushed firmly into the other's side. Their eyes wandered across the bulk of Ruadh Stac Beag, a mile in front of them. More sandstone rock drenched in swathes of white scree.

'So, over there, that is little red mountain, and where we are sitting is the big version?'

'Yes – although my knowledge of Gaelic is hopeless. But roughly that. I know it's a bit crazy, because that hill is pretty huge too.' They were quiet for a moment, thinking about the hills, thinking of what they had been saying. Thinking of how long they had known each other. Peter felt this was as good a moment as any to give Sue the memento he had for her. 'Anyway, talking of red mountains, I have something for you I've picked-up on the route. Something I have often looked for actually, but only found today. Serendipitous maybe.'

Peter fumbled in his rucksack, which was lying just alongside. Eventually he exclaimed when he found an object that had clearly got buried in amongst other things.

'I hope you don't think this is silly Sue.' He paused, a wave of deep feelings suddenly surged up through him and it caught him off guard. He put a hand over his eyes, the emotion of the moment suddenly getting at him. It had been rising all day and now broke over.

'Oh no.' said Sue, putting an arm around his shoulders. 'What's brought this on? I can see the signs Pete.' She tried to tease him. 'You are starting to bite your lip!...' Peter had lowered his hand and they looked at each other intensely, expectantly, trusting. The affectionate feeling they had for each other flowed between them. '…and now you've got me doing it too.' She paused. 'This has been a big day for you and me hasn't it?'

'Sorry.' Peter found a handkerchief, dabbed Sue's eyes then his own.

'Don't bloody apologise Peter! Please stop doing that sweetie.'

They were now pressed close together, surrounded by the wild beauty of Torridon all around them. Peter took her right hand with his left, and held it tight. They looked at each other intensely, both of them moist-eyed. 'Sue, I want you to have this…' and he held something hidden in the palm of his right hand. They looked at each other for what felt like minutes but must have been just seconds and then he dropped it into Sue's other hand as she opened it.

She could feel from its texture and weight that it was a rock. Her eyes searched his, so close now. Then she looked down at the stone, which she recognised immediately as a piece of Torridonian Sandstone. Peter was starting to explain he had been looking all day for the right piece, and on other days, and he had, at last, found this in the gully up to the ridge. Sue didn't really listen and found herself crying gently now because she recognised the shape easily and could feel its smooth edges.

Through a few tears himself, Peter said it had been very difficult to find the right shape, but he hoped that the roughly triangular and rounded edges of this piece of Torridonian Sandstone were good enough - as close as he was going to get anyway - to the shape of a heart.

They held each other's eyes again. 'I want you to have this Sue.' Peter just about managed to say, quietly. 'Keep it if you will. It's to remind you, for a long time hopefully, of the special friendship we formed in amongst these lovely mountains, long ago.' They hugged then, a long, warm and familiar hug that went on for a very long time. 'And this is the most I've seen you cry since Chamonix.'

'It's your fault! You total sweetheart.' And she kissed him on the lips, and they stayed kissing like that for a little while. 'I will never, ever, part with this rock Pete.'

Eventually, they pulled apart and got themselves up, putting their rucksacks back on.

'It's going to work-out Pete, isn't it? For you and Mike I mean, well, and for me and Ian?'

'Course it is!' He said. 'Come on, let's get back to them.' And they headed off at some speed, downhill now, towards the top of the descent gully, using momentum to shift their mood. Worried that they had been taking a long time away from the other two, they scrambled down as fast as they could, both agreeing that maybe it was better not to overthink it or they would slow right down.

They found Ian and Mike by the place they had stopped earlier. Ian gave Peter a look with raised eyebrows and then turned to Sue, smiling. 'Well, that was obviously a longer walk than mine with Mike. Arthur found some dragons to slay did he?'

'Something like that actually.' Said Sue, with a long sigh.

'You two!' said Ian, shaking his head slowly, tight-lipped but a smile was clear too.

Peter felt like he had been given a mild telling-off. 'It's my fault Ian, Sue had to put up with a lot of reminiscing on my part.'

'Yeah? But I suspect she didn't do much to stop you either!' suggested Ian.

'That's true.' Said Sue. 'Pete and I have just realised though that our friendship feels like it's been going on a long time. Not as long these mountains have been around, but hopefully as enduring.' And she gave Peter a kiss on the lips, underlining her feeling openly to both Ian and Mike.

'We should all have a drink to that Sue.' Said Mike, moved by what Sue had said and done. 'If we can't do that back at the Kinlochewe Hotel, then soon.'

'Our place Mike. Like I said up there.' Said Ian, pointing over his shoulder. 'Or your place.'

'Well, it sounds like we have all had a good chat the last couple of hours!' said Peter, but we need to get on. And with that, he shouldered his rucksack and led-off down the path and over the rocky lip of the corrie, thinking all the time of what Sue had said just back there. Then thinking of the conversation Mike and Ian might have had. He kept checking the descent was going ok for all of them, but found himself happy just to be alone with his thoughts most of the time.

They arrived back at the car around five o'clock. All of them realised how weary they were feeling as they struggled to make light work of changing some of their clothes and taking off their boots. They were soon heading back to Kinlochewe though, with Sue driving again. Everyone was just feeling a bit too tired to talk much and Sue summed it up from the driving seat.

'Well I'm pleased you boys are quiet. It means less banter about women drivers and this one in particular.'

Ian, already half-asleep, just said, 'whatever Sue. Just wake me when we get there. You just keep straight on by the way, steady speed and we'll be there in no time.'

'You see,' said Sue, 'You can't stop doing it even when you're trying not to!'

'I just want to say thank you Sue. I really appreciate you.' Was Mike's comment. Sue caught his reflection in the rear view mirror and blew him a kiss.

They were soon back in the Kinlochewe car park and grouped beside Peter and Mike's car. They were all fatigued enough to know they just needed to move on but each of them also had strong feelings arising from the day's walk and it was hard to part.

'Your original estimate was right Pete. We will be in our B&B by six-thirty and the same for you to your cottage.' said Sue.

'Yeah, but I underestimated it really.' He pointed to the huge northern prow of Beinn Eighe, its triangular form looming high behind the village. 'We would still be up there if we had stuck to my plan A.'

There were gentle nods and Ian said, 'It's good you left us something to come back for Pete. And I reckon we all will too.' There was then a brief conversation about when that might be. It was a bit inconclusive, but they all agreed that they had just experienced a unique day and it had been more than worthwhile to meet-up. They said they would all meet again later in the summer for a day trip when back down south. It felt like polite conversation but the feeling of shared friendship was much deeper than their wearied words could express properly at the time. It only remained then to say their goodbyes.

'Let's get on with it then.' Said Peter, sensing a general reluctance to bring this particular adventure to a close. He thought to himself that it really was like closing a chapter of his life, and turning over to a new page.

Mike spoke first. 'This isn't a speech, but thanks for your company both of you - and especially for your shepherding me up there Ian. I loved it and felt very safe.'

'Don't worry about that, I really enjoyed your company.' Said Ian, and Mike could feel the truth in those brief words. 'It was an important talk we had.' He added.

'Thanks for coming out with us Sue,' said Peter, determined to keep dry-eyed. 'It was really special to be with you both right now.'

'I agree completely.' Chipped-in Mike. 'Can't thank you, both of you, enough for making me feel so normal.'

'Aww, you two are always going to be my special boys now.' Said Sue. 'We should do this again. We will do it again. I know we will.'

And then they all exchanged hugs and Sue got kisses from Mike first and Peter last. She whispered to Peter 'Thank you for my Torridonian heart.' Then paused a second, before adding, 'if you ever need me, I will be right here.' She said, pressing a forefinger into the centre of Peter's chest.

He couldn't reply, mostly because he couldn't speak without sounding a bit choked, but simply tried to allow his feelings to emanate from his body into hers. The unspoken affection just flowing between them.

Mike and Peter continued waving at Ian and Sue's car until it disappeared out of sight along the road to Gairloch. The two of them then looked at each other and hugged. 'A very special day Pete.' said Mike, for which he received a tightening of Peter's hug.

In the car, Ian was driving this time. They had gone a few miles alongside Loch Maree without anything being said, both feeling weary and content. He talked with Sue about meeting the other two, that he'd invited Mike to visit them He was pleased Sue seemed enthusiastic about that too.

He then asked 'What's uppermost in your mind then Sue?'

'Other than getting my boots off?' she joked, Ian laughed along with that. 'Oh…actually my mind was just off on a very, very big wander Ian. It might seem daft, but I was thinking of some distant future date – maybe when I'm sixty! When Pete's sixty too.'

Ian was taken aback. 'Blimey Sue – I thought you were just sitting there quietly, being in the moment! Not looking into the next century!'

They both chuckled. Sue stroked Ian's arm, pleased they were both in a good and cheerful place. 'Yeah, I know Ian, but it was feeling a bit like a premonition really. I could see us all, us four I mean, coming together then. A bit greyer, maybe slower – but the same people otherwise.' Ian nodded. 'I really think that could happen you know.' She said finally.

In the other car, heading back southwards to Shieldaig, Mike felt honoured to be given the chance to drive for a change. He took it as an indicator of Peter being relaxed and that felt just great, as far as he was concerned. They had both been quiet for the first few miles after leaving Kinlochewe. Mike could feel the settled and calm mood enveloping the interior of the vehicle.

'I hope the car doesn't feel too heavy, by the way, does it Mike?'

'Er, what?' Mike thought it was a strange thing to suddenly say. 'Why should it be heavy Peter?'

'Well, I have sneaked a few rock samples into the boot! The car park we used for our walk is built into a drumlin and I managed to find some great samples while we were faffing with our kit before we set off, and also when we came back down. Sue helped me load them quickly and then transfer them. There aren't many but they cover all the main rock types of Torridon, and of my mapping area really. It was pretty easy to spot them and just grab them – for me anyway.'

'You are more familiar with the rocks here than anyone else in the car park, I would imagine – maybe one of the few who could do that. Do they make nice souvenirs then?' asked Mike.

'Yes, they do. Of course. Very special. The samples from my student days ended up in the lab and they were much smaller anyway.' Peter wanted to add something else, 'Also, I mainly thought they could go nicely in our rockery!'

'Our rockery?'

'Yes, you know.' Said Peter. 'When we get back from this trip, we should get on with the idea of getting a house together, I think. I thought the rocks would be good, somewhere in the garden of our new home.'

Mike found himself slowing the car and realised he might have to pull-over any moment, now also remembering a similar moment from the previous summer. "Our rockery…a house together… our new home." He shook his head a little, keeping his eye on the winding and undulating narrow road ahead. 'Damn it Peter, you shouldn't have said that while I'm driving.'

Mike managed to manoeuvre themselves into the side of the road, hoping no vehicles would come along while he quickly dabbed his eyes. 'Those were lovely things to say. I'm sorry to be a bit like this - it's just been a very special day.'

'Yes, it has.' Agreed Peter. 'We were so anxious weren't we? Setting out this morning. Seems more than a few hours ago. I think maybe they would have been a bit worried too. Those two are going to be friends for life though, don't you reckon? Our first true friends – to us as a couple I mean.'

They looked at each other for a few seconds, both thinking about the day – all the walking, the bits of scrambling, the hard effort involved, the lovely company they had shared, the moving conversations that had taken place. All of it had taken place while they were immersed in, and surrounded by, the vast, ancient and spectacular landscape of the North West Highlands. They were silent for a while then, arms round each other's shoulders, running the day through their minds, reflecting on what it had meant for them, and what it must also have meant for Ian and Sue.

Eventually, Peter expelled a large breath and simply said, 'I think it's love Mike – it's simply all about love.'

Afterword and acknowledgements

As with my first novel, The Faultline, this story is a mix of memory and imagination. A lot of things in this story happened but not necessarily in the same places, times or in the same order. Meeting old friends in Chamonix really was a thing back then and so was, and hopefully still is, the ability for a group of young people to collectively run into the sea naked and then have a disco party in minimal clothing.

The geology and landscape are real and enduring and I have again tried to convey accurately something of the wonder and beauty of the Savoy Alps and the North West Highlands of Scotland. Part of my soul continues to wander across the latter, forever waiting patiently for the next reconnection with the rest of me.

And that's what this story has primarily been about – people connecting and reconnecting with each other. People finding a way through the twists and turns of friendships and relationships that can last a lifetime. The constant ebb and flow of friendship, attraction, affection and love.

Throughout the production of this novel, I have been dependent upon, and valued so much, the steadfast support of my partner Dave and my authorial assistant and agent, Katharine Douglas.

As with The Faultline, this novel would not have been possible without the help and encouragement I have received from friends in so many ways – sometimes without them even realising it. Special mentions must also go to Angie Avis, Emily Ayling, Joe Bendon, Sue Bowie, Nik Crane, Paul Cresswell, Sheena Duncan, John Graham, Mair Graham, Pete Harrison, Clare Holland, Bob Kenney, Lisa Merrell, Kitty Odell, Lucy Payne, Liz Pearcy, Mike Ruiter, Mark Squires, Pat Stephens, Chris Varley, Tom Watson, the Walters family, Mike and Matt at Café 1b, Dan and Stuart at Westbury Inks.

John McLellan, 3rd March 2024.